i

This is a work of fiction. The major characters and story line are not based on actual people. The South African raid into Lesotho on December 9, 1982 and the historical figures who spoke at the funeral for its victims are, however, portrayed accurately.

Mabbs-Zeno, Carl C.
    A Witness Too Silent / Carl C. Mabbs-Zeno
    ISBN 978-1-7331262-0-5

A Witness Too Silent

Carl Mabbs-Zeno

Peterborough, NH
2019

A Witness Too Silent

Contents

I. Mosele's Moment (1973)

Strong, fast moving, thick-skinned fingers; accustomed to work; with the clean soil of the field adhered to her hands by the moist glue of her sweat... They have been pulling stray plants, weeds, usurpers of water and nutrient resources that she would devote to her vegetables, from dawn to midday in a hot African sun. At the end of each row she stands upright and stretches her back to prevent cramping and looks toward the sun to measure the progress of the day although she does not work to the hour but to the hectare. The field she is working is not vast, small really, as measured by the standards of modern agriculture or by the needs of her family. It is one of many plots terraced onto the mild slope, reflecting the history of inheritances scattered among children of prior generations. She has other fields, that is, her family does in her father's name. She sees him only for the plowing in the spring and for a drunken spree at various holidays.

She knows which plots are theirs as do all her neighbors and finds comfort in knowing there is probably enough land for survival, and if her father brings in money from working the mines of South Africa and does not drink it all up, the family might even prosper in its way. At least until her parents get old and new hands are needed in the fields and the mines. It will be her responsibility to provide those hands although the one thing she knows for certain about the future is that she will not have a husband. Children she wants very much, but even a baby would not be enough if he or she must come at the cost of having a husband to beat her and drink away the family's reserves. She will have a baby, she is sure. She will need one to become an adult.

More than the ceremony that marked her first menstruation, having a baby would mark her majority. It would allow her to start her own household. Without a child, everything she grew would be shared with her present family of seven including three useless boys. How did her mother do it?

Mosele stood up straight and leaned to each side to stretch the ache out of her muscles. She looked over two fields to where her mother and sister were toiling. Even at that distance, she could see the pain in her mother's movements. She knew her mother had a sore back that hurt whenever she was bent over. It occurred to Mosele that a longer handle on the hoe would allow her mother to stand erect while she cut the roots of the weeds between her rows of pumpkin vines. There were no trees near the village and she had never seen a long-handled hoe for sale at the Fraziers general store. And then she remembered seeing a neighbor with a broken broom. It might have gone into the fire by now, but she would ask about it tonight.

The neighbor's broken broom turned out to be no use, not because it had been burned but because the broom was nearly as short as the hoe, consigning the woman who swept her floors every day to yet another task while bent over at the waist. But the idea stayed in Mosele's head and she had an eye out for something to serve as her mother's hoe handle until a week or more after she first had the thought, she noticed there was a pole lying under the collapsed thatch of an old rondavel, a ruin where a witch had lived so now no one went into it. She carved the pole into a long handle for the hoe, but she was not satisfied with the theory of her invention. She practiced with the new tool and twice had to reattach the head so it would have the right angle for the work and many times had to reattach the head to ensure it was strong. She examined how the metal head was attached to the normal hoe and saw that she could not duplicate that on the pole. The usual hoe was made from a branched stick so there was a support for the head, and yet she tied and tarred and carved and twisted until she had a way to secure the head to her pole. Then she had to learn how to use the hoe. She spent a full week on her experiments, smoothing the pole and shortening it to a convenient length and diameter, hiding near the witch's hut where no one would see her, until she was ready to present it to her mother.

Finally, on a day when Mosele knew her mother would be weeding all morning, she casually brought out her tool and explained how to use it, how she could stand up straight and use the power in both arms to do the work of chopping through the roots of the weeds and lifting them into a pile beside the pumpkins. Her mother was amused by the new tool but she was unconvinced that the established ways of weeding were in any way flawed. She used it for an hour before returning to her short-handled, one-armed, bent over style and when she leaned into her first familiar stroke, she felt the pull in her lower back and the strain on her right shoulder and knew this was the only way for her to work.

Mosele looked to her mother from time to time and noticed when she put down the new hoe. She was disappointed but not surprised. She worked her way over to the side of her own field closest to her mother and called to her, "Mme!" which means "mother" in Sesotho.[1] "Mme! What's wrong with the hoe I made for you? Does it hurt your back?" She was sure it did not hurt but she wanted to force her mother to acknowledge it.

"Your hoe is perfectly wonderful my darling child," she answered in Sesotho. "I will pick it up again in a few minutes. Right now I have an especially hard bunch of roots to dig out."

"I can't hear you, Mme. I am coming over," answered Mosele although her mother had a big voice that traveled well across the fields. And then, up close and more quietly, "Mme, what is wrong with the new hoe?"

"I just need to get used to it. It is not my usual movements. I miss the weeds with it."

"You don't want your usual movements. That's what hurts you. Please Mother, try it a little longer. I used it and it took out the roots. You can do more

---

[1] "Sesotho" is the language of Lesotho. A person from Lesotho is a "Mosotho." The plural is "Basotho" and "Basotho" serves as an adjective referring to anything from Lesotho.

because it has a long handle that helps you hit the soil harder and you can use both hands if you want more power. Please try it a little more. You will like it."

"*Kea leboha hahulo*, thank you very much for showing me how to hoe the weeds that I have been hoeing all my life. You know I am the mother and you are the daughter, so I decide how I want to work." Mosele's mother was getting irritated now and she refused to pick up the hoe again, not until the day had darkened and the work in the fields was being replaced by the work of preparing dinner, and yet Mosele's mother was proud of her daughter's idea and her desire to make things better. Nonetheless, she sincerely believed the new hoe must be flawed in some way that she could not quite see.

The priest, however, knew much less about turning up weeds and he could be convinced that the hoe was a wonderful invention so on Sunday when she was leaving church she made a point of boasting to him of her daughter's brilliance. She did this just to stand out in his mind. She was not sure why that should matter since she understood he was only a vehicle to salvation and not in any way holy himself. She thought it was not vanity to boast on behalf of someone else although it did feel wrong somehow. She was very surprised at his interest which she thought demonstrated his lack of knowledge about farming more than anything religious and then even more surprised when he asked if Mosele could come see him in his office sometime soon.

Mosele went to the church that afternoon. She was supposed to pound maize between the church service and dinner, but her mother thought it important to respond to the priest's invitation. Mosele had studied the catechism with the nun and seen the priest during those classes in addition to seeing him in church a couple times, but she had never spoken to him directly. She was normally self-confident around adults so she was surprised by the butterflies in her stomach when she knocked on the office door of the priest.

"Come in," he said in friendly tones, not as heavy as his teaching voice. "Mosele! Thank you for coming to see me."

She muttered a few incomprehensible syllables because that was all that would come out of her paralyzed throat.

"Please sit down. I enjoyed hearing from your mother this morning. I think you and she are very regular at services, aren't you?"

"We are believers."

"Yes, I can see that. Very good. She says you are a smart girl. Have you done well in school?"

"I was a very good student, but I finished last year."

"Did you finish high school then?"

"I finished but I did not need to graduate. I was a good student and learned everything in ten years."

"I see. But you only learned what they can offer in your school. You could go somewhere else and learn more."

"No there is no other school. I can already write clearly and speak English and do maths."

"Yes, I was noticing your English is very good. That is why I looked for a way to get you into another school, into the district mission school. Would you like to go there?"

"That is in Morija. It is too far from our fields. I would not have the time to go there every day."

7

"I might be able to get you a place to stay in Morija. We could get you food and books. Your family would not have to pay any fees."

"What is this? How could I go to school and not pay fees?"

"I am not saying I can do this, but I might be able to get you a scholarship. First I have to know if you want to do it."

"No. I am too busy already. I am needed at home. My mother needs me in the fields and around the house. I am not a child anymore."

"No, of course you are not. I can talk to your mother and see if she can let you go for a term. It would be so good for you. Think of where you could go with a diploma in your hand!"

Mosele could not think of how a diploma would help her get anywhere. This Catholic priest from France had a very odd view of what was important among the choices open to her. She would gain nothing from more school except the dubious honor of placing "Dpl" after her name when she signed it. Did the church not teach against such vanity? Now that she could see he was not well informed on local needs, was not as omniscient as the nun and the catechism suggested, her self-confidence returned to normal levels.

"I think I see what you mean, sir. Please let me discuss it with my mother and come back to get more facts about it if she thinks it is a good thing for us."

"Your mother was right about you. That is very smart. But don't take too long to get back to me. I only have one slot and I need to fill it soon."

Mosele did not really discuss it with her mother. When her mother asked what the priest wanted, Mosele simply said "He wanted to send me away to school."

Both she and her mother thought it was a very kind gesture on his part but neither seriously considered it. Not until two weeks later when Mosele and her mother and almost everyone she knew was rehearsing for a wedding. The rehearsal, which consisted of two days of singing, was as much fun as the wedding although the food was not as good.

In between songs, no one rested her voice. There were too many stories to tell to the girls they had not seen since this year's crop and this year's weeds had emerged. She did not think of it as gossip-- the concept of sinful interest in your neighbors' affairs was not present in Basotho Catholicism or anywhere else in their society. One story in particular held her attention and she asked for details from everyone who claimed to know about it. Their versions differed from one another, adding to the attractiveness of the anecdote. A girl she knew from a village she knew had gone to the National University in Roma. Roma was not mysterious, merely irrelevant, until now. Now, however, it was something to understand. What Mosele most wanted to know was why the girl had gone. Why would someone like herself want to do that? The prevalent answer was that it was the best place to meet a boy who was going to be important. The sons of chiefs were very common there. Most of them went straight from high school to college, never working in the mines. They had, therefore, not picked up the bad habits from South Africa. And with so many young men, the girls there were all considered very attractive.

Mosele was dubious that the bad habits of men came from South Africa. They were too pervasive. And she was not interested in going somewhere to find the son of a chief, and yet the concept of college at Roma was hard to put down. There was more to the place than finding a mate. Between the lines of the rumors her friends repeated to her, she saw this as a path to being important for a woman. If you could write "BSc" at the end of your signature, you would be telling whoever read it that you were somebody of substance, not just a village girl, not just living the life everyone in the village lived. Maybe you could go to France and see what made the priest that way, or go to England and see the British Queen, or go to the Post Office in South Africa and get a letter that the white postal clerk would have to hand you with respect for being more than he was.

II. Pheta's Prospects (1973)

Fingers raw and stiff from the cold... Snow is falling. It is coming in chunks and blowing into the boy's face. The sound of the wind howling in his ears isolates him from everything but the storm and his discomfort. He shuts his eyelids hard against the assault, protecting himself but unable to move without his sight. The wind is strong and the snow abrades his cheeks like hail. His arm is too heavy to lift for protection so he turns his head away from the wind. The movement wakes him. He has been dreaming, but the cold is real. The gravel under his face is painful on the soft skin of a child; it gave his dream the idea of hail. He had slid off his blanket during the course of the night. The day is dawning and will not be painfully cold once he gets moving. The January nights are cold in the dry air of the arid mountains of Lesotho but not as cold as they will be in winter when snow really does fall. Pheta has been through the winter in the mountains and he does not want to do it again in his bare feet and no more than ragged shorts underneath his wool blanket.

He sits up to feel the sunlight on his face. The boys will not light a fire for warmth. They must move the herd to pasture. He wakes quickly, surprised at how light it is already. Pheta stands up and rubs his legs to warm them. It does not have much effect but he is young and will not be stiff for long. He looks around for the other boys. There are three others working with him to feed and protect the goats. He sees all of them sleeping in a pile, gathering warmth and probably some soft comfort from each other. He plucks a handful of dry grass from the ground and sprinkles it on their faces to wake them. No one stirs. He smiles at the situation, at his superior position for the moment. He picks up a handful of sand and considers how to prolong his humiliation of his friends. He drops one grain on each face. Still no one stirs except that Thabo opens one eye. He rolls his eyeball around until it is focused on Pheta. Pheta sees it and laughs quietly as he stumbles away to find something to eat. Their cache of provisions holds a plastic bag of mealies, of cooked maize, for each of them. It is bland fare both in taste and nutrition but it is all Pheta expects. He takes his morning portion and washes it down with water cupped with his hand from the stream. As he drinks, his foot presses on the cold, wet rocks along the edge. He hardly notices the numbness expanding into and beyond his toes, so he does not move his foot away— that is just how things are in the morning.

"Pheta! Pheta! Take them up the mountain!" Thabo was yelling, in Sesotho, as if Pheta were far away although he was actually so near all three boys were able to hit him with clods of dirt to emphasize the order. They had a good aim for throwing things. They controlled the goats by throwing pebbles at them all day long, but the clods of earth were not as sturdy as stones and they would not withstand a grip firm enough to toss them more than a few meters. It was not a violent gesture on their part. They only hit him on the legs. It was a reserved approach, almost friendly in the insulting way of boys living on their own. Pheta was the youngest herd boy in their group. It was appropriate for him to draw the least desirable duty, getting the herd out of the kraal every morning. Appropriate, he knew, but that was not enough to make him accept it. He was smarter than them, he was sure. And he would grow bigger until he was their size someday, not far off, and they would still be dumber than him.

One of the clods hit him hard in the lower back where it hurt. It probably had a stone in it which Pheta felt was not fair and he almost began to cry. He held back his tears not because he was afraid they would be seen-- he was far enough from them to hide them-- but because he needed to focus on his revenge, on getting back so they would not take further advantage of his temporarily smaller size.

To get away from their attention, he did as they wished and started herding the goats out of the kraal. He pulled back the pile of thorns they used as a gate and then counted the herd. He did not know numbers, having had no schooling, but he had a pocketful of pebbles that corresponded exactly with the number of goats in the herd, with dark ones representing the mohair goats and light ones representing the others. He dropped a pebble into his pocket as they went by until all the goats were out on the hillside and all the pebbles back in his pocket. He had noticed lately that he did not really need the pebbles—he could feel the quantity of each kind of goat. It was a simple problem to account for them, but he wanted to be careful so he used the pebbles every morning. All the boys kept pebbles in their pockets for throwing at the goats. Pheta used his left pocket for counting and his right pocket for ammunition.

He gathered the herd on the path to the upper fields and looked back to see what the others were doing. They had settled in slowly for a leisurely breakfast. Pheta walked into the tall grass along the side of the donga[2] until he spotted a grasshopper pop up. He grabbed it quickly by reaching front of it where it was about to flee. Then he walked quickly back to the others. Before they could ask what he was doing, he placed the grasshopper in Thabo's bowl, pressed it into the mealies. Thabo was disgusted but he was not about to throw down the bowl with his breakfast. He yelled and the others all stood and made happy disgusting sounds directed equally at the grasshopper and at Pheta. But Pheta was not finished. He reached back into the bowl and grabbed the wriggling insect, and held it to his own mouth where he bit off the half with the head. "Mmmm, good. A little sauce with the mealies today." The remaining part of the grasshopper continued to writhe. Its legs were equipped with sharp spikes, so Pheta placed it very carefully in his mouth and squashed the legs in his first bite and ground them into a harmless mush. He chewed with his mouth open so the other boys were sure to see what he was doing. They squealed and looked back and forth among themselves but were otherwise paralyzed, and Pheta headed off with the herd without any further attack.

Pheta laughed to himself as he climbed the mountain with the goats. His bare feet felt no more through their thick soles than the goats did through their hooves, and his legs warmed from the effort of the climb.

---

[2] An eroded gully.

After an initial hurry to be safe from a counterattack, he climbed at the pace of his whims. His revenge had been so easy. It had not been as daring as they imagined. He had learned to eat grasshoppers and other small creatures and plants while lying on the rocky slopes of the sparse pastures he shared with the goats. His experimentation and courage accounted for his robust health despite the meager rations he was allowed by the other boys.

The way up the mountain was a zig-zag without any dominant path. All the slope was about the same: same angle to the horizon, same sparse grass and bushes, same expanding view of the interior of Lesotho, same cloudless sky above. The goats showed no preference except that they clearly wished to avoid the sting of the rocks from Pheta or the other boys. They munched on whatever was nearby, ensuring the slopes stayed nearly bare. It was the task of the herdboys to make it uniformly barren.

Pheta did not think of the mountains as barren. To him, they were home. He had always been in the mountains, but he was aware that there was something else in the world and that the alternative was inferior, lacking in pasturage and peace for the goats. More than that, beyond the mountains were innumerable people with competitive, possibly violent, ways. He was not aware of the austere beauty of the mountains. The dewy mornings were just cold on his ankles and the red sunsets and pale sunrises did not impress him much since the slopes where he lived faced the north, so the rise and fall of the sun was accomplished out of his view. Beauty to him lay in his family and in their sharing meaty food with him on holidays and telling stories in the evening and protecting him from whatever the witches in the next village were plotting.

After a couple hours, with the sun well up in the sky and beating hard on him through the thin mountain air, he saw the other boys approaching. They were calling out his name and he wondered if he should hide the herd from them. Maybe they were planning to torture him further—it was not an inevitable part of their relations-- but it might be fun to torture them a little more in their search for him. This time, however, something seemed different. Their calls were more persistent than normal, not the desultory, separated calls usually made in the mid-morning when they joined him. He had always thought of their calls as being like the cheeps of ducklings keeping track of their mother in the reeds of the reservoir. This image would cast him in the role of the mother duck so he never answered their calls although every day they called again. He lay hidden in a small gully and watched them work their way up the slope, marked by horizontal trails every meter or so all the way to the top, contours carved by goats on the upper and the more barren slopes, and by sheep lower down although the generations of herdboys had added their share of footprints to building the texture of Lesotho's mountains.

They were headed one slope away, with a small valley between them and him. He could hide and keep them wandering all morning, but he was curious about their enthusiasm for finding him this morning. If they were planning ill, they would not be so loud—they were not sly enough to give him such a false lead. He sat up and whistled with one finger from each hand between his teeth. He saw Thabo's head turn sharply in his direction a moment later and remembered that sound takes time to travel long distances, more time than it takes light to come back. The three boys began running along the contour path toward Pheta, yelling some message that was not clear to Pheta until they had passed into the valley where their voices were lost entirely and were absorbed by the side of the valley. Thabo arrived first as he was the fastest. He was saying "*Mme!*" which is a hard sound to say loudly enough to be heard across the valley. It means "mother," which in this case was to say his mother had come up the mountain to find him. Pheta ran loose-limbed down the mountain, his youthful joints absorbing the energy in his steps. He called a single note as he ran, "Aaaah Aaaah," a note just to say he was moving and it came out louder each time the shock of another running step shivered up his body. What could she want so much that she came up in the middle of the morning? He would be coming home within a few more days anyway. It was his turn to pick up food for boys.

Once his mother saw Pheta running toward her, she stopped climbing and moved over to a small rock outcrop to sit down and still she was more out of breath than Pheta when he arrived in her lap. She was a large woman as is common among the Basuto.

"What is it, mommy?" he cried in Sesotho, as he first became aware of the tears streaming down his cheeks.

His mother, Mapheta, laughed and hugged her youngest boy. "Pheta, your father has sent us money! It is for your schooling. You must go to school tomorrow and today we must buy you some things." The other three herd boys looked down at Pheta being held by his mother as they worked their way over to the goats. Mapheta had not said why she wanted them to find

Pheta but she had not seemed sad so they were not worried, but then when she and Pheta walked away and back toward the village, Thabo asked aloud "How will we know if we have all the goats if Pheta does not come back?"

III. Bretton Begins Again (2003)

He rubbed lotion into his hands and then checked that his fingernails were well trimmed, holding his fingers bent with the palm toward his face like a man. The lotion had come to him free in a small plastic bottle with the name of the city where he last stayed at a Sheraton Hotel. He read the name, Lusaka, and could not be sure if he had been to three countries since then or four or five. Maybe he had put the lotion in his carry-on when he stayed in Lusaka on an earlier visit which would have been two years ago. He did not really need the lotion at this moment. Putting it on was just a ritual he had adopted to mark the moment when the pressure of doing all the little steps necessary before starting an overseas trip were replaced by the long uncomfortable respite of the flight.

He read the fine print saying the contents included palm oil. It might have come from Ghana where he had watched young women turning a heavy press inside a concrete casement under a thatched roof to squeeze the oil from the farm's small, hard red clusters of nuts. He had stood beside the operation as if he understood something of it, as if he could help. He was assessing the project that built the press. Yes, he could see oil was being produced. He knew it would be exported or, if the international price was low enough, would be used within Ghana. If it stayed in the country it would be used for cooking, not for lotions. Was one of the uses better? That was not a question for him; he was only to say if the project was benefiting someone worthy at a rate sufficient for the United States to fund it for an additional three years.

He rubbed his now well-oiled hands across his face. The smell of the lotion was pleasant and the touch of it softened his skin although he had not realized it was so dry. Following his travel routine further, he closed his eyes to take advantage of the few minutes while other passengers boarded, those minutes when he never did any reading since he liked to take advantage of the time to review the situation he was leaving behind in the office. This was also a pleasant step as there were mainly petty problems in the office that would have taken up his energy with little prospect of permanent resolution. On the trip, he would be free, for the most part, to focus on a separate set of issues.

It was satisfying to realize the number of people who valued his counsel. Brenda and Angie would be unable to work effectively with him away because they would fight over which of them should take every step, the two Richards would be paralyzed by fear of making a mistake so they would delay finishing anything until he returned to reassure them or to edit their work, his boss Maggie would waste time finding staff appropriate to whatever tasks she was devising. He started to count the people who depended on him, not from vanity exactly, more because he tended to count everything.

The power of the plane accelerating down the runway, pressing him to the soft cushions of his high-backed seat confirmed command of the machinery of man to his purposes. In all too few moments after lifting

19

miraculously, flight was always a miracle despite its familiarity, the view from his window seat lost its reality. That crowd of people who depended on his inputs, who fit on his part of one floor in a huge building, shrunk to a speck and then disappeared over the horizon. Within a minute of departure, the buildings that housed everyone who knew him in the Washington area had diminished to insignificance. His house, his street, his city, shrank below him until the parts he controlled or influenced, the parts that had driven his passions or given him heartburn over the past weeks, were suddenly no more significant or durable than a few tiny waves in the ocean. Yet there were signs of countless people below him, people who never heard of him and who cared nothing for his work. They did care much more, he could see, about baseball and swimming since ballparks and pools were always in sight. He saw absurd toy towns vaguely like a map of the area he knew around Washington, and soon thereafter the view contained a remote, abstract canvas of colors reflecting the season.

Suddenly and predictably, he was over the Atlantic and there was nothing more to see for six hours. He was at that point an anonymous passenger among too many crowded inside a tiny speck of technology, dangling far outside his control or influence. As he settled into the flight, his thoughts inevitably turned toward the assignment at the end of the flight for which he always felt unprepared. How could the cost of this technology that would carry him over the ocean in near comfort be justified by whatever he might do in the next few weeks in a country he hardly knew? Apparently he had fooled his employers (they were the American taxpayers); had he fooled himself too?

Back in the airport, he could accept the familiar illusion of his importance, dressed in stylish international attire; reclining in the first class lounge he had earned by his mileage, not by paying exorbitant fares; reading magazines that mentioned issues he had studied and on which he had opinions; always near one or another nicely made up woman in well-fitting clothes.

It had been easier when he was starting out, when no one expected much of him, when he could not use the first class lounge, and when he did not pay any attention to the cost of travel (it was not then his responsibility to allocate travel money). Like most of his contemporaries, he wanted to travel, saw it as enhancing his career, as an investment by his employer, and a job benefit. He lay back in the seat and closed his eyes to recapture those heady days as a young economist.

"Where is your home?" The question came from close by. Bretton opened his eyes and turned to the man sitting beside him. He was almost certainly African, not Afro-American. His conservative suit was too inexpensive and his tie too garish for an American who could afford an overseas flight. He was thin with isolated curly grey strands starting to grow in his hair. He smelled of soap and aftershave. "Myself, I am Ghanaian. This is my first trip to the Republic. Our company would like to expand into their market. We must see if that is feasible."

I have a conversationalist this trip, Bretton thought. *He is well spoken so that might not be so bad. It's a long flight. Maybe I can learn something of his business in South Africa. I wonder if his business is based in Ghana. If it is seriously going into South Africa, it is more likely an American firm.* His thoughts delayed his answer as he recovered from the nap he was about to take.

"I meant, are you South African or American?"

"When I am asked 'where is your home,' I am inclined to say, 'we moved around a lot,' and no one likes that answer. To simplify matters, I answer that my home is Monroe, Ohio, that town wherein I passed adolescence, where I graduated from high school, where I last lived with my siblings and my parents. But I do not wish to call that place my home. It does not feel like the place where I began or like a place that formed me. I have never gone back to it though I pass it on the highway nearly every year. What feels like home is Maseru, the capital of Lesotho. There I could never speak the language well. I fit in so poorly that there was never a moment when I or anyone I knew forgot that I came from elsewhere. Yet it is Lesotho's name that warms me when I hear it. It is Lesotho that I would love to see again. It is Lesotho where I can most easily imagine there are people who stayed behind and kept a memory of me."

"You understand what home is. That is not an American's answer."

"America has a lot of different answers to any question you ask."

"But you are South African then, with an American accent. Lesotho is in South Africa, right? A black part?"

"Southern African, maybe. Lesotho is its own country. You are right that it is surrounded by South Africa, but not one of the homelands set up by the Republic as phony countries during apartheid. Very odd geography... I have been to Accra. Are you from the city?"

"From Keta; on the coast closer to Lomé than to Accra. But I want to know how is it an American can call Lesotho his home. It is very strange."

"My first job after school was in Lesotho. I went there to teach at a technical college. Teachers often speak of the frustrations of their profession but they always close with the admission that the students are wonderful and the teachers are always right on this last point. My students were wonderful. They lived in a poor country with no hope of substantial economic progress. They mainly hoped for peace, but that did not come during my years there. The students never spoke to me of the bombings in the capital or the constraints on trade and employment imposed by their neighbor. My students talked about agriculture and business and machinery. Reluctantly they sometimes talked about mathematics or English or their grades. In the evenings I could get them engaged in conversations about their girlfriends or boyfriends. The boys would talk to me about football, but they spoke only of the game itself, not the national teams or the professionals for these things were not familiar to them. Their evenings played no TV and little radio. They held dances and put on plays. They talked among themselves a great deal. Their culture was built on deep social interactions with a small group of people, creating a people immensely talented at being friendly.

"Of course I could never fit in, not as if I came from Lesotho. I tried to learn the language and the culture. I learned how to wear a blanket, how to tie it like a man and not like a boy. I learned a dozen ways to say hello with their associated hand movements. I learned what to expect at a party. On the latter point, the expectation was: not much. They drank and talked. The young people, even up to my age, would play music, and an individual or two might dance at a favorite number. The big song when I lived there was Marvin Gaye's 'Sexual Healing.'

"After I finished my private language lessons from a Peace Corps tutor, I could not speak Sesotho well enough to understand the radio or to say anything with subtlety. I could say enough that my students seemed to believe I could understand them. Nonetheless, they never spoke to me in Sesotho, even if I asked a question in their tongue. At the college where I taught, they were far more comfortable in Sesotho, but they had been drilled on how to treat people like me and there were some elements of that lesson I could never overcome. I noticed that when they were laughing about something as I came in the room, they would see me, quiet down, and switch to a new topic. I liked the fiction that I could follow their colloquial exchange, so I would smile or nod as if I overheard the joke.

"I recall my first day of teaching in Lesotho. I wrote my name on the board in classic fashion. I underlined my first name as I introduced myself and said this is what they should call me. Near the end of the day, a group of Basotho teachers came to me, 'Basotho" means people from Lesotho, and they said it was inappropriate for students to call a professor by his first name. Apparently, my status reflected on their status. There were only three or four Basotho teachers in our school who had themselves any college training. My PhD created, in some minds, even more distance between myself and those around me. I was searching for ways to diminish the gap. However, having the students call me Dr. MacNamara was not comfortable for me. It was the opposite of Sidney Poitier saying 'They call me Mr. Tibbs'.

"The male students were typically close to me in age. The students at our technical school had not been good enough to gain admission to the only regular university in the country. Therefore they had gone to South Africa to work in the mines after high school. Apartheid prohibited their settling near their work or having their wives or girlfriends there. They endured a bachelor existence for years at the mining camps. Their salaries were paid to their families in Lesotho. This ensured they would return home. On holidays, the few border crossings would be backed up for miles as the miners waited on foot to enter Lesotho.

"After some years of this, a few of the young men longed to return to their families or to start new branches of their families, and they returned to the underemployment of life in Lesotho. Work as a government agricultural extension agent did not pay acceptably or reliably, and it required attending our school for two years, but fifty or so young men a year managed to put aside their other commitments and came to us for training. They still wore the heavy rubber boots they were given to work in the mines. I did not sense a pride in the boots, just the practical matter that they were solid. ...Uncomfortable, unhealthy, impractical in the dry surface world of the school, but solid. I could not say to these men, 'give me my academic title'.

"I had to choose, I feared, whether to identify with the students or the faculty on my first day. I asked for an appointment with the head of the college. I did not know yet how to handle political matters in this culture, so I just said I had been approached about how formal to be and I wanted his guidance. The Principal derived his power over the faculty not so much from his position at the school as from his rank as a traditional chief and his connections to the national ruling elite. He had no concern for accommodating the sensitivities of his faculty. He listened carefully and asked a few questions to be sure he understood my problem. Then he relaxed visibly, secure that my issue was utterly insignificant and pleased for that. Casually he said, 'ask the students to call you whatever you like. Don't be concerned what the faculty thinks.' It was just the answer I wanted and he was entirely right, as proven by the lack of any resentment later from the faculty for my having ignored them.

"During my years of teaching in Lesotho, my students laughed at me when I greeted them in Sesotho and when I wore a blanket as they did in the winter. They called me by my first name and sometime, very rarely, by my Sesotho name. They sometimes slept in my class and cheated on my tests. Many of them put little effort into my homework and they must have seen, at times, that I was asking them to learn useless things for any life they were likely to experience. I was an inexperienced white man in a country surrounded by apartheid, a country where all the largest commercial enterprises were owned by South African whites, yet a country with no white citizens. In this politically and emotionally stressful environment, there was not a single incident during those years when any student, including those who were not in my courses, showed me even the slightest disrespect.

"My officemate told me once that his only knowledge of white people when he was a boy was the excitement of seeing them drive past his village. The village children always had an eye out for the cars of the white people. They would run to the road and shout "*Sequoea! Lipongpong!*' which means "white person! Candy!" Sometimes, the people inside the car would roll down the window, briefly letting the dust inside, and toss wrapped candies onto the road. He asked me to never give candy to the children. He asked me to never toss anything to anybody in his country. He also tried to interest me as a partner in a vending machine, but I was insufficiently interested in becoming rich to participate.

"After leaving Lesotho, I was stationed in Washington. Lesotho remained for me a unique, early professional experience to which I compared all subsequent assignments. It was my professional starting point, a home where I easily made my professional mistakes within an uncritical and forgiving crowd.

"After five or six years, however, I managed to find an assignment that would briefly take me back to Lesotho. I wondered what I might recognize and whether I would find anyone I remembered. The visit began auspiciously with a landing at the new airport. I drove to town on a new road. This beginning to my trip, however, ended my tour of new economic development. There was a new bank in town, but I never went inside. Otherwise I could discern no advance amid the considerable decline.

"The roads that could not become any worse were no worse. One of the two international hotels had changed its name, having been bought by the other international hotel. One of the two movie theaters had closed. I was surprised that the better of the theaters was the one that failed until I learned its failure was due to its proximity to the headquarters of the opposition party. People stayed away so they would not be associated with politics. I had always thought the theater was a hazard because its ticket window consisted of a sheet of glass with the center-bottom broken out. To buy a ticket, the customer had to place a hand through the ragged glass hole. I was certain someone would slit a wrist someday. The less worthy theater, i.e., the one that had stayed in business, had so many broken seats that it was difficult to find even two adjacent ones that were habitable. In that theater, I watched *Easy Rider* when it was unbanned by South Africa, ten years late. It was a cold day so I was wearing a blanket and sipping coffee from a cracked porcelain cup, like everyone else in the theater.

"When I returned to Lesotho, I stayed at the local hotel on Kingsway (the main street), next to the movie theater, rather than at one of the two international hotels. I washed my face, changed my shirt, and walked outside to see what I would remember in town. I was not past the shadow of my hotel when I heard my name called from across the street. As I walked the length of town that afternoon, covering less than a mile but more than two hours, I was accompanied every step by some friend. Most of them were former students whose names I did not remember. They told me tales about other former students and where they had gone. They told me of every member of the college staff, most of whom had not gone anywhere at all. They insisted I tell them of everything I had done, and consoled me for my lack of children and for the long delay in my return.

"I cannot recall what I saw of town that day. I remember only their faces with the clean, dark, smooth skin of healthy thirty-somethings in southern Africa. And their constant, excited chatter. They seemed desperately happy to see me and they were confident that I wanted to know about each of them, whether present or not. I was conscious that they were not happy to see me because my unexpected arrival had broken their boredom. These urban graduates, the ones working in town, were mostly employed and relatively busy. I felt as the prodigal son, which was surprising because I had never been part of the family."

My seatmate had remained awake and attentive through my speech. "It is a beautiful answer to my poor question. So you are going back again to your home?"

"Unfortunately no. Close. Johannesburg is close but I am changing planes for Windhoek. I have work in Namibia for a couple weeks."

"As you say, you will be close. You could take a weekend off to visit your friends."

"I would like to think I still have friends there. I have not kept in touch with anyone. I was there before the internet. The mail was never good enough for the kind of friends we were. If I do not go back, everyone will still be young, even me. My dog will still be chasing chickens on the farm. If I do go back, it will not be to the place I knew."

"That is how home is. My parents are late. My children are scattered across the globe looking for the most expensive colleges I can afford. But I have new family every time I return and they all need to know me and I need to know them," the Ghanaian added.

"Where are you living now? Do you get back to Keta regularly?"

"I live in The City." The man laughed to himself but it came out as a chuckle. "New York City, I mean. It's not the only city but we are egocentric enough to think that way most of the time. I travel for my work.

Always to Africa and back. I get to Ghana many times every year. I go to Keta once or twice. For me it is a large village. I visit my chief. I bring presents for the children. I sit and talk to people I have always known and any new ones who are visiting like me. Of course I have no farm. There is nothing for me to do there except be part of the place. I will always be going back there."

"You have a beautiful answer too."

The man leaned back and Bretton took that as the end of the conversation for the time. Eventually, the air hostess came by to take drink orders. Bretton perked up as he did not like to miss any distraction during the long flight. He ordered a ginger ale and she handed him a small packet of pretzels.

"You could take a few days off?" was inflected as a question.

"I should; you're right. No time. I have to get back to DC. My trips are almost a separate job from what I do in the office and the office work builds up when I am away. If I am gone for two weeks, I return to a nightmare of demands. If I am gone three weeks, I have missed deadlines and people are starting to work around me. I don't want them to know they can get along without me."

Their drinks arrived and the man held up his glass. "On to Windhoek!"

Bretton clinked his plastic cup onto the man's and answered, "Say 'hello' for me to the peace and security of Keta!"

There was more they could have discussed in the next nine hours of flight. They had much in common and an ability to communicate. Perhaps they did not want to spoil the closure of their toasts. Perhaps the Ghanaian did not wish to exclude the man on his left for he turned that way to converse after dinner but right then Bretton was too sleepy engage further. The exchange with the Ghanaian was not forgotten, however. With his eyes closed, leaning back as far as the airline would allow, Bretton regretted that he would not be seeing friends, except for the nagging hope, a hope he had hardly admitted to himself until this period of leisure, that a woman he used to knew and was now stationed in the Namibia office might remember him and regard him as a friend. She might show him around Windhoek and who knows how it might turn out?

IV. Namibia (2003)

Anjali met him with the Embassy driver at the Windhoek airport. She kissed him once on each cheek and smiled broadly and genuinely. "Now I remember why I liked you so much," he told her. "How generous you are to meet me at the plane! At my level of the bureaucracy, I am used to seeing only the driver for the first 24 hours."

"Nonsense, Bretton. Your trip is a top priority for our mission. We will do everything we can to impress you."

"Well, I am impressed. How much budget should I be recommending for next year?"

Anjali was just as slim as he remembered, perhaps too slim for some tastes but she looked very interesting to Bretton. She was a tiny woman with dark, very clear skin and long raven tresses. He knew she was from South Asia, but was not clear if she was from Bangladesh. That would have been his guess except that he would not guess. He used to know and it would be insulting to show that he had forgotten. It had been just over three years since she left Washington. He had known her there although they had not worked together. She had asked his advice on her career, regarding him as a mentor, a role he did not accept although he answered her enquiries as well as he could. This was her second posting. Her face had matured nicely. They had lunch together a few times in Washington and exchanged a few e-mails when she first went overseas. He had enjoyed her company, enjoyed being near an attractive young woman who hung on his every word as if he actually knew how things worked. There was nothing to tie them once she started her career. He was no mentor for full-time overseas work.

"We will drop you at the hotel so you can recover from your flight. Then the driver will take you round to see the office and meet with the Mission Director for a few minutes. If you feel up to it, my husband will pick you up later for dinner. You have to see our little Nina. I hope you don't mind eating at our home. She is too small to take to a restaurant."

Hearing she had a husband and a daughter was comforting to Bretton and he felt some unrecognized tension escape from his chest as he settled back into his seat more comfortably.

"You have a daughter? Congratulations, Anjali. I am sure she is a lucky girl."

"You never came to visit me when I was in the Nigeria mission. I have been busy."

"It's hard to keep up with you folks in the foreign service."

"True. But we know that so we keep long memories."

"I want to see your girl as soon as possible. Of course it is not possible to see her until I wash up and put on some clothes that have no memory of me and the two guys pressed against me for the past ten hours. What's your husband's name and what time should I meet him?"

"We will pick you up at the hotel at seven o'clock. I remember why I liked you so much. You are funny in your own dry way."

"Hmmm," was all Bretton answered with a wave because he did not want to end the conversation with something that was not funny. She did not mention her husband's name.

At the office, Bretton was met at the security gate by the Mission Director which seemed to be a good sign. He shook Bretton's hand without looking him in the eye which was a bad sign. He gave his name without any further courtesies, "Hamilton Scott," a name destined for power. He was too young and too handsome. It was a small Mission with only one area of programing, fighting HIV/AIDS. He was less happy than Anjali about Bretton's arrival. The Director spoke of work while they walked to his office. Bretton had expected small talk, even looked forward to it. This was the moment when he might be invited to some social event to set the relationship up in friendly fashion. That the Director saw no need to be friendly, even though he did not know Bretton, was a sign that cooperation was not going to be good. When Mr. Scott was older, if he was successful, he would know that people like Bretton deserved a modicum of respect. They were there to serve him. Bretton would have to teach a portion of that lesson over the next two weeks.

"You know how much time we spend writing reports for Washington? Every year Congress says the paperwork has to be reduced but it only changes and gets harder because we have to learn the new system. We only have four Americans at his post and handle as much per person as any Mission in the world and that is why we can't get into the field for six months of the year-- endless writing reports."

Bretton knew this and he understood the Mission Director did not want to hear sympathetic words from Washington's representative. Bretton was his listening post for now,

"I'll see what I can do to adjust your reports to the new requirements without bothering you with questions. Don't worry about the requirements right away. Let me see how the data you have fits."

"What do you know about what we are doing here? Do you have some ideas on how to do things better? Has somebody else figured out how to get the clinics to treat women with the respect due a human being?"

"Maybe the annual health conference is the place to share those ideas. I am just here to cut into those Washington requirements. We've got to convince the AIDS Coordinator first of all that you are doing it right and then we have to convince the Secretary and then we have to convince OMB and then we have to convince Congress. You know, it won't be that hard. You're not trying to start something new. Let's just keep the flow going. You know how it works. You've got me as one more clerk working here for a couple weeks."

"Can you stay until the report is finished? Are you going to write it?"

"I don't know enough to write it. I can do some of the busywork. You know, there is plenty of that. I can give you a draft of some of the Director's commentary. I've seen a few of them before. You can correct it however you want, obviously. Some Directors find that having a draft in the right format helps them think through what they want to say. You won't have as much to worry about in the structure of the report, you know."

The Mission Direction was taken aback. This is what he wanted to hear although he had not realized it. He would not admit that this Washington bureaucrat would be of use other than to acknowledge the requirements for a strategic plan were stupidly conceived and oppressive so he moved on to explaining how things would work as determined by the Mission Director, i.e., himself. Anjali would be Bretton's control officer. Anything Bretton wanted would go through her. She would set up appropriate meetings with implementers and government officials. Bretton was not to meet with anyone except through Anjali. He could use the secretary for office matters but should avoid bothering her to the extent he could, and so on though minutia Bretton had heard before although he kept his attention intensely focused of the Director's words and took notes as if there was some gripping news in them.

The time approached 5:00. The Director made a point of saying he would be in the office for some hours yet but he understood Bretton would expect to be going back to the hotel soon. The Mission had a van that dropped off American staff at their homes for a modest monthly fee. They all lived in the same area of the suburbs, but the van could take him to his hotel without any charge. Bretton said he noticed the hotel was only five blocks away so he would walk. He liked disallowing the Mission Director from doing him one more favor.

At 7:00, Bretton was in the lobby to meet Anjali's husband. They recognized each other easily, two men looking around the room for a contact. Anjali's husband was on the way from his work to home. Anjali had already been home for 90 minutes and had dinner nearly ready when they walked in the door. The house was fragrant from the cooking. Her household help, she hesitated to call her a maid, had prepared the table and watched the baby girl while Anjali cooked. Bretton had tried little curry in his life but he trusted Anjali and found her enthusiasm for food, as for every other part of her life, infectious. He managed to eat more than she and her husband combined, and suspected that was a complement to the chef although he had only eaten what his taste desired once it met her cuisine.

《 《 《 《 ☒ 》 》 》 》

On his first morning in Namibia, Bretton was still running on adrenaline, pumped into his veins from the small glands on top of his kidneys as a result of his fear of failure. Coming to a new post always brought out his insecurities but long practice had enabled him to project calm confidence, temporarily fooling himself as much as anyone. He took his drug, adrenaline, and hoped it kept him going long enough to know what he was doing and to earn some confidence that it was going well. His morning routine was so well practiced he did not have to be aware of which four-star hotel was his home this week. The walk to the office was already familiar from his two passes the day before but still fresh enough to command his attention so he could put off

36

worrying about the job until he had returned to the Mission.

The secretary showed Bretton the TDY[3] desk. It was just a small wooden table in the hallway. There was not enough room for a person to pass by without leaning against his chair. He had access there to some Mission files. They were easy enough to navigate without bothering the staff further. It was an insult to offer him an accommodation so Spartan, doubtless an intentional slap in the face to "Washington." The U.S. government could afford better. If he complained, he would be regarded as insensitive to ask time and effort be dedicated to his comfort when they could be used to save lives. That is not the tradeoff he saw. He was there to ensure an accurate and persuasive strategic plan. He would save the Mission many hours of work, more hours than he would spend in the country. He was part of the machinery that saved lives. The person who contacts the American public and its elected representatives, the benefactors, is no more nor less essential to the outcome than the ones delivering assistance. It was not his comfort at issue, rather, his efficiency. Nonetheless he would not need to compromise on the quality of the report. He could do most of the work from his hotel room once he downloaded last year's working documents and the current year's performance data.

Once he found the files that would get him started, his confidence surged. This was familiar territory. Within a day he would be so immersed in the local data on HIV/AIDS, he could talk with the Mission staff and sound as if he knew their operation. The Mission Director was unlikely to acknowledge it, but he

---

[3] TDY – temporary duty

would notice. Bretton kept a low profile for the first day or two both to avoid making a fool of himself and to short-circuit any claim that he was taking up the staff's time. He took the outline he brought with him of an ideal report and inserted comparable sections from last year's Namibia report. He could then simplify the draft by removing irrelevant sections. With only one objective in Namibia, reducing HIV/AIDS, much of the outline could be truncated. He praised the computer for its ability to generate a draft so easily. He was about to begin inserting the new data into the draft when Anjali came by.

"Do you have plans for lunch?" she asked.

"My only plan was to skip lunch. I was completely sated last night. Besides, the hotel breakfast comes with the room so I eat everything for the day before getting out into the world. But I'd be happy to have a tea or something with you if you are offering."

"We always eat at the Embassy café. It's not bad. We can just go down whenever you're ready and we'll probably see some of the staff you need to know."

"I would be good to have a few minutes to talk with you while you're wearing your control officer hat. Are you ready now? I can stop this any time."

Bretton had a slice of pie to go with his tea so he would seem relatively normal about lunch. At least he did not worry she would be insulted by his light fare; a woman so slim could not be eating full lunches every day. Besides, they had eaten lunches before and she knew his habits.

"I'd like a meeting of all the project managers on Wednesday. I will be ready by then to ask a few questions."

"There are just three of us. How much time do we want for each meeting?"

"No, just one meeting with everybody. I doubt it would take an hour but we should schedule it for an hour anyway. Can't be wasting your time you know."

"Oh don't worry about Hamilton. He's not serious. He knows we need you here."

"I'm not worried about him, but I want to make him happy. Don't you know I want to make everyone happy?"

"More dry irony."

"I plan to insert a generous portion into the strategy. Think anyone but you and me would notice?"

"I don't know. It might it easier to read."

"You know no one in Washington will ever read it, not the whole thing, that is? Someone will read every part, but not the same someone. Most of it will only be read by one person. That is what we want to happen, only have one person read each part. If a technical reader passes something on to someone else to see, it can only be trouble for us. The cover letter, that's what gets read. It has to be good, instill confidence in your mission by the layers of decision makers, provide some pithy quotes that can be used to prove to various players in Washington that you know what you are doing."

"Hamilton says I should set meetings for you with the government right away. Is there anyone you know you want to see or should I just work that out with him?"

"Let's not do that. Don't worry about Hamilton."

"What do you mean? You want to do it later?"

"I don't want to do it at all. I'd say let's just do one with the Minister you know best, Finance or Health. Include Hamilton and he can say he brought in

Washington to see the operation. Fifteen minutes in the Minister's office. I'll wear a starched shirt for Hamilton's benefit."

"You don't want your own meetings?"

"Just me and my laptop. I don't have time to learn Namibia. I trust you guys and your data. But I will check the data, mainly for consistency. If I have any spare time, I will devote it to getting to know my friend once again. You know, work my way through Nigeria and two years down here. Also, I'm doing research on what to see on the weekend."

The day passed quickly. He hardly talked with anyone after lunch. He was getting ready for the meeting with program staff when he would make his request for more data. They knew what went into the report so it would only be a formality to ask for it. At 5:00, the Mission emptied out, local staff went home to their families and the Americans caught the van on its scheduled run. Bretton walked back to his hotel and continued to work on the report. He wanted a complete draft before the weekend so he could devote his second week responding to the comments from the Mission. His schedule would put pressure on the Mission Director. The Director would have the draft late Friday and could not get comments back before Monday. If he took the weekend off, he would be holding up the report and Bretton would have to take the weekend off to await feedback. At least it would feel that way. Bretton wanted to get out of Windhoek for a couple days. He might never get to Namibia again. The little fantasy he had allowed himself of a trip upcountry with Anjali was long gone but a memorable solo expedition was still in the cards. Comfortable countries are all alike: every uncomfortable country is uncomfortable in its own way and Bretton was ever intrigued to see the way in each country he visited.

By 11 pm his adrenaline had run out, his glands were drained. He bought a cola at the machine in the hall and took a chocolate bar out of the minibar for the last meal of the day. The draft was over a hundred fifty pages, about half of which related to Namibia and the rest stolen from other country reports. He would get it under a hundred pages by Friday. Cutting pages was much easier for him than adding material. He could sleep without terror. Maybe the next day would descend into routine. He did not look forward to meetings. He preferred the job was just between himself and the data.

Friday arrived much as he expected, but soon fell apart. Anjali came quietly down the hall to his desk and put her hand on his shoulder, breaking his focus on the computer screen. "Hamilton needs to see you right away. Something's up. I don't know what."

"Bretton." Hamilton stood up to greet Bretton for the first time since he arrived. "How is the strategy going? I heard you have a draft already."

"I have put together what your staff prepared. I should be able to give you a rough draft today." He was going to continue to brief the Mission Director on his progress and hoped to instill a commitment by Hamilton to work on the weekend, but Hamilton was not interested at this moment in the report.

"I got a call about you. You're going to have to leave early." He was going to continue, but Bretton knew it was his place to object to this proposal.

"We are on track to get this thing done. I can't cut it any shorter than it is."

"The *Chargé d'Affaires* in Lesotho says you're known there. Minister of Finance is a friend of yours?

The *Chargé* says he is not cooperating and he wants to talk to you. Asked me a favor on behalf of the Ambo but, of course, it is your call. There's time to get back here and finish up if you can stay out a little longer."

"I don't know the Ambassador in Lesotho. Haven't been there in years. I heard a former colleague became Minister of Finance but I doubt he would remember me. Pshoene, that's his name. Very bright guy. Albino and blind as a guy could be that still drives. If he is still alive, he must have stopped driving."

"Yeah, Pshoene. That's what he said. Some kind of negotiation and he wants you there tomorrow. Sunday at the latest. I said we would get you there. We can do that, right?"

Bretton wondered what the Lesotho Ambassador had to offer Hamilton Scott in exchange for this cooperativeness. Lesotho was a tiny country and the Ambassadorship did not go to powerful people. But Hamilton was suddenly impressed and Bretton found that amusing. Going to Lesotho would be fun. Being called in suddenly meant he was not expected to take anything, therefore he could not feel guilty for his lack of preparation. He did not promise to deliver whatever the Ambassador wanted so it would be a low stress visit. He had made arrangements for a driver and a car for the weekend, but that could be rescheduled.

"OK. Sounds like a mystery. If you can live with some delay in the strategic plan, we can do this, whatever it is."

"The *Chargé* said you speak Sesotho."

"I learned a little when I lived there. Enough to get along with the students. I can't imagine how that would have reached the ears of the current Embassy."

"Well, someone obviously remembers you. I sure did not offer you up. It's gonna mess with our schedules around here. I already moved everybody around so they'd be available to you. But we are all on the same side here so let's send you out to Pshoene, out to our Ambassador in mighty Lesotho."

Mighty Lesotho? wondered Bretton to himself. Namibia was 3.1 million population to Lesotho's 1.8 million, hardly a difference supporting ridicule. But Hamilton's jibe renewed the question in Bretton's mind of why Hamilton was being so supportive. He considered asking Anjali to see if she could worm some hint from Hamilton about why he was kowtowing, but he quickly dismissed this idea. Anjali was far too honest to possess the guile needed for that question.

"So," he said to indicate he was taking a new tack, "do you know this Ambassador? Any hints for me?"

"I haven't met him yet but I know about him. Very young; well-connected apparently."

"Well-connected doesn't get you to Lesotho," Bretton said. *Or Namibia,* he thought.

"It does if you're young enough. He's just warming up."

"I suppose that is a tip of sorts. I would not want to run into him and assume he's the Fulbright Fellow." *And I will expect him to assert himself excessively to show he is the boss,* he added but not aloud. *Maybe that is enough to explain Hamilton. Maybe he is impressed by the potential influence the Lesotho Ambassador could exert in the future. And maybe Pshoene's request explains the Ambassador. But why would Pshoene want me after all these years?*

On his last visit to the country, Bretton had not met Pshoene, probably had not even given him a thought. They had liked each other when Bretton lived there but were not close at all. On the other hand, as far as Bretton knew, no one had been close to Pshoene back then. He was too serious to be enjoyed and too strange, being albino, to be absorbed automatically into the group. *I wonder if I know anyone in Lesotho with the craftiness and the stature to figure out Pshoene's angle.*

Saying goodbye to Anjali on Saturday afternoon, Bretton sincerely regretted leaving her. She had lost the potential, never realistic anyway, to become intimate, but she was a pleasure to be near. It was refreshing to know people in his business could survive with her innocence. Dedication to the job of assistance was typical, although not universal, but it was usually motivated to some degree by dreams of career enhancement or public glory. And the work was often made tawdry by corrupt partners in the recipient countries. The innocent do not rise to the top in any country, and seldom rise at all in the poorest countries.

"Much too quick a visit, Anjali." He shook her hand and held on to it for an extra moment. Kisses on the cheeks were probably the right level of departure ritual but he felt self-conscious about an intimation of intimacy. "I hope I can get back here after a quick trip to Lesotho but, as you have seen, I do not control my own time."

"What do you mean, you might not come back? I can't write the report. What are we supposed to do?"

"Anjali, I'm not abandoning you. Go over the draft I left for a few days and then I will know what Hamilton has got me into. No matter what, I will be helping with it. I was never going to provide the program substance. I can do the format stuff via e-mail."

"I shouldn't say this... Hamilton is very good at some things, but he can't really write well. He probably pretends it does not matter if you are here or not but he is counting on you to justify our budget for next year. Maybe also to justify a big job for him after Namibia. He told me you know the decision makers in Washington."

"You surprise, Ms. Anjali. I did not know you were watching the politics of our little bureaucracy."

"I'm not. It's just what he said."

"I was referring to your understanding Hamilton's pretension as braggadocio."

"I would never say that."

"No, you are too nice to say that although you understand it. You are absolutely right not to say it. Never say bad things about your boss. Or your employees. Or your colleagues, I guess. But keep your eyes open and see them for what they are."

"You better come back. If you can't make it next week or this trip, come back anyway. I need to get you into the bush."

"I'd love that. Next time."

V. Back to Lesotho (2003)

Back in Jo-burg airport after 20 years, Bretton did not feel the urge toward enmity that had underlain his passage through the airport back during the apartheid era. His plane was not met this time by an armored personnel carrier or men carrying automatic weapons at the ready. This was the first time since 9/11 that he noticed an airport where security had declined.

45

When he lived in Lesotho, there were few flights from Jo-burg and it was customary to spend one night in the airport hotel before catching the morning run to Maseru. It was a good arrangement when coming from the States as it let him catch up on lost sleep and begin his adjustment to jet lag. Connections were more frequent now and he was scheduled for a 90-minute layover before the final short flight. Coming from Namibia, he needed no recovery from jet lag

He waited for his luggage to come down the chute. Lesotho had long been in a customs union with South Africa, which collected the duties from travelers and importers to Lesotho, and passed along some portion of it to the Basotho government. During apartheid, everyone in Lesotho was suspicious of everything associated with the South African government and suspected the South Africans made excessive profit on the customs union, but no one was in a position to monitor the revenues so it was not a public issue.

On most of Bretton's trips to Lesotho, he had carried only his personal items and paid no customs duty but there was one time during his second year of teaching when he had taken a vacation to Hong Kong. The exchange rate for a person whose wages were paid in dollars was extremely favorable and he bought two extra suitcases to carry all his purchases. Most notably, he had bought a serious camera, a Bronica 2¼ x 2¼ with loads of accessories. He had studied camera magazines for months before the trip and knew all the prices in New York. In Hong Kong he was paying about half as much. He had also bought several cheaper cameras for students at the college. He had started a photography club and loaned his camera to the students, none of whom had a camera. He bought two inexpensive cameras for students who asked him for this favor and two cameras for the club to use and two cameras to be given as prizes at the end of the school year. He was not sure what the students would need to do to earn a prize but he was sure they would be excited when he announced the cameras.

In the Jo-burg airport after the Hong Kong trip, he took his luggage, now three suitcases, to the hotel for the night. He put the most expensive things he had bought into the smallest suitcase so he could carry it on the plane and not check it. Lost luggage was common in those days. He had the Bronica and its lenses as well as a large set of oriental silverware that weighted down the small case to the limit of its capacity. He planned to carry it smartly so no customs agent would look at it too closely. The next morning, he had breakfast and returned to the airport lounge to await his flight. Not surprisingly, he met a couple Europeans he knew in the lounge, also on their way back to Lesotho. He was regaling them with his stories of bargains to be had in Hong Kong when two customs agents came up to the group and asked for him by name. Very politely they asked to see his luggage. They had the customs form he had filled in saying, as usual, that he had nothing to declare.

"Of course," Bretton said. "I have plenty of time before my flight," and he looked toward one of the European men standing with him, a savvy Belgian with no sympathy for the RSA, and rolled his eyes toward his small suitcase. The Belgian took a step over to the small, heavy suitcase to show he understood and Bretton marched off with the customs agents carrying his other two suitcases. The younger agent, thin, white and shy, tried to help by carrying one of them, but the older agent told him not to touch the suitcase, as if that would invalidate whatever contraband might be inside. They stopped in a small, empty room just off the main hall.

"This is just a formality, you understand," the older agent said and then he motioned to the younger one to do the inspection and he wandered off. Bretton unlocked the suitcases. The young agent opened them, side-by-side on the floor. They were neatly packed, largely filled with new things in unopened boxes. There were also several shirts and a jacket with price tags attached. Bretton stood while the agent kneeled beside the suitcases and gently pawed through them. *No guns or drugs or booze or pornography or political pamphlets. Isn't that what you are trying to find?* thought Bretton as if his thoughts could carry into the boy's head, but he said nothing aloud.

"Is any of this stuff new?" the agent asked.

You may be simple but you cannot be stupid enough to wonder that, thought Bretton. *So why are you asking? Are you giving me a chance to admit my false papers?*

"Let me see. It has been a few days since I packed my bags. I got most of this in South Africa before my trip but I never got around to using it. But now that you mention it, I did buy a couple cameras for friends. I forgot about them. They should have been on the customs form, I guess."

"All right. Close up the cases. We will write a revised form." Bretton paid $14 in customs and he never knew if the boy was too nervous to demand more, or if he was afraid of Bretton for some obscure reason, or if he just had mercy on the American passing through. Bretton always thought his projecting confidence might have induced the older guard to move on to more likely quarry and whether admitting to something might have offered the boy a way to save face with his superiors without inciting a confrontation.

Now, years later, he filled in his form again checking "nothing to declare" but he would have paid whatever customs was due since the apartheid government was gone and he had enough income now that the duties would not have been felt.

This time he saw no one he knew in the waiting room or in the Maseru airport. A driver from the Embassy was holding a sign with his name and thus connected quickly. He was in his hotel less than an hour after departing from Jo-burg, with nothing to do until morning and still too early for dinner. Was this home then? ...As he had claimed so romantically on the plane? He had not forgotten his claim. It had been hollow when he made it although it was an accurate impression when he made that first visit back to Maseru. Fifteen years since then eroded the memory. Bretton did not want to walk down Kingsway, the main street, because he knew no one would be running out of any shop calling his name.

Nonetheless, it was nice that Pshoene remembered him. Pshoene would not be likely to recognize him, assuming he could see at all. Bretton was no longer thin as a teenager or lithe as an athlete. His balding pate might be a surprise. Pshoene, however, would be recognizable. His kinky blond hair might have given way to baldness without changing his appearance significantly. He was already walking with a stagger and a stoop when he was thirty. Bretton could not imagine him without his coke-bottle glasses and pale, scabby skin. More fairly, Pshoene had done well, as well as someone could do in Lesotho. Minister of Finance was a responsible and influential position. Bretton was sure his former friend had earned his way to his position with competence and perseverance. It spoke well of the government that it had chosen Pshoene.

Bretton went down to the bar to kill a few minutes until he was hungry. Maybe eating a few salted nuts would give him an appetite. The décor of the hotel had changed since he knew it as the Hilton. It was the Avani now. The huge basketry chandelier he remembered hanging above the lobby was gone, and he regretted that. The management was still trying to make the place look African although the operation was thoroughly European in concept and execution. The late sun filled the lobby through two stories of windows. When he went into the bar where it was dark; he was blind for a few moments. No one was sitting at the bar but a white couple was seated in a booth. They sat on the same side of the table, apparently because that made it easier to snuggle. Bretton was disappointed. He calculated his odds of finding someone he knew in the bar of the principle hotel in an Anglophone African country at about fifty-fifty.

What'll you have?" the bartender asked when Bretton did not immediately make his request.

"I don't want anything in particular, but I would like something. What do have that's simple and short? No, don't tell me. Just give me one."

"Ntate MacNamera? You have come back!" The bartender sounded very happy to recognize Bretton.

"How could you tell who this old man used to be?" Bretton looked into the face of the bartender and shook his hand. "How did I know you, Ntate?"

"You taught me maths. You used to race with us; your brain against a class full of calculators. You almost always won. What a brain!"

"I was trying to show you that you don't need a calculator. I only did very easy problems in that contest. It is faster to see the answer to an easy problem than it is to type out the numbers without thinking. Especially for the students back then when calculators were new things. I was trying to get you to think. Do you remember that?"

"Yeah, yeah, yeah. You always said we should think. We should not just believe everything. In fact, you said we should not believe anything. We should always figure it out for ourselves. You are the only teacher who ever said these things."

"I was an idealist."

"Maybe that works for you but it does not work for us. We need calculators."

"And now you work at the Avani. Is it better than farming?"

The bartender smiled broadly. "Good times."

"Do you know what the other students are doing? How many are farming?"

"I know where everybody is." He spoke as he poured a whiskey for Bretton. "Some have farms. Not too many do it very much. Women do most of the farmwork. For men it is just part-time."

"Did the agriculture college turn out to be useful for the students?"

"Do not worry Ntate Bretton. The college was very good. We are happy we went there."

"Yes, I bet you are," Breton responded in an atypical slow, subdued drawl. "Is anyone teaching farmers things from the college?" He wondered if the agricultural extension services they had envisaged existed into the present.

"Yes, Ntate. We are all teaching sheep husbandry and poultry and agronomy. We don't teach any maths though. We use the maths. All of us do."

"Do you use my maths in the casino?"

"Oh no, Ntate Bretton. We do not go in there. We do not have money to throw away."

"I hope you do not throw it away... I am sorry. I forgot your name."

"No you did not forget it. You never knew my name! I was only in one class with you and I was very quiet. You see I am not quiet any more. I talk to people all the time. I think I got confidence when I got a degree."

Bretton worked his mind to recall how to ask in Sesotho for a person's name. It must have been one of the first things he learned, but it would not come to him. "I have been away too long. Please your name."

"M. Phaki." They shook hands.

"What does the 'M' stand for?"

"Just call me 'M'. I was always just 'M'."

"All right, M. Good to see you again." Someone else came into the bar and M went to his table to take his order. He repeated the order through a window to the kitchen and returned to Bretton but did not say anything.

"You can get dinner served here?" asked Bretton.

"Yes. We have a good cook. What would you like?"

"*Moqoene.*" Bretton had asked for a small patty of flour cooked in lard. It was the Sesotho version of a donut.

M laughed. "We only do Western food. You must visit your Sesotho friends."

"I could get a hamburger?"

"Just like Wimpy's!"

"I'd like to eat. Just order something for me."

M went over to the kitchen window and ordered a dinner for Bretton.

When he returned to the bar, Bretton asked "Do you know where the college staff is these days?"

"Who would you like to see?"

Bretton knew the answer to that question instantly but he hesitated. He did not want to give his true answer. It would not matter in the least if he gave another name or two. But the answer was so certain it lingered on his tongue until he gave it.

"Pheta. I'd like to see Pheta."

M did not react immediately. "You were still here when they found him, but maybe they did not tell you what happened. We do not tell foreigners everything. You knew him. You should know. The night he disappeared, you see, a couple nights after the raid, he went out cattin'. He always had a girlfriend on the side and what a beautiful, wonderful wife he had. His wife did not catch him that night. It was the boyfriend of the girl. He was waiting for Pheta. Didn't know it was going to be Pheta but probably would have done it anyway. They cut him up, maybe before he died. Kept some parts of him for witchcraft. You know which parts. Ones with special power. Ones no one wants to lose. It was hard on his wife to have him go that way. She was hurt publically. Makes it worse."

"I'd like to see his wife. Is she still around?"

"Don't think about Pheta. His wife does not want to think about him again. She's forgot him by now. I think you would rather see Matseliso."

"I don't remember a Matseliso."

"Oh sure you don't," the bartender mocked sarcastically. "You probably already saw her. It doesn't matter to me. What I see in here! Who cares? She doesn't have a boyfriend now. Lives with her daughter. Oh wait; she was not Matseliso after you left. She was Palesa when you were here. Didn't you hear she had a baby?"

"So the baby is named Tseliso?" Bretton knew the custom some Basotho mothers adopt of calling themselves after their children. The prefix "ma" means "the mother of."

"Don't worry. Tseli was born more than a year after you left. We all noticed that."

"You are right. I do remember a Palesa. I won't be looking for her. I would rather remember her as she was and have her remember me as I was."

"Yes. We always knew you were smart. You don't need that person now."

Bretton did not like M's way of speaking about Palesa. He might need her more now than he did when he knew her but he was sure they were not the same people they had been. No one was after this many years. Suddenly he did not want to talk to or, more precisely, listen to this stranger who knew so much. His dinner arrived and Bretton took it to one of the dark corners of the room.

Like so many hotel bars and cafes across Africa and Asia and Eastern Europe where Bretton spent evenings alone, more nights than he spent at home in Washington, which he never regarded as home, the

Maseru Avani offered quiet privacy more valuable than its innumerable drinks or unimaginative dining. Bretton relaxed for the first time since leaving Namibia. There was nothing he had to do until he retired for the night. He would eat slowly, savor his hamburger with its local peculiarities of bun and condiments, and think back on Palesa, pleasant thoughts he had not called up for some years.

VI. Palesa (1983)

Lesotho was known in the foreign service as the country of bald, fat women. Bretton doubted that was a fair characterization but in his first trip around the town of Maseru he understand how it got that name. He did not realize at the time that there was a custom of shaving one's head on the first anniversary of the death of a loved one, usually a parent. And if the loved one particularly deserved commemoration, one's head might be shaved on the second and other anniversaries of death. It was never clear to Bretton, no matter how long he lived in Lesotho whether the hair of most Basotho women grew very slowly or if it was extreme kinkiness that kept it always close to the scalp.

As for fat, the women were not obese in the way some Americans get, but it was true that the women were commonly heavier than would be considered stylish in the West. This was a product of the hard work they did and the very starchy diet of mealies, that is, ground corn. With very carefully worded questions to avoid insult, Bretton had asked a few men, once he got to know them well, why the women of Lesotho were so broad while the men generally remained thin. He never got an answer to this question because everyone he asked was perplexed. As far as they knew, that is simply what women and men are like.

There were exceptions. Palesa was tall and tight. She would have been fashionable in New York City or Hollywood, particularly with her almond eyes and smooth black skin. After a few months in Lesotho, Bretton did not think of her hair as short; it was a mini-Afro. In fact, her hair was longer than most, "deeper" might be a better term for her kinky mat, since she had not lost any important relatives. Palesa was troubled by her figure and asked Bretton confidentially one day if he, with his store of Western knowledge, knew of something she could do or take to make her fill out more. Bretton made an effort to look serious when he wanted to laugh at her question. She was the local beauty and neither she nor her peers knew it.

That moment, the question and his respectful and supportive answer, was a shared intimacy. After that Bretton felt more comfortable in looking at her, not ogling her, but noticing her and enjoying her to himself. She noticed him and waited for him to do something more. Even though she lacked confidence in her appearance, she knew there was enough about her to interest men and had some experience with what men do about that. They did not talk much but were consistent in greeting each other more vigorously than basic courtesy would demand. Bretton saw her as too beautiful for him. Despite her question to him that day, and he knew it to have been a sincere question, he could not imagine she would take him seriously as a partner. As a foreigner, a relatively young, tall, and minimally athletic one, he might be an interesting thought to her. He must have seemed rich although he knew otherwise. But he had the insurmountable handicaps of being skinny as an adolescent, boney-faced, very poor in speaking Sesotho, and entirely unfamiliar with local styles and practices. By any measure, he was socially awkward even if there were good reasons for it. Rather than demonstrate his weaknesses, be kept his distance. It was better, he believed, to enjoy her glances and imagine her interest than to prove to her how misplaced her interest was.

However, Bretton was no longer an adolescent and he refused to be a victim of his personal insecurities or to accept a celibate life over the next two years so he looked for a quiet moment and screwed up his courage to have a personal conversation.

"Palesa, we should talk more." It was not a clever line for picking up a girl at a college mixer but it was a modest and clear line for the situation. They already knew each other. Palesa did not seem to Bretton to be a girl who would respond well to someone trying to be cute, if he could even pull off cute in a foreign culture.

"We don't need to talk, Abuti Bretton." "Abuti" meant "boy" and was used in lieu of the more respectful "Ntate," meaning literally "father," but Bretton knew it was used to indicate familiarity among the students, perhaps the way "brother" is used in some American subcultures. He was not sure if it was meant in a good way from Palesa.

"Yes, we do not need to talk, but I would like to talk with you. I would like to know you better."

"It is very dangerous for me, Abuti. Basotho do not want me to be with you."

Bretton wanted to ask her why and whether there was something he could do about it and what she wanted and how serious this objection was but she melted away before he could get any further question out. He looked down and continued walking across the parking lot to his car with a sense of relief. He had spoken up. He had been clear and she knew what was on his mind and that he was not afraid of her or of women generally or of Basotho women. But if he was so unafraid, why was he relieved to find she was out of reach and why was her simple statement accepted so easily? *Never mind. It is good enough to just look at her. Maybe another woman will turn up.* He believed his thought but it was Palesa he wanted.

As literature claims, love will have its way and as nature demands, sexual attraction will work its magic and as history teaches, close contact between young men and women will find a path through any silly interpretations of social grace. In this case, whatever it was, was advanced by the woman. After more than a month of coy glances unbecoming to adults of Western or African origins, Bretton happened to ride the college bus into Maseru to do some shopping. He rarely took the bus since he had a car, but it just struck him one day as a good idea to share this small experience of the students. He was one of the last to get on the bus and the first thing he noticed was Palesa sitting near the back. The seat in front of her was open so he went right up to it, knowing he would have a chance to smile at her from nearby when he sat down. He felt bold and made a small joke to her by muttering "*Khotso,*" as he took his seat. It was an excessively formal greeting for them, meaning "have peace." He liked sitting in front of her, knowing she was looking at the back of his head and, he hoped, thinking of his presence. And then he felt her hands on the back of his neck. She began to massage him. His first sense was fear but that soon passed. What was there to fear? It was just a beautiful woman touching him. Why had he been so secretive with her up until then? Was he unsure of her, of whether she was interested in his intimacies, or was he unsure of himself, if he had the courage to work through the inevitable difficulties of another culture? Something felt wrong in it. He could not relax. He simply felt he should have talked to her more directly, more personally, before touching in public. In addition, it was in front of the students and would be certain to cause a stir to see one of their teachers doing this with one of the other staff, even apart from the nationality issue. And yet there was no stir, not that Bretton could detect. No one looked at them. No one whispered. Bretton had seen students touching in public, just as they do in America, but he had not seen anyone older than student age doing so.

Bretton got off the bus at the first stop, the grocery store. He would walk back to his home after making his purchases. Palesa did not get up and barely looked at him when he rose. He smiled at her but refrained from thanking her. He left with a sour taste, wondering what he should have done differently. He could not see what might have been better. Why had she no smile for him when he left? The meaning of her touch was a complete mystery but nearly all the possible explanations he could imagine were positive, up to the point where he might have fallen short somehow. There was still a lingering idea that she might have been mocking him or just playing with him to show she could.

They went another week without speaking directly although they saw each other in the staff room at morning tea and passed in the hallways from time to time. Bretton always looked at her and she always looked back and Bretton told himself this was necessary and acceptable. He was not especially surprised or excited when Palesa invited him to a party in her rondavel. She made it clear there would be other people there. He knew which rondavel was hers and knocked at the door. No one came to the door but he heard voices inside. He looked around quickly to see what was appropriate. They were wearing shoes although the floor was covered in cloths, thin ones, not rugs, but in layers softening the whole place as if it were a bed. He wiped his shoes carefully on the mat at the entrance.

Palesa rose to greet him formally. He was surprised but not shocked when she introduced one of the guests, the largest Basotho he had seen, as her boyfriend. He was a very polite man who apparently spoke no English, although it may have been a choice to avoid a language that was not comfortable for him. He was also introduced as a policeman. Bretton liked being clear, knowing where he stood. Palesa had liked him enough to invite him and she had finally told him she had a boyfriend. This made sense of her earlier claim that "they" would not like her to be with him. "They" was essentially this fellow. Whether large or small, he had a prior claim on her which she showed no sign of repudiating. Bretton looked forward to an evening in a local rondavel. He had been to parties in Lesotho, lots of them, but never to one among people at this stratum of society. This would push the boundaries of his experience, not in the way he would have chosen or fantasized, but a learning experience.

Her rondavel was one of the staff houses situated along the campus boundary. They were identical on the exterior although Bretton did not know this as he had never been inside any of them before. Palesa's was modern in its way, with a small refrigerator, a hot plate and a sink in the area that served as her kitchen. A single bare electric bulb hung from the ceiling and an extension cord looped from the light socket to a hook on the wall to service the kitchen and a desk lamp that was not lit. A set of shelves covered with a curtain held whatever clothes she did not have hanging on hooks on the wall. Everyone sat on the floor which must have been common practice since the only table was knee-high. A wire was strung across the room to support a curtain in front of the bed although the curtain was open. The room was round, of course, so the curtain drew a chord across a small part of the circle. Altogether, the space was adequate, reflecting the smallness of her life, whether driven by small ambitions or accommodation to her reality. Even with eight people at the party, the floor was not crowded and no one sat on the bed. There were small bowls of nuts and cooked vegetables which the guests noshed absentmindedly in between much more serious draughts of lukewarm beer in liter bottles.

Bretton carefully picked a place to sit where he would not be physically isolated because he anticipated, correctly it turned out, that the conversation would be entirely in Sesotho, colloquial, rapid, and incomprehensible to him. It was not an unpleasant situation. He was contented basking in the acceptance of these modest people. They were accepting him partly because he was invited by their hostess and partly because they knew him or his reputation as a fair-minded visitor to their country.

Perhaps they spoke to him when he first arrived and he did not understand them; maybe not. After a few minutes, he could see he was being ignored, which was not an insult, merely a practical reality. Bretton did wonder, however, why he had been invited if no one was going to speak English. Eventually he realized conversation was not especially important in this gathering. There were other silent people in the room. In fact, silence throughout the room was not uncommon and was not an embarrassment to anyone. Drinking beer was clearly the main activity but Bretton reached the inescapable conclusion that all present regarded companionship as an important adjunct.

After thirty minutes of steady drinking, light conversation, and silence from Bretton, his legs were tingling from constrained circulation and he began to consider leaving, having fulfilled his social obligation. He felt like the village idiot to be sitting amid the banter and comprehending nothing while no one expected anything else from him. Palesa was sitting on the opposite side of the group, partly shaded by the sink. He was looking at her less than normal because he did not want to offend her boyfriend and because there were so many people in the room he could not be sure who was watching his eyes at any moment. He tended to watch the boyfriend as he was the most unusual person there. He knew all the others from the college staff, two secretaries in addition to Palesa, one cleaning woman, and three young male laborers from the college farm.

Out of the corner of his consciousness, he saw movement from her shadow and he allowed his attention to drift her way. She was looking down at her bare breast and fondling it like a pet animal. She had dropped her blouse on one side exposing the breast and one shoulder although her arm remained in her sleeve. There was enough light on her to reveal the exquisite softness of her plaything. She laid it on her hand, pointing the nipple forward and looked up at Bretton, smiling slightly. Bretton's nerves reacted in unison to electrify his entire body. He was amazed that he did not actually move and worried that the thrill had been revealed in some other way. He checked the grin on his face but it was only normal. He gave his eyes an extra moment to memorize the vision of Palesa and before tearing his attention away from her to see how the rest of the room had reacted. No one was looking at her or at him. Their chatter and quiet laughter continued in the same boring way it had since he sat down. A bared breast did not have the significance in this culture that it did in Bretton's. It left him doubting the validity of his fascination although he would not trade it for a more rational view on nakedness. The policeman, who was sitting closer to Bretton than to Palesa, turned toward Bretton for no apparent reason. Perhaps someone had mentioned him. The boyfriend stared for a moment before smiling at Bretton. He said something that might have been directed at Bretton or been about Bretton or had nothing to do with Bretton except that he then turned to look at Palesa. He definitely said something to her. She immediately looked back at Bretton and laughed a little before slipping herself back into her blouse and leaned back on her hands, leaving her small but firm breasts to show themselves distinctly, but more modestly under her thin garment. Bretton did not know what any of it meant although he felt it had much to do with himself. He did not like being the idiot even if it was in the company of Palesa's bare breast.

Bretton stood up to indicate he was leaving. Everyone suddenly focused on him and apparently everyone was distraught at the idea of losing his company. Bretton could hardly make his fake excuses for leaving given the language barrier even though he knew the secretaries, at least, were capable of speaking English. So he mainly gestured and said, "*Kea leboha,*" (thank you) over and over as he backed his way to the door. Palesa rose slowly and came to him at the door. She pushed him outside and he nearly fell on the steps because he was facing backwards to exit. She shut the door behind her.

"Why do you leave? It is still early."

"Palesa, I enjoyed seeing your home but I cannot be part of your party for long. I do not join in the conversations. I just sit there."

"No, you can speak Sesotho. Why do you not talk to anyone?"

Bretton could see the beer was having an effect on her speech. "You know I cannot talk Sesotho."

"You can. You use Sesotho with the students."

"*Khotso, lumela, ho jong, u kae.*" Bretton said "hello" in the various ways used in Lesotho.

Palesa understood his point. She stood very close and held his hand. She slowly pulled it toward herself and around her waist. She leaned forward to lean against him.

"He is not really my boyfriend. He just likes to say that. You can see we are not together. He is a nice man but not my boyfriend."

"It doesn't matter, Palesa."

She answered angrily. "Yes it does. It matters. I don't have a boyfriend."

"All right. You don't have a boyfriend. You are the most beautiful woman in Lesotho and you do not have a boyfriend."

She pressed against his chest. "Abuti, can you buy some more beer and come right back?"

Her firm curves felt good against his chest. His hand was still wrapped around her waist and he was surprised at how narrow it was. She did not wear clothes that brought that out. The side of his hand felt the swell of her rump, an attribute highly prized in southern Africa. He did not caress her but he kept aware of what lay close to his touch. He wished her last sentence had been in incomprehensible Sesotho. The flush of desire she had brought out converted into a flush of anger but it passed as quickly as it had arisen. She was drunk. None of it meant anything. She was a beautiful woman he could never understand and who would never understand him. He was in Lesotho but an ocean remained between them.

He extracted himself from her sloppy embrace. "Okay. I'll get some beers. I should have brought some when I came in the first place. But I don't speak Sesotho so I'll just drop them off when I come back."

She muttered something in an indeterminate language as he strode off to fulfill his mission. She did not come to the door when he returned and they did not speak again that night but there came a night not much later when she invited him inside her home again and there was no light on, when he found her on the bed and her breasts were bare to his touch, softer than he had known was possible for human flesh to be.

VII. Pshoene (2003)

"Thank you for coming on short notice. You understand we would never ask someone to change his plans unless it was truly a pressing matter. The PM relies on Pshoene to run things inside the government. Neither one of them cares much about the people, you know. This is Africa. Now that Lesotho is doing better, you know with the water and all... you know about that?" The Ambassador interrupted himself to be sure Bretton knew something about the economy.

"You mean the Highlands Water scheme? It was starting just after I left, but I came back for the World Bank and did a short term research thing so I saw a little bit of it."

"Highlands Project. Yes. Biggest project ever around here. It made this country. Brings in money from the South Africans. What I was saying is the PM uses Pshoene when he wants to say 'no' to something. Claims Pshoene is just looking at the technical side. We want this education reform to go through. The IMF says the money is there but Pshoene says it's not. Doesn't want to bankrupt his country, he says. That's a good one, doesn't want to bankrupt Lesotho, right?"

"Right. You and the IMF want money for the schools. The PM wants it for something else. Pshoene says the money isn't there. Why me? What can I do?"

"Look, don't try to talk Pshoene into anything. You're here because he asked for you. Just do what he says and let me deal with the politics."

"I don't do politics. But I don't see what he could want from me."

"It's just a delaying tactic. He heard you were around and used it to make another demand. He will have you doing some busywork but it will be good for us because we got you here right away. We gave him what he asked for. He will lose leverage with the PM 'cause it won't delay much. I'll get the education money as soon as the PM says to do it. He makes the decisions. Pshoene is just blowing smoke for the PM to see how serious we are. It'll be a simple job for you. You just have to show up. Remind him of what buddies you were back in the day. Hang around while I take on the PM.

Keep Pshoene busy, maybe, so the PM can't use him for more distractions. You can just look at the IMF report if you want reassurance on where the money is. Can you handle this?"

*Brash. That's what you are, young man. Well connected men can sometimes go forever in denial of their actual shortcomings but you are so conceited, blind, and prejudiced you will someday implode spectacularly. Africa? You know Africa and disparage her? Africa is more beautiful than you will ever know. And Africa will eat **you** up. I don't want to be on the plate beside you when it happens.* "Should I set up a meeting with Pshoene then?"

"I'm taking you to see him. Got to make the point that we did what he asked and now he has to spend time using you. 10:00. Okay?"

"Sure. 10:00 is fine."

"Good. Our economist is coming too in case Pshoene wants to bring up any technical things. You won't be ready for the smoke he could blow over the problem. Said you taught farm accounting, right?"

"That was a very long time ago."

"Anyway, let's hope you remember some of it. 10:00."

"Right. See you then."

Bretton met the Embassy economist at the front gate. They were both a little early but neither would admit it was to please the Ambassador. Bretton liked the economist, but he could see he was very inexperienced-- mostly he had been a good student. Lesotho was his first overseas post. Bretton also recognized during the conversation in the car that he was not only a better student than Bretton had been, he was not as green as Bretton had been on his first trip to Lesotho.

When the three men arrived at the outer office of the Minister of Finance, the Ambassador did not sit down when the secretary offered him a chair. He was signaling that he was not going to wait for long. There was a whole language in diplomatic circles built on arriving for a meeting early or late. Bretton had first seen it in Lesotho at the college graduation ceremony after his first school year. The program for the event indicated when each rank of person should arrive. There was a very firm statement that all students should be in their seats by a certain hour. Faculty were scheduled to arrive 30 minutes later. The College Principle came 30 minutes after that. The last arrival was the King. Bretton did not sit in his seat for the allotted 90 minutes indicated on the program. When he was stretching his legs outside the auditorium, he saw the King's car was parked nearby, waiting from his own time to arrive, wasting his own time as well as everyone else's.

Pshoene came out as soon as the secretary told him they were there, but he played his card in the game by going directly to Bretton and greeting him first, leaving the Ambassador to stand in the background.

"Ntate MacNamara! Welcome back to Lesotho. We have been missing you."

Bretton answered respectfully, *"Khotso, Ntate."* Bretton pronounced *"ntate"* with a "d" sound for the second letter to match the way Pshoene said the word. It was not the way Bretton usually heard it but he suspected he heard it as a "t" sound only because he knew the spelling. Saying it like Pshoene made it sound like the English "daddy," a fitting companion to *"mme,"* which sound a lot like "ma." The similarities tied Bretton to the Basotho in a fundamental way with a global culture dating back to antediluvian times.

69

Pshoene shook hands once and slid his fingers down to hook Bretton fingers in the simple dap students had used when Bretton lived there. It was an extraordinarily friendly gesture to be coming from a man he had never known well and who had always been stuffy in his manners. Bretton's hand remembered the dap and played it properly. Bretton gave a small laugh to recognize the gesture. He doubted it mattered that he stared into Pshoene's face as they shook because Pshoene's visual focus was somewhere indeterminate.

Pshoene was better dressed than Bretton expected, not only better than when they were both young college faculty, but better than any government official Bretton had met in Sub-Saharan Africa other than South Africa. His suit was probably not terribly expensive, but it was a suit and it was pressed and unfrayed at the cuffs. It was lightweight wool and might have been considered fashionable if Bretton knew more about men's fashion. Pshoene had always been gaunt but his frame served well for hanging up the suit. His tie had a simple pattern and coordinated in color with the suit. Bretton had a vague memory of Pshoene's wife, a village woman. Either she had taken on urban skills or Pshoene had taken on a new wife. Second wives were allowed, a custom Bretton had always thought demeaning to woman but which he saw at this moment might have preserved the status of the first wife better than the Western custom of divorce.

Pshoene did the proper thing then in greeting the Ambassador and inviting him into the inner office leaving the two in his entourage to be assumed invited as well. However, his delay in greeting the Ambassador had been noticed by all and the Ambassador was looking for a way to reassert himself. As they were seating themselves in the office, the secretary lingered until Pshoene offered tea. Bretton and the economist declined but the Ambassador said it was the right time for tea, displaying his knowledge of local practice. Bretton felt it was past time for tea. They had left the Embassy at ten, tea time, and Bretton had found tea time was more precise than any other time in Lesotho.

"Yes, it is a custom we learned from the British. I am never sure if Americans will follow it when they are here." Pshoene did not take tea. This placed him up two in score over the Ambassador who drank his tea alone. He tried to save face a little by asking the secretary to take back the biscuit she had put on his saucer.

"We have delivered you an accountant, as you requested."

Pshoene turned to Bretton. "Are you an accountant now?" Another point for Pshoene.

"I will try to help you however I can," answered Bretton who had never claimed to be an accountant and did not want to appear to be one.

"We will see what you can do for us. When can you start?"

"He is available to you immediately. We rushed him in here and put aside his other responsibilities. I hope you will not need him for long." The Ambassador was desperately trying to head his own delegation.

"We have a desk for you here in the Ministry. My staff will give you an orientation. I am hoping you will teach them some of your tricks." Pshoene continued to address Bretton.

"Is a week enough?" asked the Ambassador, legitimately insisting on an answer to his question.

"A week? Probably. But we should let Ntate MacNamera tell us how much he will need once he has seen our problems."

"Ntate Pshoene, I hope you do not imagine I have learned very much useful to you in the years since I was a teacher here. Maybe I can identify some technical expertise we could bring here."

Pshoene reached across the table and took Bretton' hand. "I think you will be fine for us. I remember you well. We will meet today to go over everything." On the last sentence, he squeezed Bretton' hand and continued to squeeze it in the silence until the Ambassador spoke again.

"Don't you want to go over that with our economist here? You do remember meeting him before."

Pshoene dropped Bretton hand and turned to the economist. "Of course I remember him and I appreciate that he can clarify problems of an economic nature. We don't have that kind of expertise on our own staff. For the present, however, that is not our priority."

"Yes," inserted the Ambassador. "It is exactly the top priorities I wanted to discuss with you. The PM assures me that he supports the education initiative, but he says you are holding up the appropriation."

"Please, not at all. I cannot hold up funds. The PM makes the decisions. We all agree education is the priority. You see how I have asked to have a teacher come visit me to help? The funds are in process. They are not delayed. In our country, just like yours, it takes a little time to move money. We are in process."

Bretton did not know what the conversation was accomplishing. He interpreted the squeeze from Pshoene as a wink of the sort Pshoene could not do with his eyes. Two men holding hands was not unusual in this part of the world, but the squeeze was something. He would be quiet until he could speak candidly with Pshoene. He could tell the Ambassador and Pshoene were not frank with each other. Pshoene was disrespecting the Ambassador and the Ambassador was smart enough to be irritated by it but not smart enough to end it. Bretton thought it was consistent with the Pshoene he remembered, the one who had few friends at the college and did not seek any.

The Ambassador stood up. He meant it as an insult to initiate his departure abruptly, having accomplished almost nothing by his presence. He made one further effort to salve his ego.

"Dr. MacNamera will be at your service, but you let me know if you need anything further from him. I will be seeing the PM later today to make sure the education project can go forward now."

Pshoene hesitated before rising, letting the Ambassador have his say while he listened, leaning back in his high-backed desk chair. He answered as he slowly rose. "Thank you for coming. It is always an honor to have you in our ministry." The secretary came in the room unbidden. She must have been listening. Pshoene and the Ambassador shook hands. The economist started to turn to leave and Pshoene stepped up to him to shake his hand too. Bretton hung back. Pshoene spoke to the secretary. Please accompany the Ambassador to the door and then come back to show Ntate MacNamera his office. The Ambassador followed the secretary out without a word toward Bretton.

Pshoene was smiling as he sat down. "*Lula fatsi*; please sit. Do you remember your Sesotho?"

"I recall that phrase is literally 'live on the ground' and harkens to a time when sitting was not in chairs."

"And I recall you were a scholar of our culture."

"Ntate, let us be fair. I was no scholar and I never knew that much Sesotho. Just enough to put on a good show. The Peace Corps kids all knew more than me."

"We were supposed to speak English at the college. I am sorry to have brought you here. I know you had better things to do."

"Please do not apologize. I am very happy to come back. I have been looking for an excuse to get someone to pay my way back here for years. I don't get to choose where the government sends me."

Pshoene sat silent. Bretton remembered silence was much more acceptable in Lesotho than in America. Basotho were comfortable being with each other while nothing is happening.

"Ntate," Bretton let some time pass before speaking. "I am very curious. Why me? I don't know what technical services you need but I doubt I am the man for them."

"That is just the kind of statement I would expect from you and it is 'why you.' Are you the same man you were before?"

"Looking back, I think I was barely more than a boy then. Are you the same? Is anyone after this many years?"

"Some men are the same, some are changed. I would like some help from the man I knew. That man was not a slave to his President. When your President invaded the tiny country of Grenada, you started a petition among the Americans here to protest it."

"You heard about that?"

"Oh yes. Genada is much smaller than Lesotho so we like to think we are its big brother. We did not speak of it to Americans, but we were disappointed that your country would care to invade it. We thought at that time you were more respectful of sovereignty. It was a lesson for us."

"I would sign that petition again. I might not start one like that. I have other ways now to make myself heard. They are not especially powerful, but they are better than sending a letter. Or maybe I am not the same man. I have worked for many Presidents since then, and I did basically what I was asked to do, regardless of what party or person was in power." He allowed silence to fill the room before continuing. "I was never asked to invade a country. A bureaucrat in foreign assistance makes many compromises but does not do direct harm to anyone, not that he notices anyway, not in the short run, and in the long run we have moved on to a different country."

"I asked you here to help me with this Ambassador."

"He said he asked me here to help with you."

"I am not surprised. You do not believe, I assume, that I am opposed to education? We were both in education and both believed in it. That is why we worked hard back then and why we were disappointed in our colleagues who were less serious."

"At that point in my life, education was all I had ever experienced. Everything I had ever been told about it was positive. I don't think I have changed my view much since then. I know I loved the students. We had the worst students academically.   The agricultural college was not for the bright ones; that was NUL. But we had not an arrogant soul among them, not that I noticed with my minimal language awareness. Our kids, well, some of the boys were as old as me, our students were anxious to serve their families and communities. No one came to us to get rich or to pass the time. Our school was transparently working toward skills that applied in Lesotho villages. ...Maybe except for some of the classes I taught."

"You taught maths which everyone needed. And you taught them there was a world beyond Lesotho and beyond South Africa. After you, we sent several students and faculty to university in the United States. There were none before you."

"I wish I had something to do with that. I was only here a couple years."

"Your Ambassador is not like you. I cannot talk to him. We tell him we want to fight over education. Then we give in and he feels like he got something. Do you know what we are really trying to understand?" It was a rhetorical question but he waited a few moments before answering it himself. "China."

"Okay, okay. I might know something about that. China's role is full of controversy across Africa these days. I take it the U.S. has a position on what they do in Lesotho."

"I knew you were the American to bring here."

"You remember when I was here, Leabua Jonathon went to China? They gave him a party and a parade and when he got back he gave the Taiwanese a couple days to leave the country. I think the mainland Chinese got their Embassy building."

"No one else could use it with that big Chinese gate out front."

"I read about riots over Chinese shopowners a few years later."

"That was very unfortunate. We did not mind so much when the South Africans owned everything important in our country but when the Chinese bought the shops, we were very resentful. It's not too hard to see the trouble with that."

"What is it you want from me?"

"I heard you were very useful in Zambia a couple years ago. You remember that trip?"

"I have been there a few times."

"The important thing I know is you have added many years of experience with the government and, if you are still the man I knew, you would advise me properly on the Chinese no matter what the Ambassador says."

"What do the Chinese want?"

"That is a good question. I wish I could answer it. Your Ambassador says they are only going to do what is best for them. He says the project they have offered is just to give jobs to their workers. Says we should not accept anything from them unless we want them moving in again. Says there are lots of people on the move in China and just one village is big enough to overrun Lesotho."

This characterization of Chinese assistance was familiar to Bretton. "It is likely any project they are offering has a direct benefit for China. There is also a lot of controversy about how much of U.S. assistance is simple generosity. I cannot say what you ought to do but I am willing to look into it more. I expect there is not a simple answer. Maybe you can modify their proposal to reduce the parts you do not like, include local jobs, maybe. Maybe you should take it just to assure our

Ambassador that he does not make decisions for your government. If you are not certain what they want in return, are you clear on what they are offering?"

"They will improve the road past Butha-Buthe. The World Bank says the road will be valuable for tourism."

"You and I might agree that road may not be the best possible investment for Lesotho, but it is hard to see how it would be bad, I mean, if someone else is making the investment and the World Bank sees merit in it, why is the Ambassador against it?"

"I don't know that either. You see why I need you?"

"Not really. I don't see why any of this matters much. But I can look at the World Bank report, talk to the Bank staff although there probably aren't any in Lesotho, ask around at the Embassy. I doubt the Chinese want to discuss things with me, but I could sit in on a meeting between their staff and yours. I have seen some very productive relationships at the staff level on Chinese assistance. They tend to have very strong technical skills and good internationalist goals once you get the political figures out of the room. Like us, only more competent on average."

"Did you forget you are talking to a politician?"

"When I said 'like us', I meant like Americans. Basotho politicians tend to have a whole different kind of weirdness. I wouldn't know what politics is like here now."

"We do have an office for you. You will not expect it to be very fancy. You have already given me a work plan. I will have the secretary give you a copy of the Chinese proposal. Oh yes. I hope you will take it as a complement that we can talk openly, yes?"

"I am very pleased you still regard me as your friend."

"My wife says I should invite you to dinner, but I do not think you would enjoy sitting in our house with just the two of us. Maybe after you are here a few days, you will find a girlfriend and then we can have you visit."

"A girlfriend! Ntate, I am here to work. I do not look for girlfriends on trips like this."

"I meant you might find a girlfriend from before."

"It is extraordinary that you remember me at all, Ntate. I doubt any woman I used to know would care that I came back after all these years."

"Maybe not, but I think Miss Palesa would like you to visit. She is still at the college, I believe. My wife also remembers you well enough. Do you remember her? She taught at the college in the home economics section. She was known as Mme Mahasa back then. Mosele Mahasa."

VIII. Mosele (1983)

When Bretton first met her, Mme Pshoane, nee Mosele Mahasa, was a large woman, in the way common in Lesotho although she was no longer a farmer and did not need to subsist on high carbohydrate corn mealies. She probably knew she was large and carried herself with pride that showed no modesty about her imposing appearance. She typically wore the colorful fabric prints that constituted formal dress across Sub-Saharan Africa although she only wore a matching turban on formal occasions. Mme Mahasa had been the head of the home economy section of the technical college, young for holding so much responsibility. Bretton did not know where she had been educated but the accent in her careful English was neither American nor British, so he surmised she was locally trained.

During morning tea one day when Bretton was still new to the school, Mme Mahasa asked if he was going into Ladybrand any day soon. Ladybrand was the small town in South Africa nearest the Lesotho border. Expatriates spoke of it often as the place to buy things. He had no intention of ever going into Ladybrand, he was not even curious about what he could see there, but her question was either a polite request to have a ride or a check on whether he was boycotting the Republic. He studied the expression on her face. It was not severe exactly, but was farther from soft than from hard. She was always officious in his presence. He suspected she was more relaxed among people she knew better and might look very nice in that circumstance. It was still early in his tour and he did not know any Mosotho except those with a business reason for knowing him. Mme Mahasa was an especially respectable figure at the college and a drive into the Republic might build up a friendship and give him some insight into the local culture. So he hoped she was sincere and he offered to go any day in the coming week.

"I will thank you to let me know when you decide to go," she answered stiffly, refusing to suggest a date or to acknowledge he was doing her a favor beyond allowing her to sit in a vehicle that was going to town anyway. That was all right with Bretton. She was a respectable person and would warm up to his sincere generosity. He looked forward to the challenge of thawing her and imagined she had been smart enough to set up the game that way, to have him angling for her favor. It might be in her personality to keep it always that way, to control the relationship, always cool but close enough to be approached. The pay-out for her was not sexual, of course, just as her allure was not. It was a matter of power. She had influence in the college and she would have more if he was supporting her, even if the basis for his support was only his desire to know a local person personally.

Bretton met Mme Mahasa at her house, a concrete block box with a tin roof in the row of identical faculty housing. Bretton's house was nearly the same although his was on the other side of campus with the expatriate faculty. He parked the car and turned off the engine. Before he could run up the walkway to her door, she was coming out. He had arrived at precisely the agreed time, having waited a couple blocks away for a few minutes to be sure he was right. They left at 6 am, which was not an odd time to be starting the day in a place dominated by agriculture although neither Bretton nor Mme Mahasa actually did any farming.

Bretton opened the door for her but she declined his offer and opened the door to the back seat herself. "I will move into the front when we are over the border." Bretton was not clear on why she wanted such an arrangement, but suspected it had to do with making it clear to anyone who knew her that she was just getting a ride, not going as a companion. Presumably she was not worried about being seen by any family or friends in South Africa. He then used the moment when she was sliding into her seat to look at her. Until then, he had never looked at her closely; it would have felt impolite. He had formed a general impression of her being heavy but carrying herself well, implying strength. Now he saw she had especially smooth skin, unmarked and fine, like a baby's. He could imagine touching it. She suddenly looked much younger than he expected. And her facial features were also pleasant, apart from her scowl. If she were more relaxed and smiling, say at a family gathering, she might be called beautiful. Still, she was too big for his taste. Within the local context, where big women were the norm, she might be quite desirable, at least on the basis of appearance. He saw the irony that Mme Mahasa might feel her behavior toward him was more controlled in Lesotho than in South Africa.

He stopped just after they were out of sight of the border to allow her to move to the front and made no comment on the seating arrangements. Perhaps he would seem knowledgeable enough to understand them. Up to that point, they had hardly spoken. With her in the back seat, it was not convenient. Going forward, he tried to engage her in some kind of conversation, taking care not to suggest in any way that he was trying to get uncomfortably close to her. He stuck to issues relating to the college. She tended to provide very brief answers in a fashion that would seem unfriendly back in Ohio but which might or might not have been appropriate where they were; he could not tell.

The drive to Ladybrand was only about thirty minutes from the border although those thirty minutes were more miles than thirty minutes most places. The road was straight and empty. Bretton was not into speeding but it was so easy to blast along in his smooth blue Peugeot with a speedometer calibrated in unfamiliar kilometers per hour. Driving hard was a substitute for talking. Bretton doubted Mme Mahasa ever drove and probably seldom rode in cars, especially fast ones.

When they reached Ladybrand, Bretton asked where to go. Mme Mahasa assumed Bretton would want to go to the grocery store and gave him directions there. He did not need any groceries and did not care to search for South African equivalents to the less satisfying items he could find in Maseru, like decent crackers or ice cream. Ice cream would never survive the ride back to Maseru anyway.

"I'll wait for you outside," Bretton suggested and immediately saw in her expression that he had made an error.

"I can hurry, Ntate. Where did you need to go?"

She was embarrassed that he had done her a favor and a little mad to be embarrassed. He could not say the whole trip was a favor to her. The only reason he had heard for going to Ladybrand other than the supermarket was visiting the doctor. He stammered to come up with a reason for seeing the doctor that would not worry her about spending time in the car with him until she suggested "The hardware shop is just across the square."

Bretton did not know if she sincerely thought he wanted hardware or if she was just relieving the tension. He did not want to give into the stereotype of men to hardware and women to groceries but there were bigger social issues at play. She would not appreciate being schooled by him in gender politics. "Excellent. I won't need to wait for you then and I can go there right away. Don't rush. It may take me some time to find what I need in a new shop." So they parted without any further plan.

In fact, Bretton thought it was a good idea to see what the Ladybrand hardware store carried. This was an agricultural district so the place was sure to offer a good variety. With at least two years of living in Lesotho before him, he would have to make repairs to the shabby house he had been assigned even if he did not attempt to raise his standard of housing.

The store was not as easy to use as he imagined. Back in Ohio, Bretton had once been in a hardware store without customer access to the shelves. You asked for whatever you wanted and the clerk got it for you. This supposed you knew what you wanted, an old-fashioned assumption in marketing. The Ladybrand store had a similar premise, although the customers could, in theory, browse the stock. The inventory was not on shelves-- it was spread out on the concrete floor behind the counter. There must have been some order to it in the mind of the shopkeeper but Bretton could see no logic to the placement of objects on the floor. It was all in neat rows with space between each item or pile of identical items. A stack of fertilizer bags sat next to a single heavy shovel which lay next to a pyramid of pipe fittings. The room was large but not large enough to hold all that an isolated hardware store ought to have. On the other hand, there were not many of anything so greater variety was possible than if there had been a substantial inventory of popular items. Bretton hung back, reluctant to browse the sparse display and reluctant to pretend interest. The clerk saw him come in but did not move to help. He was on a ladder, busy putting up a poster about the quality of chicken feed he offered. Bretton did not take offense at being ignored and assumed the clerk would respond vigorously if he asked for something. He felt a little bit foolish for coming into the shop, saying nothing and then going out. He considered saying he was living in Maseru and just wanted to see what they carried, but that was a step friendlier than he wanted to be with any white South Africans.

The door opened with a clatter from the bells hung on it and a postman entered carrying a heavy leather bag over his shoulder, and wearing a pith helmet on his head and green knee socks reaching nearly up to his khaki shorts. The South African postmen wore shorts in any season. He gave Bretton a very friendly wave and then began to tell him a story even before getting to the counter to sit down his bag. The clerk called out and climbed down from his ladder so the postman waved him closer to include him in the storytelling. He gesticulated broadly and included several phrases of onomatopoeia: booms, hisses, and kissing sounds. These were the only "words" Bretton could understand since he did not speak Africaans. Nonetheless, he listened to the story and nodded his head approvingly whenever the postmen hesitated and said "huh!" Finally the postman's voice lifted to a climax and he slapped the counter with his hand for dramatic effect and the clerk began to laugh wildly. Bretton laughed too; it was genuine as it is easy to laugh when others are, but he had no idea what the story had told. The laughter gave him the break he needed to exit gracefully. He backed out, holding up his hand to prevent protest and looked downward to avoid eye contact, all while keeping up his chuckle. The clerk was questioning the postman further so Bretton was able to slip outside without being missed.

Outside he felt the cold air anew. The inside of the shop was not warm, but the air was calm at least. He decided to wait in the grocery store, perhaps near the door where he would not be noticed by Mme Mahasa until she was ready to check out.

He looked both ways before crossing the dusty two-lane street but there were no cars in sight, not even any parked along the road. The only movement or sound in the town was the cold wind coming off the

86

veldt. He could see to both ends of the town from the middle of the road. There was not even a paved cross-street. It was not the consumer paradise the expatriates back in Maseru had lauded, although he was realizing now that their praise had been facetious, a joke on the new member of the community.

It felt odd to stand in the street, unsafe, almost illegal, and yet he could see no reason to move on. No place offered a better view. He started to count the buildings and to note which were residences and which were something else when he noticed an open metal gate along a stone wall built of cut limestone, like the town hall. It invited closer attention and he walked up the middle of the street until he was in front of the gate. Bretton was amused to look at the park inside the gate without going inside. He saw a wide gravel path through low bushes and a bench just where the path bent out of his view. Maybe the blustery air kept him out of the mood, but he saw nothing attractive in the park: no water feature, no sculpture, no floral display, no majestic trees, no exotic protea or tree ferns or other plants that might have impressed his inexperienced African eye. He went no closer and turned to go toward the grocery when a young couple came out of the town hall and headed toward him. He had not spoken to a black South African and decided to walk in their direction so he could greet them.

They were dressed in modern, that is, European or "northern" style, nothing traditional, but well-worn and almost consciously undistinctive. The young man was in faded blue jeans, faded from age and use rather than as a style, a plain t-shirt and a sport jacket frayed at the cuffs. The woman walked behind him, looking down at his heels. She wore flat shoes, a dark skirt and a sweater, and carried a large, black leather handbag. As Bretton neared them, he worried he did not know what to say. He knew how to greet people in Lesotho, and he knew black South Africans this close to Lesotho were likely to speak the same language but they did not necessarily place the same cultural values on the greetings when provided by a white man. He hesitated and then the initiative was lost. The man spoke first.

"Pardon me. It is permissible for us to utilize the park?" He pointed through the gate. Bretton was pleased that his first spoken interaction with a South African would be to permit use of a public facility although he doubted he had any right to grant permission. He was white, but not South African. No one knew he was American so he smiled his most friendly and warmly answered, ""Of course you are welcome. I just wish it were a nicer day for your walk." He felt deliciously subversive and hoped no harm came to the nice couple if they were, in fact, legally barred from using the park and were caught inside.

IX. Butha-Buthe (2003)

Bretton had dealt with politically ambitious people enough that he did not hold their ambition against them and did not expect them to have technical expertise to match their rank. He tended to admire their ambition, an attribute for lack of which his own work suffered. He also admired their capacity to forge ahead without the kind of experience or credentials he would have found comforting. In addition, he respected, but did not admire, their interest in addressing and exploiting the personalities involved in a project. Now he was drawn into playing a role he normally avoided, however, he did not mind doing this in an isolated, short-term instance. He had studied, at least observed, how it is done.

Being a technocrat, Bretton applied the formula he usually used when starting a project, outlining a strategy. The gaps in his knowledge of the situation prohibited his drafting a complete strategy, but he could draw up a plan to be modified as the week went by. Firstly, the GOALS... He asked himself what he needed to do to appease the Ambassador. That was essential to getting out of Lesotho in good time without harm to his career. He also asked what he wanted to accomplish for his own peace of mind. When he asked this question he was not sure if it referred to what he should do for Lesotho or for the United States, but it was acceptable within his planning procedures to leave that refinement until later. He sat before his laptop for fifteen minutes trying to formulate other goals but could not find any. Clear and conscious goals were important. Two goals on one project was a very small number-- his procedure did not have a requirement for more so he accepted the two vague entries as a start.

Next, he asked what tools he had. Obviously, he was not equipped with any authority. He did not speak on behalf of the U.S. Government or represent any budget. He could not convincingly play the expert who knows what needs to be done. His relationships with the players was in every case either weak or non-existent and yet each of them, the Ambassador, Pshoene, the Chinese, would suspect he represented some opposing interest. He did not even have knowledge, local or academic, relevant to the issues on which he was to intervene or advise.

The page labeled "TOOLS" bore only that single word while Bretton searched for an asset to record. If he had no tools, he should remove himself from the project. He wrote "ability to resign," because he knew that even though he might not be able to convince anyone of what to do about the Chinese offer, he could convince everyone that he was useless to them. Then he added "collegiality with technocrats, Chinese included." And he added "knowing more of others' needs than they know of mine." He was not sure this was true but it seemed there was something in it that might be useful.

Then he wrote "APPROACH," because "strategy" sounded too refined for the rough sketch he could provide at this stage. The first parts of his procedure had helped him realized he should get to know his Chinese counterparts. He would need a translator, someone who worked for him even if his counterparts spoke English. There might be subtleties in any interaction and these would require him to control his end of the conversation. He would see what flexibility they had in their program for Lesotho and to learn why the Butha-Buthe road had been selected. It might be easier for him to ask about this than for Pshoene since the Chinese had doubtless told him why already and further questioning by him could be misinterpreted as resistance. Further questioning by Bretton would look more like inexperience or stupidity on his part. He would also need to understand the Ambassador's resistance to the Chinese program although Bretton expected this would be much easier to discern. He would start with the young economist. To separate it from the education issue on which Bretton was supposed to be working, he would embed the road questions in a broader update of the situation.

Bretton went back to Pshoene. "Can you find me a translator who knows Chinese and does not work for their government?"

"Are you reading their proposals? We have them in English, you know."

"No, I want someone to listen in when I speak to the Chinese to be sure I am understanding things. I might meet some staff at my level or maybe some of the workers on the road project."

"There is no translation service here."

""I was thinking of a shopkeeper you might trust. I do not want to learn any secrets and have no secrets to hide, but I would like someone I can pay to help me."

"I think you have grown up since you were a young professor."

"No one can call me young any more, Ntate."

Pshoene picked up the phone and dialed one digit. Bretton heard a phone ring in an office nearby. Pshoene gave some orders in Sesotho and then smiled at Bretton. "I will have someone here in a few minutes. It will cost 50 rands per day. Should I get an appointment for you at the Embassy or will your Ambassador do that for you?"

"My Ambassador will not hear anything from me about the Chinese. I am here to get an education program from you, right?"

"I don't know. Should I make an appointment with the Chinese, say, tomorrow?"

"No, thanks anyway. Now I am thinking it would not be good for them to see me coming from you either. Don't worry about any appointment. Can you get me a car to use? I do not want the Ambassador to know where I am going."

"I can give you my car any time you want it. You must use my driver. It is the rule here."

"All right. I do not mind if you know where I am. Tomorrow I would like to go to Butha-Buthe."

A half hour later, a young Basotho brought Han to Bretton's office. Bretton asked Han if 50 rand per day was good pay for his translation services and they shook hands on the deal.

"May we start tomorrow?" Bretton asked. He thought he ought to examine the man to see if his English was good but was more interested in moving ahead. He was careful not to say how many days of work he was offering. He could always look for a replacement. "Is there a place in Maseru to buy some Chinese things for lunch?"

"Yes, in my own shop."

"Excellent. Please bring along something simple to eat. Nothing that needs to be cooked. Spend about ten rands and I will pay you when we meet."

In the morning Bretton had a full meal from the breakfast bar in the hotel and stuffed a few rolls in his pocket in case he did not get a chance to eat again. He was not planning to eat the Chinese delicacies. The driver was waiting outside the hotel at 7 am, as planned, with Han already seated in the back of the car so Bretton had some confidence his companions would be playing their parts in the day's exploration.

"*Lumelang bontate!*" Bretton met them with enthusiasm. He presumed the Chinese man would know his plural Sesotho greeting and if he did not, Bretton thought he should learn it. The driver and Bretton exchanged names and Bretton thanked them both for coming with him on short notice. "To Butha-Buthe and beyond," Bretton exclaimed, channeling Buzz Lightyear, knowing there was no chance his reference would be understood.

"Have you ever been to Butha-Buthe?" Bretton asked Han.

"No, not yet," he answered.

It was hard to get a conversation going, but Han clearly did understand English. Bretton asked where Han had lived in China and how long he had been in Lesotho and what he did in Lesotho, receiving always clear and brief answers until Han finally initiated a topic.

"Why do you need a translator?"

Bretton had prepared his answer to this issue. "I heard there were Chinese working on the road after Butha-Buthe and I might need to ask the workers to let us through or to suggest where the best views are. I am very cautious. Mosopha here can ask the Basotho where to go but there are not many people up there. The workers may be the only ones around."

"The workers will not know where to take pictures. Also, there are not many workers there. They have not started construction."

"Really? I thought there was a lot of work under way. I guess I was listening to someone who is not well informed. It would not be the first time. If we run into some Chinese workers, we may ask where to see the mountains or where there is a waterfall. Maybe we will not ask them anything. I just like to be well prepared. I hope you enjoy your first ride up north."

"Yes, I am very pleased to be going on this trip."

"So, you sell Chinese foods in Maseru. Are there other shops like yours?"

"No, all the Chinese come to my shop. When construction becomes active on the road, I will open another shop in Butha-Buthe. This trip is a business lesson for me."

"When do think you will start the new shop?"

"The workers will come from China in two months, I think."

"That is very soon. You need to make preparations."

"I am worried it is not completely certain this will happen."

"Why is that? Doesn't this road need the work?"

"The Chinese government has not signed the contract yet."

"What are they waiting for?"

"Maybe they want something from Lesotho."

"It is hard to imagine what Lesotho can do for China."

"Yes. I do not know what they want. Maybe something in the United Nations."

"Yeah, maybe. How about you, Mosopha, have you been to Butha-Buthe much?"

"I have been there two times but I have never been to Sani Pass."

Butha-Buthe is a mountain of historical significance to the Basotho as the place where the first king camped for two years in the 1820s when Shaka led the Zulu expansion known as the mfecane which disrupted all the peoples of southern Africa. In the year of Bretton's visit, the town of Butha-Buthe was an isolated settlement of about 10,000 people. The unpaved road after Butha-Buthe goes 250 km to Sani Pass without passing a refueling station. From the pass, the road drops precipitously down to KwaZulu-Natal, South Africa. The Lesotho portion of the road is known as the Roof of Africa and is the site of an annual international motorcycle rally. Various international commercials have been filmed on the road to demonstrate the capabilities of four-wheel drive vehicles.

The car climbed quickly up the Lesotho plateau to the village of Teyateyaneng. Bretton told Han and Mosopha of visiting it 20 years earlier and buying tapestries woven of mohair that now hung in his apartment in Washington. He could pronounce the name of the town fluently, but he called it "T-Y" because nearly everyone did. The style of tapestry he had bought, a naïve village scene displaying homes, horses, chickens, and people wearing blankets and the distinctive Basotho hat, was well known back then and now sold on E-Bay for three times what Bretton had paid for his. He wondered if the style was still known in Lesotho but doubted either of his traveling companions was well versed in the weaving market. Bretton had them stop in front of the church that had served as a weaving studio.

It was now abandoned and collapsing. He took a picture of Han and Mosapho to maintain the charade that the trip was a pleasure outing.

Bretton settled comfortably into his role as passenger, looking across the open terrain at picturesque small villages tucked into the base of the steep slopes and surrounded by peach trees and tall yuccas planted as thorny fences for ruminant livestock. The passenger window was open, letting a breeze connect him to the atmosphere of the mountains. On the higher slopes, herds of goats or sheep grazed lazily. A few dirt roads wound off from the road to Butha-Buthe but he saw no other paved roads. It was all indistinguishable from what he remembered from 20 years earlier.

It would have taken only a minute to drive through Butha-Buthe. Bretton had them stop so he could take a picture of the remote town none of the three had ever passed through before. Bretton began a conversation with a group of men sitting on the ground in front of a church, apparently just waiting for the day to pass. He turned the conversation toward their opinion of the proposed road improvements. They warmed quickly to the topic which appeared to be familiar to them. Mosopha translated.

"He says the road is very important to the town. Nothing grows up high in the mountains like this except goats. That is why the people living here are not many. If the road is made good, the men can come back from the mines to see their families many times in a year. And there will be tourists from South Africa and Europe to see the mountains. There is only one hotel because the tourists are not many, just when the Roof of Africa Rally happens. Most of tourists bring tents or caravans. These men would like to be in a modern city."

Bretton asked about the road rally and the presence of Chinese workers. Then he moved onto another group of men standing on the street and watching the first interaction. Eventually he bought a small orange from a stack of six oranges in front of a woman sitting next to the road in a row of women selling tiny amounts of things. He asked the women about the town and the road and the Chinese too.

By this time, they had heard several times of the building where the Chinese had based their operation. Mosopha was starting to see that Bretton had an agenda beyond his own tourism but he did not say anything about his suspicions. Bretton asked Han to bring along the food he had brought and he went up to the Chinese men outside the building and offered them a snack. Bretton ate a little himself and had Han explain that Bretton had been to China twice for his work and really liked the foods. He revealed some slight knowledge of China by mentioning that the foods were very different in different regions he had visited and claimed to like the cuisine of the southeast although he could not actually distinguish the foods of the regions. It was all an opening to chat about their plans and impressions about Lesotho and the road project. They were happy to chat and even drew a map in the sand to show what they would be building if they ever got started.

Eventually Bretton and Mosopha and Han drove past Butha-Buthe, but Bretton did not make much pretense of tourism any more. They spent an hour or so to see how the unimproved road looked and then it was getting late enough that they needed go head back to Maseru. Han, like Mosopha, saw that Bretton was excessively interested in the Chinese project and understood Han had been brought along to help Bretton learn something but it was not clear at all what had been learned or why it had been done in the secretive way Bretton had contrived. They understood they ought not to talk about the odd conversations in Butha-Buthe although neither had made a promise of confidentiality and both would tell their wives and friends all about it at the earliest opportunity. That was acceptable to Bretton. He did not care if people knew he had been nosey about the project. His reason for secrecy was to have the conversations before anyone official got in the way.

Besides, whatever tales they might tell would not reach American ears very quickly.

X. USAID Offices (2003)

The USAID offices were in the Embassy. With his ID from USAID/Washington, Bretton could get inside without an appointment and he asked if he could meet with whomever was running the education project. Fortunately, that person was in the office. Bretton introduced himself and then recognized the name of the education officer.

"Bill Friese! We worked together in Romania on a project a few years ago, remember that?"

"Bretton, yes, sorry I didn't recognize you right away. Didn't expect to find you down here, I guess. Yes, you did the design on that Roma education assistance. Hey, where's your hat, the black wool one. That was pretty cool."

"I don't wear that hat in the African summers. Say, I heard the project got an award from the EU. Congratulations."

"Oh you heard about that? Yes that was good. Your name should have been on it. Don't know why they left it off. I'm sure we had you listed."

"Doesn't matter. I was not there to run the thing. I was happy to have my office transfer the funding to the field. I am sure you appreciate that coming up with the funding is a challenge, even for a potential award winner." Bretton wanted to remind him that he had done critical work for the project and to suggest he was not forgiving him for leaving him off the award. "Now you are doing something here. The Ambo asked me to come by to see if I could help convince the government to be more cooperative. I used to live here and know some of them. I was a little surprised to hear about the project. I thought you just did AIDS work in Lesotho."

"Yes, that is all we did. All our program budget comes from OGAC.4 But you know how Ambassadors are. This one wants his own program, wants a legacy, you know. So he's trying to take some of the AIDS funds and give them an education angle that will be known as his idea. The health team is fighting me on this and I don't blame them."

"So the funds started at State and went to USAID to administer and the Ambo is taking them back? I don't really care about that. Is it a good idea? Is it a good use of the funds?"

"It is not what the health folks thought was the best thing when they set up our program."

"So he is not getting any extra funding?"

"No, he wants to take from our existing program. And then the Basotho are supposed to put in some."

"But you have a long term plan already approved."

"Yes, I'm not sure how the funding works. As I recall, that would be more along your line."

"I am neither an education nor a health expert, so I better have something to add. Let me look into it. But back to the program itself. Is it a good idea on its own merits?"

---

4 Office of the Global AIDS Coordinator at the U.S. State Department.

"It is good. It is not entirely his. He is mainly interested in having something with his name and he thought he could repurpose existing funds. We designed it. I believe it in it."

"What's it cost?"

"Fifty thousand a year for five years of U.S. money."

"Lesotho is a small place. It can absorb that amount easily enough but it is hard to see the effect of such a program on the OGAC annual report."

"The whole country fits within the rounding error of the South Africa figures."

"Yes, true enough. But it is our country now; yours and mine. I will make a case in Washington to fund it separately, you know, additional to the current ceiling. Can you give me three personal, intimate stories where the proposed program could affect someone? You already have this thing designed so you must have those in your head."

"I can give you the proposal."

"No, I want three stories not seen before that I can use in Washington. And I need them tomorrow. One page or less for each."

"I don't have time for something like that even if I could do it."

"You can find time. You need to give me a chance to help you. I did it before, remember, in Romania. And I have done it other places. I'll see you are credited with attracting the funds if we can get them. Come on, it will save the original program and ensure your ed program goes forward."

"Three pages. I'll give it a try."

"Knew you could. Knew you would. Do you have some pictures to go with them?"

"I'll look."

"Give me at least one about an innocent mother with AIDS and one about a child."

"Plenty of them around."

XI. The Economist (2003)

Bretton went through the security screening to the State Department side of the Embassy and then asked the young Mosotho receptionist if he could meet with the economist and she asked if he had an appointment.   He did not but he explained the economist was his control officer so she accepted that it was worth her effort to call the economist's secretary to see if he was available.   Even the smallest Embassies have layers of protocol.

As they were shaking hands, the economist skipped past the usual courtesies. "I hoped you would come by yesterday so we could work up a plan for your TDY. Didn't you get my message?"

"Message? No. Did you leave it at the hotel or at the ministry?"

"The ministry.   Isn't that where you were yesterday?"

"Yes, but I am not surprised they did not get it to me. Probably sitting on someone's desk."

"I had Khodu make up a list of Basotho officials for you; she's my secretary; very good, too; knows everyone. She will set up appointments for this week. You're going to want to see the Education Minister pretty early and there is the Dean of the Education faculty at NUL and..."

"I appreciate all that but I will go ahead and make my own appointments."

"You think you still have contacts? Khodu can get you in wherever we want. A lot has changed in 20 years."

"I probably don't have any contacts any more, but I am used to organizing my TDYs."

"We handle contractors here all the time and we know how to get them moving quickly. I've been doing this for over two years."

"I am sure you do. What works best for me is to run my own program as I have for 20 years. This assignment, like many that fall to me, is not amenable to the usual systems."

The economist saw that Bretton was not going to take direction. "OK, easier for us. If you can't get in somewhere, let us know soon so we can get started on the arrangements."

"Will do. There is some help I could use. I speak a little Sesotho but I was never good at it and forgot most of what I knew. Can I get funds for a translator to help me through the government offices?"

"You don't need a translator. They all speak English."

"Yeah, I know they do. I also know they speak Sesotho to each other and keep some of their records in Sesotho. The conversations and records I want are the ones not in English."

"I see your point. We don't give out money for this. You will have to use the Embassy contract for hiring translators. It will be easier and cheaper than anything you'll find. Just tell the secretary when you want someone."

"How much do they cost?"

"The going rate is ten rands an hour or fifty rands for a day. We pay eight rands an hour or forty rands for a day."

"Good contract. But I have friends of friends and can pay thirty rands a day and they will be happy to get it."

"Thirty? You should give us their names."

"This is college staff. They don't want to do it regularly, but I can ask them if they would like to be on your list."

"Just get us an invoice. How many days do you need this?"

"I'd like to be out of here within a week, so let's say four days for a translator."

"Sounds good."

"I'll get you an invoice." *Pshoane will give an invoice for whatever I suggest. I pay fifty bucks twice to him for Han and get thirty bucks four times from the invoice. Give the rest to M if he's helpful. Don't want any profit out of this.*

"How will you get around town? Do you want a driver?"

"Don't need one, thanks. I'll just be in the government offices, I think. They are all in the same neighborhood. I can walk pretty much every place."

"All right. What did you learn yesterday?"

"I am not really doing research here. The Ambassador wants me to get their cooperation. You already gave them the facts, I presume, so I am just giving them confidence in the program."

"You make it sound like a high level cocktail party but this is just little Lesotho. There are no big players here."

"We had no cocktails, but yes, my role is more diplomatic than technical, don't you think?"

"So how are you going to give them this confidence?"

"Let me ask you a little about the program."

Bretton asked a few questions about the education programs, questions designed to show he had done his homework and that he was not challenging the design. And then he asked what other donors were doing that might coordinate with the program. He suggested he was pursuing an angle of showing the Basotho that all the foreign assistance was coordinated to their advantage and they should not accept any part that might upset other donors. The economist liked this idea. And then Bretton brought up what the Chinese were doing.

"Oh they are not coordinating with the rest of us. They have one of the biggest programs but it is not linked to what we're doing. It is not even linked to what the Basotho want to do. It is just their usual big construction thing."

"That's too bad. What are they building?"

"A road. A road to no place up in the mountains."

"Connected to the water project?"

"Not really. The thing it, they want to wreck the Roof of Africa Rally. They see it as a Western thing, maybe a capitalistic thing. Doesn't fit their view of dominating Africa."

"And their road interferes with the rally?"

"Yeah. Well not directly. It spoils the most remote place in Lesotho and makes it into a place like any other. The rally would not draw interest if it only goes on paved roads, you know."

"Doesn't the rally go different places from year to year?"

"Some. But its popularity hinges on the bad roads up there in Sani Pass. Ambo has become a big fan; even sponsored a bike last year. He sees this as a potential big earner for Lesotho. The damn Chinese don't care about the economic impact."

"Sponsored a bike! That must cost a bit."

"Oh, he's got money. He didn't get this job on his good looks."

"Have you seen an analysis of the road impacts other than the rally?"

"There's nothing up there to take advantage of a road."

"There are people in Butha-Buthe who might benefit from better access. The returns to road improvement generally extend beyond the people and businesses already there, wouldn't you say?"

"That's not the issue here. Benefits are minimal unless you are trying to make jobs for Chinese."

Bretton did not want to argue-- there was nothing to win—but he found it curious. *Thought the Embassy economist would either agree or disagree with the World Bank analysis. How can he insist on this unsophisticated and unprofessional position? It is an insult to me to maintain it. He is trained well enough to know better than his words. He has blinded himself. Maybe it is his ambition to please the Ambassador.*

XII. Pheta (1978)

"It does have some uses. The first derivative is equivalent to the slope of a curve. If the curve is a graph of location compared to time, the slope is speed. The second derivative is acceleration. An integral is equivalent to the area under a curve. If the curve is a graph of..."

"Pheta, do you think you will remember me when you come back from the mines?"

"Of course I will, Kholu. No, wait, I'm never going to the mines. I'm going to NUL to study maths."

"Everyone goes to the mines, Pheta. You have to go."

"No I don't. I won't go because I'm going to be the Moshoeshoe scholar."

You're smart, Pheta, but you are not a scholar. That's for someone like Motsoene or Lerotholi or Mosele. All they do is study."

"I do study and you need to study too. The exam is this week and you don't have the grades to graduate unless you ace it."

"You could sit beside me. You could get me through maths and science too." Kholu swung one leg slowly to the side until it rubbed against Pheta. Pheta looked up from the book. He felt compelled to look into her eyes to see what lay in their depths, to know what she was thinking. He looked but he could not learn anything from the look. Her eyes were too dark to see much unless the light was very bright. She had smooth, shiny skin and regular features. He did not allow his eyes to drift to her body. He already knew what he would see because he had studied it already. It was better to concentrate on the gentle pressure on his leg. She was not an extraordinary looking woman, but she acted as if she were and Pheta was convinced she was the most beautiful girl in their class. He thought that fact should have made him want her more, but every time she excited him, she would demand something from him. He usually gave her whatever she wanted. She had not denied him what he wanted but she had not granted it either. He was about to finish high school and it was time for him to experience this thing everyone thought was so important. Coochie seemed the one to give him that experience. She showed every sign of willingness but always for some other time than the present.

They were sitting in a deep window sill of a stone building used for storing hay for the animals. There was no place at the mission school in Morija where they could sit in complete privacy. Seen through the window, they appeared to be a healthy young couple studying the books in their laps. Anyone would guess they were largely thinking about each other but there was no controlling such thoughts. It was considered sufficient to control their actions. Sister Florence had seen them go into the shed. She had told them in the past they could study in there only if they sat in the window where she could monitor them from her desk. She would let them sit there for thirty minutes if they seemed to be behaving and then she would ask them to move along.

"I will sit beside you at the examination, Coochie, but that is not enough. Who knows how close the monitor will be? It is too risky to depend it. Calc just isn't that hard and we still have a few days."

"Pheta, you just don't understand. I will never know calculus. No matter what. Not even if it has some kind of use for telling when two trains will smash into each other. Not even if I knew I was going to be on one of those trains. It is easy for you and impossible for me."

"Come on. You're smart. You're smarter than me in English."

The two students were speaking in Sesotho, in some version of Sesotho strewn with words young high school students of the day favored. Pheta was not worried about his grades although he always did his work. His confidence might have contributed to a more relaxed level of effort but he simply had a very strong view of who he was and he was the sort to get good grades regardless of how much he studied. Further, he was the sort to attract the best girls, the sort to win a scholarship, the sort to have the best someday. Things came to him easily. He had no reason to doubt his luck would ever diminish.

"English! Anyone can do English. Just talk to people."

"But you can write essays. You write for the school newsletter. I would hate to do that."

"So what? Are you going to get me through the maths exam?"

"I'm trying but you're not studying."

"Studying will never get me through that exam. Come on Sweetie. Let's do something else. I know a place behind my dormitory."

This idea was intriguing but it interfered with exams in an uncomfortable way.

"Let's go behind the dormitory next week."

"Let's go now; then go again next week," she purred as she pulled his hand off the book and toward herself.

Pheta did not lean forward to let his hand reach her body. She looked just as good as she did a moment earlier but he no longer wanted her. He was surprised to find his desire dissipate. For some years he wanted a girl every time he considered the idea. Here was the specific one he wanted the most and suddenly he did not want her any more. It had something to do with her trying to take him away from studying for exams. Or maybe it had to do with her disrespect for the exams that he expected would validate himself. Or even more likely, once he thought about it, he lost his passion because she was offering herself in return for cheating on the exam. He thought he was the best looking, smartest, and most personable boy in the school so he should not have to trade something in order for a girl to give herself to him. He waited for her to get back to work, to accept his help, but she only pouted, apparently believing he could not turn her down. He wondered why she was so insistent at this moment and he suspected she thought she would control him if they had sex. She might even be right about that and he worried about that. He also worried about how he could stop wanting her so suddenly. Would he always reject sex when it became available?

"If you have to go outside so bad, go ahead."

His comment did not make any sense but it shocked her for its implications. Pheta was not accepting her. She did not know this was really possible. It was not her first time with sex but she was not so experienced that she could figure out what was wrong. She had never heard of a boy turning down what she had to offer.

Pheta did turn her down that day. He did what he could on the day of the exam to help her and it was enough for her to graduate but not enough to get her into the university. She was not enough of a distraction to prevent Pheta from doing very well and getting a scholarship, just as he had expected.

Eventually, he managed to experience sex with another girl without suddenly losing interest. It was hard to find the opportunity while living under the eye of the nuns that ran the school but they tended to trust him because of his good grades and he found his opportunity. He decided this thing he had heard about so much was all that he had heard, and it was well worth experiencing more, however, with school ending just after exams, he would soon be back home where there were not many girls to explore. He worried about finding girls worthy of his attentions for the time before meeting the fancier ones at college but a problem from an unexpected source threatened to ruin his whole concept of life.

Pheta worked his way home at the end of the school term, feeling grown up because the nuns had trusted him to leave on his own. His mother had understandably not come to graduation with all that she had to do with the garden and the other children. It was not really a difficult trip but it was exciting. He took a kombi, that is, a van that served as a very crowded taxi, from the college to Maseru where he found a real bus going up into the mountains. After leaving the bus, he rode on the wagon behind a tractor for a few kilometers and then walked the rest of the way in the dark, not a hard thing when the weather is good although it was the longest he had ever been surrounded by strangers since the day he started school.

As he crested the last rise in the road, he could see the dim light coming from his mother's rondavel. He unconsciously straightened his back and picked up his pace. He had not seen her since the last term began and he was worked up to tell her about his grades and about being certain to have a scholarship to the university.

He hesitated before the door and listened. He could hear voices but they were subdued and he could not make out the words. Even so, he recognized the sound of his sisters in conversation. He threw the door open for the drama of it and stood in the doorway waiting to be recognized. His three sisters were sitting at the table while his mother sat by the stove, feeding in some coal. She turned when she heard the sound of the door and began to ululate even before she was up on her feet.

"*Mme, le gai?*" Pheta greeted his mother in a relaxed way but could not hold himself back to display the cool he thought should come from a graduate. "Oh Mme," he sighed and tears forced their way out of his eyes and he hugged his mother. The sisters ran to greet him, copying their mother's ululations. The neighbors would be by to see what was causing such noisy celebration. Four females can rouse most of a village at any hour, but coming at night without warning would bring out everyone. Pheta's mother understood this and she dragged Pheta outside to show him to the village. With her size and her regimen of hard work, she really could drag him although he did not mean to resist her attentions.

"Pheta is back! Pheta is here!" Pheta's mother screamed and his sisters followed her in this too. The neighbors soon decided it was a family celebration. They liked Pheta well enough but they did not know him since he went to school. He had no special friends in the village. A few shouted their congratulations and a few muttered their annoyance at being disturbed but the fuss was over in ten minutes.

When they had settled back inside the home, Pheta's mother continued to hold to him, standing behind him while he sat at the head of the table and started to explain how he had come.

"It has been a terribly long day, sisters. I got up before the sun. I always do that at school even on the days they let us sleep. I am used to a bed now but I do not need to spend all day on it. And today I come home to tell you the news for the rest of my life!"

The girls squealed in unmusical harmony right over his words. They did not listen closely to what Pheta had said – they were just so excited to have him turn up after so many months away. Village life does not have many good unexpected events. Their noise was exciting for Pheta, but he wondered if they were more interested in being loud than in hearing his plans. They could hardly imagine his plans would be interesting-- they never made any plans themselves since they felt no control over the future.

"Mme," Pheta continued, turning his head to see his mother but not standing up as being seated conferred a higher status on him. "Mme, you will love to see my grades. I have done my work and I have done it well. Of course I have passed the examination for a Cambridge Overseas School Certificate. This is recognized anywhere in the world. I am one of the best in my class. The nuns are very happy with me. They call me the 'candle from the mountains.' They know where our village is. They said there has never been a flame as bright from a place like this. They have great hope for my college."

"Yes Pheta. It is good, very good, *hantle haholo*, that you have been such a good student. You have always been so smart I knew you could be a scholar. I am more proud about your hard work. I know you always had your family in mind to inspire you."

"My family? Yes, I guess so. I want my family to be proud of me. There is a chance I could be the Moshoeshoe scholar[5] when I finish college. Everyone says so. Just there is one girl who beat me in high school but she's a girl so she got to her best when she was young. I'll be way ahead of her in four years. Don't worry about that."

"That is wonderful Pheta." She snapped her wrist in a way that threw one finger against the others to make a sound that brought emphasis to her words. "You will be the best scholar in four years. We will save enough pula (money) by then for you to go to university."

"No, you do not understand how good this is. I will have a scholarship. It will not cost anything for me

---

[5] The award is named for the first king of Lesotho.

to go to university. Of course I will not have pocket money from the scholarship. Maybe you can spare a little for me. I will pay it back many times over when I am a university man. I might be a lawyer or an Ambassador to some country. Or I might learn how to make a lot in business. Many South African businesses are sure to offer positions to the Moshoeshoe Scholar each year!"

"Pocket money? You will lack pocket money! Do you mean beer money? No, you will not need it because you must work in the mines first. We have waited ten years for all your schooling. We have been hungry and your sisters have little clothing because you are not earning anything. When will you help your family? Do you think you have no family just because you only come here for two months of the year? You even need your family to get your scholarship. Do you think they will pay you to go to university if your family is hungry? Look on the shelves? Do see cakes and sweeties for these girls?"

"Mme, I did not study hard and get the best grades so I could go to the mines like every other boy. You do not know what is possible for me. When I finish all my school, I will be able to support the family better than ever."

"I know what we need right now and I know you are still a boy and I am your mother. Maybe you do not care about that so I ask you, 'What do you think your father will say?'"

"I don't care what he says."

"Do you care about your sisters? Or your mother?"

Pheta felt tears in the corner of his eyes again and he blinked to be sure they did not fall. It was too dark in the room for anyone to see but he would have been embarrassed to feel them. He was confused to hear that his mother was not happy about his future. Was he not supposed to get good grades? That was not for going to the mines.

"Mme, I could die there. Like Ntate Letsie, you know, Puso's father."

Pheta's sisters became very quiet. They were nearly as shocked as Pheta at how this was turning out.

Pheta's mother felt the tension in the room. She felt it was her fault that Pheta's homecoming had gone badly. She should have shown him what he needed to do instead of shouting it out. He was a good boy. She should treat him like one.

"Pheta, Pheta. You won't die in the mines. You are the first Mosotho I ever heard who was afraid to earn a living for his family."

That was not what she meant to say. That was not sympathy for the responsibilities Pheta was suddenly facing. Pheta sat silent with his head turned down. He was not looking at the table; his eyes were shut. He was trying to escape the strange situation. He could not close his ears but most of the noise was coming from within his own brain anyway. His mother understood so little of what he could accomplish yet there was no reason to believe he could explain it to her. She knew so many things and had so many skills but she did not know anything he had learned in high school so she could not know what was possible for him.

Pheta's mother tried again, speaking softly at first but soon rising to her full voice just because she was so determined to be heard.

"Pheta, you do not have to be afraid. You will not go into the mines. At least you will not set the

116

charges if you go inside the mines. You are a graduate. They will have some special task for you. Something that uses your maths. Maybe you could be the accountant. They just sit at a desk, right? And make even more money. You are small so you must use your head."

Pheta heard in his mother's words that she knew the risks he would face. She knew, although the women of Lesotho never spoke of it, that the Basotho, that is, the foreigners in the South African mines, did the most dangerous work. Taking a high risk by the standards of a South African mine in those days was very high risk indeed. People thought of South Africa as a blessed country for having gold underneath it, but there was gold underneath other countries where no one was desperate enough to go as deep as in South Africa where the loss of human life exceeded what other countries would allow for their workers. The Basotho understood in some ways how they were being exploited but the danger had been turned into a form of national pride. It was an African machismo that served the Basotho poorly.

"Accountant? I am no accountant, I want to be a mathematician. I do not even want to know accounting. She makes it sound like being the smartest one is not important unless you are too small and too scared to be useful," Pheta said to his sisters although he had not actually meant to utter his thought aloud. He could not see the reaction from his mother but he sensed a look on her face that hurt him more than her words.

He had to recover his place with her. "Mother, it does not even matter if you are right or wrong because, as you said, you are my mother and I know you have always loved us all and only want to do what is best for the family. I will do as you say. I always have. I do not know what the South Africans can do with me but I think you may have a good point about my being small. I am not good for the hard work. I should be in the offices."

His mother put a hand on his head and rubbed him slowly, working her fingers into the dense, kinked mass. His hair felt young to her. She knew how youth may have wild and unrealistic ambitions, especially likely in a youth with Pheta's successes. She did not know what a mathematician did although she was closer to the truth on this point than her son who also did not know what mathematicians did although he imagined he did.

"We do not need to say any more about this tonight. Let us be happy to have you with us, abuti." It was not usual for a mother to call her son "abuti." It is what his pals called him, but she had heard them call each other that way for years and at this moment she felt a partnership with her son more like friendship.

Pheta slept by the fire that night. The blanket under him was comfort enough for him but he did not sleep well. For some years he had seen himself going directly to university. He had seen himself as enviable among his peers, as handsome, smart, funny, quick on the football pitch. No one who knew him at school would have thought he would be underground in the hot rock and dark mud like one more Mosotho man sending the bulk of his pay to his family and drinking what remained of it on holidays, like his own father. Yet now he had promised his mother to help the family. In his troubled dreams, he kept returning to the thought that it might not even be possible to fulfil that promise. He had not filed for a position with the mining companies. If there was anything for him there, it was probably not going to be open for some months. He felt guilty for noticing this constraint on meeting his promise, unsure if it was a good thing or a bad thing.

Early the next morning, Pheta left his home with a small packet of food and his bundle of clothes for Maseru to find the recruiters. He did not think of what he was doing during the trip to the city. He reminisced about his family, how they were when he was living at home and how they were almost strangers to him now.

The bus terminal in Maseru was a large lot, unpaved and empty of any permanent construction but with a bustle of buses, kombis, lost and waiting travelers, and venders of everything sold in Lesotho. Considerable

livestock of portable size, mainly goats, lambs and chickens, mixed with the travelers going both to and from the villages. The luggage of the travelers was often voluminous as they carried bundles of purchased goods back to their villages. Most conspicuous were the two-meter tall clear plastic bags of Cheetos that could serve a medium-sized family for six months of snacking, but were more likely destined to be repackaged and sold to the neighbors.

The first young man Pheta asked was able to tell him where the mine offices were. Pheta asked the clerk inside how to apply for the work. The clerk gave him a form and added that they were not hiring immediately. That comment was enough for Pheta and he did not fill in the form. He tucked it into his shirt, promising himself to do it later but knew he never would. He then struck out to find the home of a school friend who had offered to help if Pheta ever came to Maseru. He was surprised at how easily he redirected his steps, at how certain he was of the way to the friend's house although it had only been described to him once and he realized his mind had secretly been planning how to survive until his scholarship began. That night he wrote to his mother to explain that he had sought a job at the mines but they could not offer him any job right away. He went on to say he was educated enough to work in an office and he was too small to impress the mining company with his potential underground. He presumed one of his sisters could read the letter to his mother but he was not sure they could read. He felt badly for not talking to them more when he was home. This regret returned to him numerous times over the next couple months but was never quite strong enough to motivate Pheta to travel back home to see them.

Pheta's friend had no job himself but he managed to accumulate enough money for food and beer by a combination of petty thievery and gambling. The gambling had a degree of intimidation in it so it paid consistently if not lucratively. The operation was considered to be training for the day when he moved with his friends to Sun City to make serious money. They might have been training in the minor arts of crime but they had no idea of how to get to Bophuthatswana with papers that would let them stay. Sun City, known to young men as "Sin City," was a resort area set up in one of the ersatz countries known as Bantustans, based on the model of American Indian reservations. The South African government pretended the Bantustans were independent and forced black Africans to crowd into them where the South African government could more easily avoid providing services like schooling and roads. Certain activities, like casino gambling, that were

prohibited in South Africa were allowed in the Bantustans although the clientele was almost entirely white South African.

Pheta quickly got as job as a waiter in a café which made his friend jealous. Pheta enjoyed the envy and wished he could repay something to his friend for providing a place to sleep but he hardly made any money. There were no tips to be had and the salary was paltry. He sent all of it to his family. Pheta had gotten the job by underbidding the current waiter. He did it for the food, eating scraps from the tables he cleared. It was enough to get him through until it was time to go to the university.

《 《 《 《 ¤ 》 》 》 》

His high school performance did not lead to the glory he had envisaged. At the national university, there were more smart people than he expected so he was not destined to become the academic standout that had seemed so likely when he began. On the other hand, he was as popular with girls as he hoped and he learned steadily how to attract them and enjoy them without creating too much enmity. That phase of study distracted him from him coursework which had lost some of its luster when he realized he would not get the top grades no matter how much he worked at it.

After three years, his scholarship was taken away. The letter he received about this stated very clearly that it was being ended due to shortage of funding not due to his performance. It expressed the hope that he would reapply after a year when there might be additional funding. He went to the scholarship office which was really just a small table and a large filing cabinet next to the actual desk of the university finance officer. The scholarship clerk admitted the prospects of additional funding in the next year were slim and he suggested that Pheta look for a job in the mines so he could save some money for tuition. There was even a possibility that he might get a scholarship to finish college in Europe or America. Pheta filled out the forms for these but he knew he could not expect anything to come of them.

Pheta, like many young people, had thought that when he graduated there might be a job waiting for him although he did not have any particular concrete job in mind. Without even the degree, he only saw one thing that would take advantage of his unique abilities: teaching. He should be a professor, he thought, although he knew there were not many such positions, maybe none for someone who never finished school. He was resigned to accepting something with low wages as long as it had potential for advancement. He applied to the mining companies and the other South African firms that recruited for skilled positions from the National University of Lesotho. These firms recruited, but only took a handful of the best graduates. He refused to consider working in the mines themselves. He remained confident he was clever enough to do something on the surface of the earth where he felt safe and could see the light and could find interesting girls. His professors did respect his abilities and saw him as well above average in ability and willingness to work and these good opinions, which he had earned, eventually yielded an offer within Lesotho. Pheta recognized the irony that it relied as much on his experience as a herd boy as it did on his extraordinary formal education—he was to teach animal husbandry at the Lesotho Agricultural College. It would provide a salary and a home. He could help his family in the small way they expected and he could participate in the social life of the capital city but he would keep an eye out for something better, something with potential for growth.

XIII. Bretton Buys a Car (1983)

The capital of Lesotho was not large, not when Bretton arrived in 1981. He could have walked from the side near the national border where he lived on the college campus to the opposite end of town, also near the border which wrapped around the city along with the Caledon River, in less than an hour. Most Basotho walked everywhere. In the mountains some used ponies, but in Maseru they walked. The most common stores in Lesotho were shoe stores. In many remote villages, that is the only kind of shop. Peace Corps volunteers in Lesotho were not allowed to buy a car. They used bicycles. Bretton, however, was part of the mainstream international community and that implied he needed a car.

Bretton consulted with the American Embassy and learned there was no place to buy a car in Lesotho. A man whose job involved monitoring the local news and writing daily reports to Washington yearned for the chance to get away from the office and offered to drive him into South Africa to a dealer. It would be hard to make any deal since Bretton could not shop multiple places without further inconveniencing his kindly driver. He had a budget and would just get the best car he could for the money. Following advice from the Embassy, he got cash from the bank. No one in South Africa would take his check or credit card. There were no large bills in the bank so he counted and then carried out a stack 18 inches high. The bank clerk was worried about his walking out with such a large bundle but Bretton felt no threat and carried his cash casually in a paper bag like a bulky lunch.

The car dealer was much better than Bretton expected. Like most car dealers, he was personable although Bretton thought his prattle excessive when he promised the recent year, eggshell blue Peugeot had been owned only by an elderly lady who used it only for driving to church on Sunday. But the price was good, as far as Bretton could tell, and he had no other choice anyway.

The car was better than any he had owned in the States and served him well over the next couple years. His biggest problem with it came in his first week of ownership. He had a flat tire on his second day. The tires were not bad; the roads were terrible. He put on the spare easily enough and went to the garage to get the punctured tire fixed. But the garage near the college did not fix punctures and did not even know who did. That seemed implausible since punctures were likely very common. *Perhaps*, he imagined, *the mechanic is jealous of the garages with more capacity.* He went back to the college and asked one of the Brits where to get a tire repaired. He suggested the place Bretton had already tried but had another to recommend as well.

On the way to the second garage, Bretton was stopped by the police for not wearing a seatbelt. This was also surprising. The police were famous for enforcing nothing and safety was hardly a concern in Lesotho. Bretton suspected the ticket was only an excuse for a bribe but the policeman acted very properly and gave no indication it could be resolved by less than a court appearance. The ticket cost 40 Rand, much more than a Mosotho, even one with a car, could afford.

The second garage did not repair tires either but they did know a place that did. The directions to the third garage were very complicated so the mechanic offered to send a boy along to show Bretton the way as long as he promised to bring the boy back. The mechanic did not say how much this service would cost, but it was the best option Bretton could see at the time.

The boy was about ten or eleven, Bretton guessed. His clothes were torn and filthy. For a boy short of puberty, he carried a lot of odor. Bretton hoped the boy did not leave grease stains on the pale plastic seats of his new used car. The boy pointed out which way to go and where to turn. He did indeed seem sure of the way. Bretton had less confidence when the pavement petered out and the houses became more ramshackle and more dispersed. Eventually they were driving on a rough dirt road out of sight of any building. The boy could not be any threat, but he might have been simple. Bretton was about to give up when they crested a hill and the boy pointed to a blocky building with various broken machines in front. Bretton stopped the car and three young men came out of the building. They spoke only Sesotho and listened to the boy who suddenly spoke fluently. Bretton recognized two oft repeated words: "maluti," the money of Lesotho; and "dagga," the southern African term for marijuana although he was not sure where he had heard it. By their gestures, Bretton soon understood they were trying to sell him marijuana. He tried to indicate that he wanted his tire fixed. He tried to communicate to them and then tried with the boy. It was all a joke. The boy believed this was a trip to buy grass, nothing else. Then he noticed the word "rand" was being used and one of the men pointed to the license plate on Bretton' car. Suddenly Bretton understood. The plate was South African. They thought he was South African. The mechanics thought he was South African. The traffic cop thought he was South African. He was not welcome. Even in their poverty, they preferred harassing him to taking his money, except for the dagga dealers. Bretton drove the boy back to the garage. It was getting late and the mechanic was closing up. Bretton walked up to him and stood silently to see what he would say. The mechanic hardly looked up. He was watched more closely by several boys in the garage who stopped what they were doing to see the confrontation.

Finally Bretton broke the quiet. "Lumela." It was his only word of Sesotho. It was a greeting. "I work at the Agricultural College. I am American." He held out his hand.

The mechanic shook his hand. "You have a puncture?"

"Yes, can you fix it?"

"We are knocking off for the night, but yes, we can fix it. I will stay late for you."

"I've got to get new plates for my car."

The mechanic looked at the car and smiled broadly, showing large white teeth with a gap on the middle of the bottom row. He waved to the three boys in the garage and the whole team took on the repair. Bretton did not mind learning a lesson. He had no love for the generic white South African male either. He wished he had learned his lesson before incurring a 40-rand ticket.

XIV. The Boat Race (1983)

On one of Bretton's first Saturday mornings in Lesotho, the British neighbor from across the street knocked on his door before he was fully awake. He hated to be seen as a late riser so he pulled on a pair of shorts on his way to the door and tried to look alert.

"Hey, hey," was all he could think to say when he opened the door. A quick look with his emerging consciousness was enough to determine that his neighbor was not the sort to judge a man by his look at seven am on a Saturday. He was himself hardly dressed for the day, wearing only a low-hanging pair of shorts with obviously nothing underneath and a pair of plastic sandals. His red hair was in disarray and his sparse beard was unshaven, and had been for several days at least. His bare chest would have been a delicate shade of pink except for the pale hairs that cast their tiny shadows on his skin. With his short stature and boney body, he reminded Bretton of a leprechaun although Bretton felt bad that the racial stereotype was in his head. If he had met more Brits, he would have realized the accent was Cockney, not Irish. Bretton's shortage of words did not matter since the neighbor was in full conversation, that is, he provided both sides of the "exchange," by the time Bretton had said his two syllables.

"You're the new man for the college, right? American? That's OK. We can ignore that for the present. Sorry I've haven't been 'round before. Busy during the week, you know. I do mechanics. When I'm not teaching the buggers, I'm fixing the farm. What're you teaching? Don't matter to me. You're welcome here."

He put out his hand and as they shook, he pulled Bretton out into the sunlight. "Roger... Roger Caldwell," he introduced himself like James Bond. Bretton almost mimicked the style but decided it would be risking a bad start with his neighbor. To be friendly, he just gave his first name.

"Bretton." *Total: three words for me so far and two of them were the same word and not even a word.*

"Say, you're just what we need: a young, fit American to fill out our team. What are you doing today? Not as big as your neighbor Alan ...have you met him yet? I'll take you by... He should have come over first thing ...must be out on the farm ... but you're a good bit bigger than me so that's good. Can you row? Probably don't need to row much. It's a race, boat race. We built one. Everyone's built a boat or a raft or some shit to get down the river on Saturday, today. Important thing is to get good and drunk. But the college boat ...wait 'til you see it ...a monster ...we want it to win this year so we'll do the drinking afterwards, most of it, while we're waiting for the others to finish. You been on the river yet?"

He paused, suggesting this was an actual question.

"I've seen it. I can see it from here if that's the river you mean. Caledon, isn't it?"

"Caledon. Right. We have a raft race every year. Came in second last year to the Germans. Can't let that happen again. They have a tiny Embassy here. I think we're going to have a Basotho boat this year. I been talkin' it up to the guys in the garage. Told them they were better than the Germans since it's mechanics against bureaucrats. Got to get away from the race thing, biological race, I mean. Sensitive around here, you know. Good reasons for it. But Germans! Really."

"What time is the race?" Bretton disguised his passion with a simple question. He liked the idea of a race. He liked the chance to show off his athleticism, but more than that he liked reliving the moments of glory at sports. A race among people who were not specialists was unlikely to revive the moments of sports failure. He had more of the former than of the latter but he hated losing so much he had stopped doing sport.

"We start at noon. Got to wait for it to get hot enough, you know. Once it's hot enough the women in the crowd will start stripping down to their swimming kit so we can enjoy the drinking part more. We'll be alright. 'Bound to be wet most of the way. I want to start before the Germans. Then we can crash around the first bend until they catch up and take 'em on. Dump 'em out, tear up their rig. We've got a huge raft so we can take more men. We're not going to hurt anyone, of course. They won't even fight back. I know 'em well enough. Bunch of bureaucrats. All part of the thing."

Bretton was wary of his relationship to competition. It had evolved during his high school years from an innocent, boyish way of interacting into a master of his personality. He had not channeled his drive into performance in areas he wanted to value, like schoolwork, but he had allowed it to blossom wherever it was easiest to win which implied, in turn, where it was easy to define winning. He played whatever game was available with a fervor that carried past more talented players, having learned that wanting to win was a big part of succeeding. He was frustrated by the poor rewards of winning contests that were inherently meaningless but he could not control his attention to these games. Like a gambler, he always held out hope that winning one more thing would transform his reputation and bring widespread respect and attention, especially from girls. *If only*, he imagined, *if only I could star in one of the prominent sports, football or basketball, and be chased by colleges and the media, famous beyond our town so I could turn away from my friends and the girls around home with better prospects in the future.*

He did get into a decent college, not the one he felt he deserved and not one as good as might have welcomed him if had applied himself to the right things, but he had a small athletic scholarship and that was something. He managed to become a star in his chosen sport, a star in a second tier sport at a second tier school, a star in the eyes of the people he knew but not in his own eyes. He knew better and took no comfort in seeing through his own act. But this was only his extended immaturity and it eventually wore thin.

Bretton had been self-aware for many years but still out of control. It was getting a steady girlfriend in graduate school that broke the hold of competition on him. Laura did not care in the least about success in sports and games and yet she liked Bretton. It convinced him there was more in himself than the ability to find an angle in any situation in which he came out on top and that there were girls with higher concerns than his. It was very fine to have a girlfriend but she was too much for him. His ego could not handle this form of success either and he moved on, finally getting a focus on what he believed was best, on his books. And then his ego recovered. He stayed away from games, like an alcoholic on the wagon, and he stayed away from fine women despite the way more of them seemed to like him now that he was not showing off for them. He knew the alcoholic's mantra, "I am an alcoholic," even if it had been twenty years since last taking a drink and he felt the pull of winning some simple game and reminded himself: *I am overly competitive.* But he was sure he could return to his old form for a lark with his new colleagues.

"Come get me when you're headed out to the starting line then?"

"Now. We're going now. We need time to train."

Bretton had things to do on his first day off but meeting his colleagues informally deserved priority. Besides, the idea of a race with amateurs was very provocative.

"Let's see; you've got shorts and sandals. I just have shorts. Can I go in and put something on my feet?"

"Yeah. Don't worry about food or anything. My wife has it all. You'll have lunch with us. Lucky you; you get to meet the brats too today. You dash inside for some shoes. I'll knock up Alan and then go back for the lorry. The women and brats will come along later."

Bretton dressed quickly, skipping the shower and shave, hoping he would have time for some breakfast before Roger came back. He did not, however, mind his frantic neighbor. Rather, he admired his energy and his welcoming embrace. He liked being a part of their party and how Roger had said he was just what they wanted. He liked having something to do on his first weekend just as if he belonged in this distant land. It was like his first days in college as a student rather than as a teacher. He had not expected that. He could only hope it did not fall apart as fast as his college experience had.

He walked over to Alan's house, hoping to be there before Roger was finished rousing Alan. He was not sure why he wanted to appear ready so fast. It might have been his competitive urges arising or it might have been to reassure Roger that he was not fussy in his preparations. Roger was coming out of the front door just as Bretton was about to knock.

"Take hold of this cooler. Alan's got it full up. We need to start lightening the load. Want to pop one open for the road?"

"I usually wait until 8 am for the first brew of the day. That's when classes started at my school."

"Oooh, we don't do any drinkin' in classes. It only for the weekends. And only when there's no students around. And only when there's a race coming up, one that needs some fortification. We're only drinkin' so we can beat the Krauts for the honor of the college. Start the term off proper."

"I can see you rarely touch the stuff."

Alan and Roger and Bretton had plenty of room to share the bench seat of the lorry. Tied onto the bed in back was the monstrous college raft. Roger did most of the talking although he directed some questions at Alan who answered them simply. Bretton was content to listen and no one asked him anything. They talked about the raft and the race. They also said some things about people Bretton did not know, nearly all of whom appeared to be British. There was no mention of the college or anything else that could be identified as relating to Lesotho.

The drive to the start of the race was not far, but the miserable conditions of the road and the clumsy vehicle they were using kept them at little more than a jogger's pace for twenty minutes. Bretton could tell when they were approaching the river because trees lined the riverbank and they were the only trees he had seen in Lesotho outside of the college grounds and expatriates' yards. Roger drove to a large open area with horse jumping fences scattered around and several empty kraals nearby.

"This is the police training ground. They don't mind if we use it," Roger explained. Bretton did not find his comment reassuring. He expected police in any country to be highly protective of their assets.

"They ride horses a lot here?" Bretton asked innocently.

"Ponies," Alan interjected quickly. "They have a few real horses for show but mostly they ride ponies. They have their own breed here. Good for mountain trails. Not much for jumping, of course, but you can see from this field that they do some jumps."

Roger added "They can't do real dressage, but you have to admit they maneuver in formations very nicely. Worth coming out when they're putting on their show. It's about the only disciplined thing you'll ever see them do."

"There're into racing too. Out at the race track, naturally. The police win a lot of the races," Alan add again trying to speak positively, it seemed.

"They get the best ponies, I guess." Roger would not let a positive word about the local police go unchallenged although it would be fair to say he would not have accepted a positive word about the police anywhere else either. "If a pony turns out to be fast, they get it one way or another by the time the next races come up."

"We going to set up in the riding arena?" Bretton asked, his skepticism enhanced by Roger's suggestion of police bullying.

"They know we won't mess with any of their stuff. We go separate ways. They don't mess with our stuff either."

It was not clear what stuff Roger meant. Bretton figured it was best to listen and watch rather than ask and challenge the people in a new environment. He was taking a risk on this boisterous Brit who was running things. Wrecking the German boat, especially when based on the assumption the college raft would have an advantage in manpower, was not sporting, obviously, and he did respect sport more than war. It felt like a European form of competition with rules based on something beyond sport. It felt nasty and made him think of the soccer hooligans from Britain. The longer he followed them into this game, the harder it would be to extract himself if he felt the need to quit. He was no quitter. He had edged himself in and he was here to the end or to damn near any end. Roger did not seem vicious even if he did have a little man's chip on his shoulder and Alan seemed like a nice guy, large and sedate. It was not likely he would let Roger do anything stupid, not while he was still sober anyway.

It all looked safer as the rest of the team arrived. Two were small, quiet Basotho from the mechanical shop that Roger ran. They showed no interest in the race or the Germans. They were motivated by loyalty to Roger and the prospect of free beer. Then Ahmad, an Iraqi, came along, the one Bretton had met already and who was effectively his boss at the college since he was the team leader on the contract that hired Bretton. The Iraqi was dressed in pressed tennis whites and looked more comfortable hoisting a martini than a beer. His wife and two children had come along with him and helped set up a table with their lunch even though it was not yet nine am. Ahmad brought his family over to Bretton to introduce them. Roger cut him off saying there would be time for that later, that it was time to train for the race. Bretton was surprised that the Iraqi accepted this intervention and nodded to his wife to go back to their table. Bretton stepped quickly to her to shake her hand and then bent down to say hello to the little boy. He was not going to be caught up in a silly game. His purpose, he reminded himself, was to make friends of his colleagues, not to run a race and, more than that, to remember that the way to make friends is not to beat them in a race, not even when you are on the same side.

Once the whole team was assembled and those who wanted a beer had sucked one down, they dragged the raft over to the beach on the river. It was all they could do to launch the awkward, overweight miscreation. Fortunately no other watercraft had reached the beach yet so there was room to maneuver. Bretton wondered if the river was wide enough for the raft to pass all the way to the end of the race downstream at the college, but he did not worry about it very much because he did not feel responsible for winning the race.

With the raft tied by a long tether to a sturdy tree that looked like the broadleaved cottonwoods Bretton knew from the rivers in Ohio, the team clambered on board. Roger assigned everyone positions and tasks. Bretton was assigned a push-pole and a position on the back corner where he could jump off quickly when it came time to attack the Germans. Bretton had looked at their craft to develop a strategy for disabling it with a minimum of violence and a maxim of cheerful play. Their boat was designed for a sea crew, making it hard to eject them. He suggested tossing their oars on the bank, upstream from the attack site. Roger did not like that but he agreed the oars were their weak point. He suggested they simply take the oars and carry them to the end of the race where they could be ceremoniously and good-naturedly returned.

Roger ran them through some drills of his own invention. It all seemed full of very bad ideas to Bretton. He wondered why anyone was obeying this childish man: a distinguished Iraqi; a tall, quiet Brit; two young mechanics who might have an incentive to humor their supervisor if Roger really was their supervisor; a slim, thoughtful veterinarian from Ethiopia but trained in Bulgaria; and himself, a newly arrived American with an obsessive past in competitive sports. They were an unlikely group for a race and even less likely as a group to go beyond the rules of fair play except that they had such a wide range of backgrounds. Bretton had no good reason to expect to understand what they were thinking. He employed an old technique from his card-playing days and looked into their eyes to see what lay there and he saw they were all enjoying the game, enjoying silly Roger running things, Roger from the mechanics department which was normally remote from the college administration, that is, from strategic leadership. Bretton was curious about how far each of the others would follow Roger's craziness and which of them would resist from principle and which from fear, and further, whether they would be any good at the game Roger was running.

"Bretton will be the main pole man on the right side and Alan will be on the left so stay out of their way when they need to walk along the side. You lot will be keeping us aimed on the river, keep us pointed forward. I'll move around to fill in wherever I can. If you're not pushing, work on balancing our craft. Don't think that's a small thing. Last year all our troubles came from sloshing around and getting stuck sideways in the damn river. Now I know the main pole men will be working hard so they'll need to take a rest at some point. They will let me know when they are ready for a switch and then you reserves will take a turn. Let's try making a switch. Alan, call for a change."

Alan was not entirely enthusiastic but he did call out and then Roger tapped the Iraqi to take over. He stood up and the raft rocked out of control. He had not stood up before on the raft and had no feel for the balance of it. Bretton took a big step to keep himself upright and rocked the raft some more. He fell to his knees and scraped both of them on the rough flooring. Meanwhile both Basotho rolled over the side. Roger staggered and then he fell overboard too. The Basotho were laughing but Roger was still sputtering orders. The Iraqi managed to keep standing and he put out his hands to take the pole from Alan who just shook his head at the absurdity of it all.

"Maybe, Roger, we should keep seated. We can all do some poling." Bretton sat of the edge of the raft and demonstrated. He was not sure his way was faster but it was much more comfortable. "How long is the route anyway?' he asked.

"Well, don't you see? That is just the point. It is a long run; maybe we can do it under an hour. We have the largest team in the field. We can afford to wear out our constituent parts and put in replacements. It'll be cushy to wait your turn on the push poles." Roger sensed the hard work their practice had shown would be needed was cutting into the enthusiasm of his team. Bretton sensed it too although he was himself starting to enjoy the thing. He analyzed the team and came up with a strategy for optimizing its performance. As they were beginning to show doubts about the race, Bretton suggested it was time to relax. He looked directly at Roger to catch his eye in a way to show his complicity rather than any misgivings.

"We are trained up now, don't you think? We have a plan and we have felt the balance of the raft. Let's not show our skills to the others. Time for a beer and let's see what Mrs. Roger has brought along."

Roger was surprised at this suggestion to halt their preparations. He did not think it had gone well at all, but the look he was getting from Bretton caused him to hesitate and in a moment he was too late as all the others took the suggestion as an order and they jumped, and fell and slid off the raft and onto the sandy shore. In their sudden movement in the same direction, Bretton and Roger were left to bob high and low on the opposite side of the raft, struggling to keep it from overturning, and then they scrambled to keep it from sinking on their side when they were the only weight remaining on board. It was a few seconds of roller coaster fun that Roger nearly turned into an angry complaint against his departing crew but which, in the end, he let pass as if it were all his idea.

When the commotion had settled down a minute later. Bretton said, "If the Captain is the last to abandon ship, you should let me go. I'll see if I can disembark without dumping you in the mighty Caledon."

"Disembark? Do you Americans use words like that? What are you going to be teaching here anyway?

You know we're just a technical school. These kids need to learn something useful."

"What am I going to teach? As far as I know, I am here to teach young Basotho. Beyond that, I am open to suggestion." He stood in the shallow water and steadied the raft as Roger climbed off silently. Roger's silence and his peeve did not last for long. Before they had scrambled up the bank, he was encouraging Roger to tell his wife and kids it was time to eat lunch.

By the time Bretton had located Roger's family, they were serving liverwurst sandwiches and beer to the two Basotho who worked with Roger. Bretton was resolved to respect local customs in food but that did not extend to British cuisine. Liverwurst was near the top of his list of foods to forego although he had never actually tasted any of it. He made as much fuss as he could muster over the generosity of Roger's wife in providing lunch and then settled with a beer next to the two Basotho, feigning exhaustion that would have to delay his lunch.

"Nothing quite like a cold beer on a hot day!" he exclaimed to them as he opened the bottle.

"It's warm beer," one of them whispered.

"So it is. Part of the British approach to fine dining, I suppose," Bretton sympathized. "Do you like those sandwiches?" he whispered back.

"They're OK," one of the Basotho answered.

"I would have to be hungrier than this to try one," Bretton admitted with a wink.

"When you get hungrier," the other Mosotho whispered, "you can have mine."

After slowly consuming half a warm bottle of beer, Bretton felt disgusted with himself for being rude to his hostess and asked her for a sandwich. He held his fingers crossed behind his back when he was speaking with her, flashing some kind of sign to his fellow guests at the lunch. He did not know what his sign meant to himself much less what it meant to them but it was a way of communicating some shared courtesy they were paying Roger's wife.

Bretton was glad when the racing began. Roger drew the seven of clubs on behalf of the college team which placed them in the second half of departures. He soon located the team that drew the position immediately before the Germans and he traded cards so the College raft would be in position to fulfill his plan.

The college team sat together on the bank above the beach to watch and heckle the other teams as they began their run. A team left every two minutes and, obviously, the order of departure was noted so the winner could be calculated from the finish line.

The first two boats were not even planning to finish the race. They were just entries to make their team part of the affair. One was a boat with a huge hole just above the waterline. They had painted a circle around the hole to make sure everyone could see it. Sarcasm was the rule of the day.

"Quick, bail it out before it goes under!"

"Hold on, I've got some tape you can put over that leak!"

"I can knock a hole in the other side for the other oar if you want!"

It was swamped within sight of the starting line and sank with all four hands, i.e., four participants with two hands each, amid great hue and cry. They dragged their craft onto the bank to get out of the way of the rest of the racers and quickly retired to their beer coolers. Roger jumped up and down until the boat sank as if he were reducing their chances of winning. Geresu, the Ethiopian, and the Basotho were excited enough to cheer when the boat sank. Alan laid back, watching but not participating. Bretton barely watched the boat since it was clearly not a competitor. Instead, he watched the other contestants on the bank to see which were most serious.

The second boat was no more than a large washtub. It was made of galvanized steel and was shaped like a large oval when viewed from above. It boasted a crew of two although only one of them actually got inside with a small oar while the other held on at the back providing additional steering and locomotion. Bretton was surprised that it floated well enough to go beyond the bend in the river and out of sight. The tub came back to the beach carried by its crew before it was the college boat's turn to leave. Bretton struggled to come up with something to yell at them as they returned, something built on the question of where they had washed ashore but he could not find a way to say it that would be funny, even to himself, so he remained silent.

The third boat was a real boat but the crew of six was double its capacity and the burden was made overwhelming by the addition of a keg of beer. The keg was placed in the bow after the six members of the crew had settled in. The bell was rung to send them off but each of the crew insisted on refilling his cup before pulling on an oar and the boat was swamped by their shifting about before it ever crossed the starting line. They complained that they should have another chance to start but the referees said they had to get out of the way so the next one could leave on time. They interpreted being out of the way as being pushed up against the far shore and then spent the rest of the race sitting in the water up to their chests consuming the remains of the keg and offering a cup to anyone who would venture across the river to get it.

"How many boats are in this race?" Bretton asked Ahmad, just to make conversation. He had already heard there were 18 entries.

"I don't know overall. I'd say there are five or six that are trying to win."

"What do you win anyway?"

"Nothing. I can't even say there is much glory after the first five minutes. Roger thinks it is a memory for the whole year. Those Brits like this sort of thing."

"So the British Embassy has a boat and the German Embassy. Who else is serious about it?"

"No one is serious except Roger. He is a good man. We like to make him happy. I think the British Embassy has two boats. The Americans don't play. The French Embassy has one. The school for foreign kids has one; just the teachers will be on it; like us, I guess. Who knows where all these others come from?"

"So this is a British thing?"

"Oh yes. Like their theme parties and silly hats of every possible commemoration. They do Christmas in July, you know, 'cause it's winter here. They do plays too. Mainly Shakespeare or Sherlock Holmes. They used to run the club but some Basotho decided to become like the colonists and they have taken it over, formally anyway. The main activity apart from drinking is bowls and that's only Brits."

"Lesotho was never a colony, right?"

"Right. The Brits here still act like colonists anyway."

"You're Iraqi, aren't you?"

"Was. I'm American now."

143

"Sorry. What I was going to say, did Iraq never colonize anyplace?"

"Not lately, but the history of the region is certainly filled with someone taking control over someone else. The first cities were in the place we call Iraq today, and the first empire might be said to have been there when those cities were merged into one political entity. The Sumerians were among the first empires; the Babylonians among the most famous but no, colonialism was not practiced by Iraq or its predecessors. That is a particular relationship that came along after the people in my land had been overrun by Alexander from the west and by Hulagu Khan and then Tamerlane from the east, and then the Ottomans from the west again."

"I could use a history lesson. As you said, there is a lot of this in Mesopotamia. But don't think I am merely parochial. I don't know much American history either."

"You're going to be teaching history at the college, aren't you?"

"You know, I think I am. I have been here long enough to know our students won't tolerate anything much removed from their daily needs. I will try to get them to think about how the past affects their present. This will be the only history they study in their lives. A word or two about colonialism may creep in. Maybe you can suggest what is most critical for them."

"Soils. I do soils science. They know how important that is to their future. Soil conservation may be the most important thing they learn at the college."

"I can believe that but I am too new to know what's important so don't take my support as meaningful."

"Don't worry. You know more history than they need to know."

"No way. They will be citizens here. How they got to where they are matters and I don't know about that. What's more, if I get it wrong, I could be making things worse for them. The politics here is a deadly game."

"Like I said, I do soils. But I congratulate you for taking on every gap in our staff."

"Liberal arts degree. I know more in any subject than anyone who doesn't know anything in that subject. But maybe that's not what an agricultural college in southern Africa needs. I'll try to make myself useful in other ways."

"You have other abilities?"

"Sure. I can pole a raft once a year or so."

Every two minutes, or sometimes a little more, another boat floated off. The organizers were pretty effective at keeping the race going. They were mostly British women but a couple American women were among them: foreign service wives and diplomats' wives. The foreign women who worked in Lesotho had nothing to do with the race. Roger's wife was among the most active despite having three small children. She was never irresponsible about her charges, always keeping track of them and keeping them away from the river, but her burden was reduced by the low standards she accepted for cleanliness, her high tolerance for screaming, and her disconcern for covering their private parts from the sun or public view. They grabbed at anyone they could reach, demanding attention and annoying everyone who was not an experienced parent.

"Lesotho Agricultural College!" called a shrill female voice.

Roger did not jump up immediately. Bretton looked to him for action and saw a glaze in his grin. He had enough beer to mellow out. Alan was lounging near him and gave him a kick as he headed for the raft. Then Roger took over again.

"Let's move boys! Time to show them what we've got!"

"In the drink," shouted Alan, out of character for him, Bretton thought, but consistent with his nation's role in the affair. Alan splashed around the raft and climbed aboard from the river side. This was helpful as his weight helped offset the others climbing aboard. It was just enough to avert catastrophe.

"Next year," Bretton advised, "we should rehearse the start. It is looking like the trickiest part."

"The tricky part is around the first bend. After that, it's just following the current." Roger had not forgotten his plan to greet the Germans.

"Be ready, Ag College," she shrieked. And then "German Embassy— to your boat!"

The German team had been standing nearby, ready to begin. They did not look impressive to Bretton and he felt no particular urge to make them lose, although he stood ready to go a certain distance outside the usual rules of racing if that was the way the game was played here.

Bretton sat with his hands on the raft and his legs spread but bent at the knees to do what he could to stabilize the raft while the rest of the crew found a place to sit. Finally everyone was still and Roger commanded, "Polemen, stand at your place!"

Bretton doubted there was a real title for his position or a real command for what Roger wanted, but it did not matter; he understood and he did what Roger wanted while Alan stood on the other side.

"Ag College!   5-4-3-2-1 go," and immediately, "German Embassy get into position!"

Three of the crew pushed off the beach.   The sudden motion made Bretton take a quick step for balance, but he was not about to fall.   In a few seconds, the raft was into the current and picked up speed.   It was looking like fun to Bretton.   He rocked the raft with his weight just to show he was balanced.   He pushed his pole into the water and barely hit the bottom.   He pulled the pole back up for another try.

"C'mon there Bretton.   Give it a push!" commanded Roger but he was laughing at the joy of their movement.

Bretton saw the riverbank coming toward them and he braced himself before placing his pole toward it. He let the pole drop into the river where it hit bottom hard.   It had gotten shallow quickly.   He let the pole stick into the muddy bottom and the raft crashed against it. He pushed it back and walked along the raft as Roger had suggested.   The crash against the pole kept the raft from casting up onto the mud and they moved back into the stream.

"Bravo, Bretton," Roger called out.   Everyone else was quietly doing what he could to keep the raft in the stream although for the most part, it was out of control.   Bretton could see they would never have much control.   It caught on a rock and turned around so it was floating backwards.

"Just face the other way and we're going forward," Ahmad the Iraqi called out, revealing his own delight in the race despite his more usual sophisticated demeanor.

One Mosotho fell sideways for no obvious reason and one leg went in the water. He sprawled out to grab something and slid off except for one hand grabbing a cross member of the raft. Geresu and Ahmad both rolled toward the side where the Mosotho had gone overboard. It was not clear if they were trying to reach him or if the drop of that side made them slide toward it. Either way, they both got a limb in the water and began to grab desperately for balance. The beer cooler slid off the side. Bretton expected some factious complaint about the beer but no one else seemed to notice it.

"Man overboard!" Roger called and Bretton could see his loyalty was first to the crew, not to the race. Roger pushed with his pole on the river bank to steady the raft while Alan dropped his pole on the deck and crawled over to the Mosotho to pull him back up. The Mosotho was laughing when he was back on board. On this day, there was no complaint about getting wet.

Bretton looked back and could not see the German boat but he knew it must be there. The raft had passed the first major bend and he wondered when Roger would call for the ambush. It would not be easy to capture another boat when they could hardly keep the raft facing in one direction for long. At most places, the river was at least four rafts wide, plenty of room to pass. If the German boat was no more maneuverable than the raft, however, it might tend to push up against the shore at the same places. There would only be one chance for an attack.

Roger did not mention the Germans again. Maybe he would have if they had gotten close. He had switched the game from competition to survival, as if falling into the Caledon were dangerous, as if it had crocodiles or hippos. Most places, someone who fell out could have walked to the shore, all of which ran along the edge of Maseru so it was all familiar and all near a road. Bretton did wonder if the South Africans cared about people washing up on their side of the river but no one ever mentioned it so he assumed that was not an issue. He felt removed from his century. He had expected apartheid to be a dominating fact of life in Lesotho and it probably was but no one acknowledged it, no one among the expatriates at play that is. It was silently regarded as a mere unfortunate state of affairs in the neighboring country.

The river changed part of its character quickly. It remained always a muddy movement, always pushing whatever sat on its surface down toward a rendezvous with the border crossing at Maseru Bridge, but it pressed into the low hanging cottonwood trees at times and around the next bend rattled over gravel and rock to be followed soon by a narrow passage without anything disturbing the surface which roiled all on its own in these fastest places. Bretton stood on the South African side as he had been assigned and walked his pole along when he could get some purchase; this was only because Roger had told him to do this, not because it felt effective. The result would be Roger's responsibility, Bretton decided. Nonetheless, he worked hard to keep the raft in the main stream and facing forward.

They passed several boats, generally because the competition was caught in the tree roots and branches along the outer part of some bend in the Caledon's course. One craft had fallen apart and the crew was sitting on the South African shore to shout to the rest of the boats to give them a ride back to Lesotho.

Alan gave up his position after a few turns and sat in the middle watching the shore go by. Roger stayed in the back trying to steer with a flat board and shouting orders steadily. The others sat along the sides and pushed with their poles whenever they could reach something.

It was hard work for Bretton, mainly because he was constantly fighting for balance. After a half hour, he was exhausted and, more troubling than that, his hands were getting blistered. He stopped for a moment to assess the damage to his skin and suddenly saw himself as silly. He was acting as if he had a special ability for winning the race when all he really had was a vulnerability to Roger's encouragement.

"Ahmad, you look much too relaxed. Take my place and watch out for the blood I have left on the pole.

Bretton wobbled to his knees and crawled to the center of the raft where he rolled over and laid straight, facing up to the sky. Suddenly he no longer had to balance himself and he relaxed. The race no longer mattered to him and he was glad for that, like an addict who has turned down a fix.

In retrospect, Bretton thought he understood the Brits. They were living their lives. Going outside Britain was merely exploiting a job opportunity. Colonialism was ended-- they knew that-- but a legacy remained in their culture. Working class people needed jobs and the Brits had skills that were useful wherever in the world machinery needed maintenance and repair, or animals needed husbandry, or any of the other nearly timeless operations of practical life were ongoing. They were not conscious of exploitation or any of the other characterizations of the colonial relationship. Their leaders were likely aware of the implications of overseas posts but that was too esoteric to gain attention in Lesotho. These Brits would go home sometime, probably at the end of their working life but in the meantime they were home here.

He had less opinion about what Lesotho meant to Ahmad or the Ethiopian, and at the time of the race he still had an open mind about what Lesotho would mean to himself. He suspected he had come to this distant land for adventure but he hung on to the hope that it was to do some good. It was clear enough that doing good would be hard for him in the United States. There were useful things he could do in theory but he felt his greatest skills would not be applied to any job he could find. A PhD in economics from a mediocre school qualified him for an academic job at a third tier school or, if he were lucky, to something buried deep in business. In Lesotho, his PhD made him a curiosity even if it did not indicate any locally useful skills. No one knew what he had done to earn it. He was surprised when he was given the job. He figured the contract company was expecting him to provide an energetic adaptation to local needs. It also figured an established economist or other social scientist would not take off for a few years to teach students on the global periphery. *Maybe*, he conjectured, *established economists had a certain personality that got them established professionally and that is why they would not go to Lesotho where they would be out of sight professionally.* Bretton respected what the economics profession could offer but he was already sure he would never rise very high in its ranks. So had he gone to Lesotho because his prospects looked boring or because he could be of more use? He did not need to answer this question as he was already in Lesotho and it was time to make the most of it, but the question did bring up a related issue: what were his skills, what was it he could do that would make

Lesotho better; how could he earn his salary? These matters need not be answered while riding a clumsy raft on the border river.

Bretton took one more turn at poling from a standing position. He consciously let up just before the finish so the raft would rotate round and cross the line backwards. He did it just to show himself he could, that he was the one controlling the raft even though Roger was trying to steer and others were doing small parts too. No one on the raft or on shore was very excited about the race at that point. It had not become tiresome so much as it had changed from a competition to a pastime on a hot weekend day. Roger's family had ridden their truck to the finish line and had set up a table and some chairs. Bretton was invited to join them for drinks. He preferred a Kool Aid to a beer at this point but could not bring himself to join with the children immediately. He accepted a beer and then gave it to one of the Basotho.

"I need to get some liquids inside me," he explained to Roger's wife. "It's not as hot on the river but the air is still dry and Roger was working us hard. You have anything wetter than beer?" She passed him a plastic tumbler of lemonade. He clinked glasses with Roger's kids, and tipped the glass into his maw until it was empty and then went back for more.

XV. Novice Professor (1983)

Bretton had no training to be an educator. Only hubris could account for his accepting the job at the Agricultural College. He had taught classes to under-graduates when he was in graduate school, but never dealt with any students at the level of the young Basotho men and women. More troubling, he had no training about or experience with their agriculture. He had not misrepresented himself on his application. He had been hired on the basis of his apparent enthusiasm to help and the apparent paucity of competition among recent PhD graduates to live in the tiny backwater kingdom.

He did have enthusiasm, the sort that is not uncommon after 18 years of being a student and finally having the chance to use what he studied. He had already realized he learned far more detail in his field than was useful for any student he was likely to encounter, whether in a U.S. undergraduate program or a technical college in a country he had never heard of before seeing the announcement for the job he took on. What would matter was to find a way to help his students. He firmly believed a farmer could benefit from certain math skills, from some basic accounting practices, and some universal economic principles. He could help them learn English to improve their access to textbooks and geography to make the international news more comprehensible. He needed to know his students and their situation. Unfortunately there was no time for him to learn. He was in class a few days after his arrival. In his first days, he was mostly concerned with finding his way to the supermarket, buying bedsheets and towels, and learning what classes he had been assigned. Then the rush of classes took over and he was busy trying to stay one day ahead of the syllabus.

In his second year of teaching, Bretton was much better prepared. He did not feel guilty for his failures in the first year although he felt sorry that the students had not been better served. He had tried, he was sure. And he would try no less hard in the coming term. He would rewrite the lesson plan for every class he taught before. He would devise new tricks to engage the students and hold their attention. He knew much more of their needs. He would remove the irrelevant discussions from the first year.

One year in any economy or culture is insufficient to understand it. An entire lifetime is usually insufficient. Bretton could see that he was still a novice as a teacher and as a Mosotho, but he could also see he was far more capable than he had been when preparing his first lesson plans. He had some successes in his first year; these he remembered less easily but he reminded himself of them from time to time, compiling a mental list that became so routine that he abbreviated the anecdotes into phrases he could almost chant to himself: the arithmetic contest against the calculator, the African map exercise, the group writing assignment, and so on. Good resolutions are important and his for the second year led to some worthwhile adjustments in his classes, but he continued to bungle the more sophisticated lessons.

His experience in a successful economy and his stories of political science emboldened him to take on the South African question. He was no ideologue; he never used the word "apartheid." He could not be called a radical or a revolutionary or be said to incite resistance, although he wished he could have been or done those things. He was a teacher paid under a contract to the U.S. government so he was as subversive

as he could be without using any words that could be
held up against him. Rather than rant against the South
African relationship to Lesotho, he spoke of the
importance of having a strong ethical foundation in an
economy. He tried to sneak up on his class, getting them
to decide fighting South African policies was worth a
struggle. He had to use arguments they had not heard.
He would not base his lesson on nationalism or racism
or tribalism.

"What would you like for Lesotho? How do you
want it to change?"

This question engaged them. It was not asking
them to recite some fact they probably had not studied
or to reach some conclusion from facts and techniques.
In their technical school, as in their traditional high
schools, they were not often challenged to think on their
own and were never asked for an opinion.

"Lesotho should be more like South Africa."

Wrong answer, thought Bretton, but he could
not say so aloud.

"What is good about South Africa?" he asked.

"More like the United States," someone else
stuck in.

"Do you imagine you would want to live in
America? Do you think you could get a job there,
competing against people who had lived there all their
lives, competing against people whose families owned
businesses and homes and property? Would you want to
live where people did not sing for weddings, far from
your families and your history?"

He wanted an argument. He wanted to hear
why they would go to the United States. After he
convinced them that was not good for them, he would go
on to show how to value their local traditions. He did

not want to dissuade them from immigrating; he wanted to break down the idealization of America. His country had just invaded Grenada on the weakest of pretexts. It seemed an obvious attempt to distract the electorate from the disaster of the U.S. troops killed by the bombing in Lebanon. He was mad at the President and at America for accepting this ploy.

But no one argued. He called on individuals, starting with the most talkative.

"No. I don't want to go there. I have a cousin who went. Like you say, he couldn't get a job. It was really cold."

No one wanted to go to the United States. It was not a viable option and they knew it. They did not live in fantasy and hardly understood how to hold a hypothetical exercise. They wanted Lesotho to be more like America.

"How would you like Lesotho to be like the United States?"

"It has more things to buy."

This was an answer Bretton could use.

"Yes, more things to buy. The shops are full of variety. That variety can be a terrible waste, making things even more expensive and requiring more work to survive. The economy wastes its resources on making useless things. It does not just make toothbrushes in every color. It makes electric toothbrushes that cost 50 times what a regular toothbrush costs and does nothing more for you. It just vibrates so you do not need to move your hand up and down to clean your teeth. It makes strings of colored lights to put on your house for two weeks in the year at Christmas. It makes five different kinds of drink like Coca Cola all of which taste the same so they spend millions of dollars to convince you they are different. It makes sticks carved on the end like a hand to scratch your back and clothes that only last for one year because they become out of style and toys that break on the day they come out of the package and cars and washing machines that fall apart after three years when the warrantee expires."

He doubted they had ever heard of an electric toothbrush. They would appreciate its absurdity. They might claim he made that one up.

A dozen hands went up for permission to speak but some people could not restrain themselves and spoke up anyway.

"You are exactly right. That's what I want: a car and a washing machine."

"I'll take one of those electric toothbrushes. That would be boss."

"You understand. An electric toothbrush doesn't do anything more for you. It just costs more."

"Yeah. I don't care. I'd like an electric one."

"Me too. If she gets one I need one."

Bretton had lit a fire he could not control. He had laid his trap poorly. He had not prepared his examples, although he thought electric toothbrushes should have been absurd to anyone who had not been softened up by advertising. He had lost track of what he was trying to accomplish. Consumerism was too bright a glittering charm to be attacked lightly. He beat a retreat before his defeat could be noticed; back to something based on facts.

His second year of teaching was much easier. Although he rewrote all his lesson plans, he had a base on which to build them. At least he had an idea of what he would try to accomplish and an idea of what was possible, given their limitations and the college's and his own. For every minute he saved by reusing some piece of the previous year's lesson plan, he lost a minute and a half to a new responsibility. He had been left alone in his first year to find his own way through the classes assigned to him by their title and nothing else. He was accomplished and adept in his second year: more travelled in the region than any of the local faculty (since he had a car); known to speak Sesotho (actually merely thought to speak Sesotho); published on the subject of Lesotho politics (for a First World audience who was hearing the country name for the first time); favored by the students (for his American informality, his athleticism on the football pitch, and the ambience of his foreign post-graduate degree); and other fundamentally irrational reasons.

Busier than ever, he tended to accept each new job. To do otherwise would be to deny they were right about the capabilities his year of experience had instilled in him. Beyond his academic responsibilities, he became the boys' track coach for the meet on the King's birthday, and the senior class counselor. He traded teaching English, which went to a highly qualified local woman named Mosele who had been the Moshoeshoe Scholar when she graduated from the national University in Roma, for a class in geography and one in history.

All this made him so busy he refused on a certain day in early March to end class early in accordance with tradition when a hailstorm came. Hail had an outsized place in Lesotho concerns. It was capable of ruining an entire crop in 30 minutes. There was no defense from it except through magic. It was common in the mountainous country, and it was important because of the widespread dependency on crops. Oddly, in Lesotho, it typically destroyed only a small area each time, leaving neighboring areas entirely unaffected. Witchcraft was invoked both as cause and as protection. This was so well recognized that even Bretton knew about it. So when he was told class must be cancelled when hail hits the college, he took it as superstition. The first few times there was hail, it was just a quick flurry that passed before anyone could argue that class ought to be dismissed. On that March day, however, Bretton learned what Basotho mountain hail can do.

It hit like an explosion soon after Bretton began class. He was in front of the room facing the blackboard but turning his head frequently to ensure he was keeping contact with the class. His brain was fully engaged in teaching. Wham, wham, wham, wham... With the recent history of violent revolutionary activity in Lesotho, Bretton thought an attack had begun. He fell against the blackboard, facing the class. The students jumped up and ran to the windows. It was so terribly loud because the roof of the classroom was a single layer of galvanized steel. Bretton shouted for the students to move away from the windows. His shouts were unheard. Within a few seconds, he realized it was hail. He shouted for the students to wait for it to pass. They could not hear that either. They were gleeful as they should be when nature reveals its power so dramatically and, in the case of the college, harmlessly. The pounding went on for a few minutes. Finally Bretton gestured to the students to leave and they danced out the door. The class time was wasted. Bretton would be farther behind. He sat in one of the student desks and tried to work on the lesson for another class. The noise continued for thirty minutes, making coherent thought difficult. Finally it abated as quickly as it began. The hail was two inches deep. Bretton looked across the campus. No student was in sight. They would not come to any more classes this day.

Bretton started his walk home thinking the storm had wasted his time but it was offset by the gift of time to work on upcoming lesson plans. He began to prepare a mental schedule of what could be accomplished in the time that had been saved from classes, but his reverie was broken by the signs of damage around him. His route home went through a Eucalyptus forest for ten minutes. The trees were tall, with straight, mottled trunks one to two feet in diameter. The hail had stripped them of leaves. At his feet was a deep mixture of ice and Eucalyptus. It was a disaster he could never have anticipated. He hated to think of losing the forest. It served no purpose but to shelter him from the sun and sky on his commute to the college. Before he could absorb the magnitude of loss, his mood began to lighten. He was lifted by the air itself, air saturated with Eucalyptus oils. It was the most beautiful scent he had ever experienced although it made him think of an exaggerated version of Herbal Essence Shampoo. He sucked it in deeply. These were breaths to memorize for late in life. He strolled slowly through the grove, enjoying, guiltily, what he feared was its death throes. But the trees were more resilient than he feared and by the following spring were completely recovered.

XVI. Ed (1983)

When Bretton first arrived in Lesotho, he was too young, or at least too immature, to follow the rules offered by people who knew the terrain better than he. He had been raised and educated in a way that taught him a lengthy set of rules for Ohio and he had been shy enough to start out by following them in most situations. A child of the Sixties, he did not believe the social rules were always right, maybe not even often right, although they were usually the easiest way to proceed. He acted with the same sloppy logic when he came to Lesotho even though the social rules he knew might not apply and the cost of misapplying them could be very high.

Like driving at night... It was in no way unacceptable to drive at night back at home in Ohio. One would have to be very paranoid to worry about it unless you were a mother. He had been told in his opening days in Lesotho by his expatriate colleagues to never drive at night. The list of reasons for this precaution was long with some very good arguments behind them yet the rule was so broad and some of the reasons so exotic, he could not absorb them so deeply as to actually fear them:

------ All the roads are in such poor repair, you could lose control of the car in a pothole or a bridge could collapse or the road could slide off the mountain with you on it.

------ The Lesotho Liberation Army could stop you and take anything they regarded as valuable.

------ Thieves could block the road and attack you.

------ Animals, that is, domestic animals like cattle or sheep, could be wandering on the road. Wild animals had been exterminated from Lesotho.

------ The other drivers may be unskilled or drunk.

------ You could get lost.

It was an impressive list of realistic possibilities that sounded far too much like his mother talking for him to obey. Were not all these hazards also present in the daylight? So he did not worry much when he pridefully accepted an invitation to dinner well outside of town with Ed, one of the students, knowing it would require driving at night.

Ed was the old man of the class. He was old enough to be father to most of the others, even to Bretton. Despite the tradition of honoring age in Lesotho, Ed was modest in his relations with the other students, acting as if he were their inferior, presumably in deference to their superior mental facility. Ed was not mentally quick although that was not uncommon among the students at the agriculture college. It was a trade school for young men and women who had not made it into the national university.

Ed was tall and bent over, bent not from age but from a habit of work. The bones in his face and limbs were heavy, giving him the appearance of strength over speed. What Bretton noticed first and always was Ed's teeth, not that they were white and well formed, although they were, but that they were so often on display in a broad grin. His smile disarmed anyone with a heart who looked upon him. Although he was innocent of trying to manipulate people with his appearance, one would have to be blind to be unaffected by the happy glow from his face. Ed had spent many years in the mines doing hard labor and the rest of his life farming maize in a highland valley. He rarely spoke up in class but in addition to a ready smile, he always did his homework. Bretton was saddened to see his first test. His handwriting bore the shakiness of an unpracticed hand. His answers were so poor, Bretton doubted he could read the questions beyond a few words that gave him a general idea of the subject. But he was such an appealing personality that Bretton found ways to talk to him after class, always informally, but effectively to hold a tutoring session. Ed appreciated the extra effort and worked hard to understand whatever Bretton was trying to communicate. Bretton watched him when the students were working in the college fields and saw he had some good practical skills. Unfortunately, Bretton taught only classes where practical skills were not valued. He felt compelled to give Ed poor grades since he did not demonstrate much knowledge in the subjects Bretton was teaching but Ed never seemed disturbed by the grades. It was another point in his favor that he accepted what he had earned. It may have been this point that made Bretton continue to seek Ed's approval. He broke his own rule about spending too much time on one student, particularly inappropriate when the student appeared to benefit so little from the extra attention. Ed nodded appropriately while Bretton spoke and he repeated whatever Bretton asked him to say to show he was listening. He even remembered things well. But he lacked the ability to assemble facts into principles or to draw likely facts from principles. In this way, he was Bretton' opposite. Bretton was extremely slow to absorb new facts but he was gifted at deriving valid conclusions from the principles he retained readily. Their quiet partnership was also driven by their similarity, both of them being unique in the college and therefore outside the usual and automatic social contacts of the staff and students. They were both invited to parties appropriate to their status, but neither fit into the flow of the college life. Neither was surprised or bothered by his social separateness although there were times when Bretton found it tiring to be isolated in the midst of the crowd.

Thus, Bretton was very pleased to be invited by Ed to his house between terms, perhaps especially because the arrangement took him outside the range of safe travel. He had been to Basotho homes before, although never to a student's home. He had been to villages in the countryside many times. But he had not eaten in a rural Mosotho home and had not visited a village after dark far from Maseru. He tended to avoid taking local food, not from finicky taste but from what he regarded as legitimate caution for the health of his Western digestive tract, however, he resolved in this case to relish whatever was put before him except homemade beer, if that turned up. He especially disliked the locally made brew he had seen at parties, with soft green things floating in it and everyone's lips pressed on the pot rim.

Ed made his way home at the end of the term with the understanding that Bretton would come along on the weekend. The directions to Ed's village were not very clear, but Bretton was already used to that in Lesotho. As long as he knew the name of the nearest large village, he could find his way by asking anyone he found along the rest of the way.

He left early on Saturday morning, driving his blue Peugeot up the long road to the mountains of the interior. Lesotho was not a large country but the roads were so poor, travel was slow so it was a long way to some places as measured in time. The road narrowed and climbed steeply as soon as it was past the small plains around Maseru. Bretton did not fear the drop from the road to the valley ever farther below him. There was no guard rail, but he had been this way before and trusted the road to hold. Most of Lesotho sits in the mountain region, but the mountains are not very high despite the steep rise from the Caledon River floodplain. Once he was through God Help Me Pass, he was in a rolling grassland that rose slowly to the east up to an escarpment marking 100 kilometers of the border with South Africa. There the Caledon River slides lazily from the west of a marshy plain on the start of its trip to Maseru and beyond, while from that same marshy plain, the Senqu begins a decent to the north where it soon becomes the Orange River of South Africa. But most dramatically, the marshy plain drains the Tugela River to the east where it soon emerges to leap down more than 3000 feet in a notch that virtually hides one of the tallest waterfalls in the world. Bretton had not been to the marshy plain but he knew of it and planned to see it someday and to toss a pebble a vertical kilometer.

The trip to Ed's village could not be shown on a map. In his area, there was no landmark known to those who published maps. The dotted line that indicated the gravelly remnant of the road that brought him into the mountains meandered imaginatively after its last named village. Bretton stopped at the general store, named like all the other general stores "Fraziers," and asked a young man wearing a blanket and sitting on a pony for the village of Sebetia. He smiled at Bretton and explained in proud English "You have a good auto there. You will have no trouble getting to Sebetia. Follow this track

until you come to Makhorana (it has two shops) and then keep to your right after that. It will be the first big town you find. You must be going to the mission nearby."

"*Kea leboha*," thanked Bretton. He was about to ask how far it was to Sebetia but he already knew the man would answer in the only way Basotho ever answered that question: not far.

"I will have to drive slowly, I think. Maybe I will be there by mid-day."

"No problem, Ntate. I could be there on my pony before half one."

Bretton could not remember if that meant twelve-thirty or one-thirty. *"Sala hantle,"* he said in parting, meaning "stay well."

"Tsamaea hantle," the man answered, meaning "go well."

The road was noticeably more rugged beyond Fraziers, getting worse with every mile. It continued to consist of two tracks a constant distance apart, indicating use by wheeled vehicles. The buses likely ran no farther than Fraziers so the only vehicles on this stretch were tractors pulling wagons and Land Rovers, and now Bretton's blue Peugeot.

Bretton was very pleased with the day. He felt independent, like an old African hand but not in the way of a colonial. He was going to see a friend in a real village, far from the peculiarities of Maseru, from the most obvious insults of the powerful apartheid regime. There was something unspoiled implied by this remote location. He was going somewhere no one he knew from home had ever gone, living a story to tell his children and doing it in the comfort of his Peugeot, which he would not necessarily make prominent in his telling of the tale.

He was not surprised or disappointed when he came to a place where a dry stream cut across the track so deeply he doubted his car could continue. He got out to look at the angle of the road to see if he could limp through or put in a few rocks to make it passable. He decided he could get through but that there was no good reason to drive farther. There would be a worse place soon and then he would have to stop anyway. He saw no nearby village but, as usual, some herd boys had turned up as soon as he stopped the car. He knew he was well off the normal path of foreigners when they did not try to sell him any colorful stones they had found on the hillsides and saved for the purpose. They were shy and said "*Lipongpong li kae*" with little enthusiasm, asking for candy which they had heard white people would give them but they had never seen it happen. Bretton did not carry candy for them. He had been asked by his office mate, who had a college degree from England, never to toss such treats out the car window. He remembered in his childhood that all he thought of white people was the hope they might throw a few pieces of plastic-wrapped candy on the ground for him to fight over with his brothers.

After quickly exhausting his Sesotho with a greeting to the boys and telling them he worked at the agricultural college, he asked if anyone spoke English. "*Sekhooa?*" The word for "English" was also used to denote white people so it appeared to the boys he was asking for a white person. They answered "no" in their way. Bretton thought they were saying no one spoke English rather than that they had not seen another white person, but the answer would have been the same anyway. Then he tried the name of Ed's village. One boy seemed to recognize it. They were all laughing and screaming as they had become more used to Bretton and did not see him as a threat so it was hard for Bretton to sort out any meaning from the group. With a smile, he put a hand on the shoulder of the boy that might have known the village and put his finger to his lips to quiet the others. They understood his gestures, but then the boy he authorized to speak for them prattled on without indicating any direction. The boy might have understood the meaning of the word used for the village but not associated it with a village. Bretton looked at his watch and saw he was not terribly late yet although he could not afford to go far on foot if he were not getting closer to Ed's.

Feeling a little frustration, he asked in English, "do any of you know Ed, tall fellow about yeah high?" and he held his hand up close to his own height. "Ed," is not a Sesotho name. Bretton did know the other students called him "Ed," so it was not a name adopted to simplify speaking with foreigners. Bretton had guessed Ed had picked it up in the mines. The boys ignored his English, chatting to each other and speaking sometimes slowly to Bretton to patiently explain something and then from the cacophony Bretton heard one boy say "Ed?" Bretton put his hand on the boy and said, "Yes, Ed." And in Sesotho, "Do you know Ed?" The boy held his hand as high as he could and said Ed again. Bretton nodded encouragingly. Soon all the boys were chanting: "Ed, Ed, Ed, Ed." Some of them started to dance. Was this just a nonsense syllable to them or was Ed's unusual name known farther than the name of his village?

Bretton could not get their attention to his question but he noticed the dance was drifting along the road ahead. Then they began to beckon him to follow. Bretton gestured to his car. He did not want to abandon it. He could be sure it would not be stolen if he took the keys with him but he expected it might be stripped of all removable parts. These were highly traditional people out in the mountains. They probably never stole anything from each other and probably could not have gotten away with it if they had, but his car seemed a temptation someone might be able to exploit. He did not want to distrust them but he did not know them personally. Besides, even in the mountains, these people were familiar with the modern society of South Africa where petty crime was common and resale of auto parts would have been routine. More than this, they were very poor. The herd boys cheerfully calling him on were barely clothed and none of them was shod. Two of them grabbed at his hands and when he pulled his hands back, they grasped his pant legs and tugged him onward up the road. Bretton kept smiling but he resisted going farther. He pointed to his car. The tallest boy came back and started to chant "No problem, *Sekhooa*." The others took it up, mixed with a chorus of "Ed, Ed, Ed." Finally Bretton gave in. *I live here now. I am not going to live in perpetual fear for my possessions*, he vowed to himself. If the car was stripped, he would deal with it. He was no dancer and could not sing more than one note of the scale, but he joined the celebration as well as he could, knowing they were not judging his entertainment skills. He took a bundle of things for Ed, that is, for Ed's wife, gifts for the dinner, and rode the flow over the hill. His decision to leave the car was at least supported by the quality of the road going forward. It was not for vehicles. Cattle and goats were its main users. They had not abused the route, but neither had they repaired the damage of hooves and flash floods. The paired lines worn by vehicles onto the ungraded countryside had given way to meandering animal tracks. Ed had not warned him of this but Ed did not travel here in a vehicle so he had not noticed where the way had become inaccessible.

The boys laughed with him for a kilometer or so when they began to argue among themselves. Bretton worried that they might be plotting to strip his car or to direct him to harm, but in fact they were arguing over who would go back to watch the herds of goats. They started to push each other in ways that look familiar to

Bretton from his own boyhood scraps. The biggest boy was not dominant; there was more than size at issue in their relations. One boy tried to reassure Bretton whatever was under discussion should not matter to him, but it all looked bad to Bretton. When three of the boys headed back, Bretton nearly went with them to the car. But his resolve to complete his journey came back to him. He wanted to be the sort of adventurer who went forward and dealt with the consequences. Avoiding every risk was the formula for missing out.

If it weren't for the stress of his fears, Bretton would have enjoyed the walk immensely. It was a beautiful day, cool and bright as is common in the Lesotho highlands. Small villages were constantly in view, generally placed, Bretton noted, where the land became too steep for crops, a picturesque pattern. The third dimension, the elevation, of the landscape was especially apparent. The land went up as down as much as it went left and right. It was not as dramatic as, say, the Alps. These were a friendlier form of mountain; every mountaintop was remote and wild, but accessible. The track they were taking kept to the lowest part of the slopes. Above them, the treeless expanse showed contours the animals had worn onto the slopes over the years of grazing in horizontal pastures, one head wide. Bretton tried to focus on the pleasure unfamiliarity brought rather than the insecurity it brought. It was only another thirty minutes, but felt longer, when they all began to point to a certain small group of rondavels and the chant of "Ed, Ed, Ed" was revived.

The chant faded away as they approached. The boys would not go the last hundred meters to Ed's home. They crowded around Bretton and reached for his pockets and made signs that he understood to mean they were looking for money. He was disappointed that they saw him as a source of tips. He was sure they would have guided a Mosotho without any thought of compensation. He did not want to think of them as "spoiled." He could see their relatively primitive state, comprised of uneducated poverty, was not entirely isolated from the larger world. Certain expatriates said Americans were too generous in tipping and created inappropriate expectations in local people. They had begun with cries for candy and were ending with pleas for money. He would give them neither out of respect for their proper behavior to help a visitor. They had not been surprised when he gave them no sweets and he doubted they would be disappointed if he gave them no money-- they were not professional beggars such as are found at tourist places in poor countries. It was tempting to distributed a few coins—they would sing his praises for it-- but the coins would do them little good and years later, when they were the age and experience of his officemate, which was unlikely but possible, everything is possible in the future, they might appreciate that he had not furthered the patronage relationship between the races.

Bretton acted as if he did not understand their interest in money. He thanked them as he would thank an adult. *"Kea laboha hahoolo! Tsamaea hantle boabuti."* Thank you very much. Go well, boys. He patted their wooly heads as he went down the slope from the road to the rondavels.

"Ko-ko" he called from the swept yard between the rondavels. It looked like a family collection of buildings of varying purpose rather than a true village. There was a small building on blocks, which he presumed to be for grain storage, and one with a hole on top which he thought might be the kitchen. Another of the same size had a sheet metal roof which he thought should be the main living space. The metal might have been a good choice for the room with the cooking fire, but he knew it was the most prestigious construction material. A large woman ran out of the rondavel and began ululating. She threw her arms around Bretton. Bretton kissed her on each cheek although he had to lean away from her to reach them with his lips, she was pressed so close. She was followed by a stream of children of various ages. There were too many, it seemed, for them all to be Ed's unless he had more than one wife. This was possible in Basotho culture but not likely for a man of Ed's position. Yet Bretton admitted the four-rondavel assemblage was more than he expected in Ed's estate, assuming it was all his family's.

Finally Ed came out of the rondavel. His slow stride was the same as always but looked more distinguished here in his home. He looked like more than a father and husband-- he was chiefly. Bretton extricated himself from Ed's wife and shook hands with Ed. They exchanged greetings in Sesotho followed by Ed's switching to English which made Bretton realize Ed knew Bretton's Sesotho was very superficial, something most of the students, who heard him sounding facile and colloquial in his greetings, did not understand.

Lumela, Ntate! My family is pleased you visit us today. Welcome here. My wife is happy to see you. I have tell her about Doctor Bretton."

Bretton turned to Ed's wife and bowed ceremoniously and shook her hand saying, in Sesotho, "My name is Bretton. Greetings to you and your family."

She held onto his sleeve and pulled him into the rondavel with the metal roof. The inside was cool and dark although Bretton' eyes soon adjusted to the light and could see things well enough. There were two small windows in addition to the door which they kept open to admit light. No electric light or lantern or candle helped show him the room. A collection of unmatched and well-worn wooden chairs surrounded the round table in the middle of the room. A row of three beds lined one wall, hardly enough for the crowd of children in the room unless at least three slept in one bed and two in the other. Bretton looked at their sizes and genders to see if it would work and decided it would.

"How many children do you have, Ed?" he asked.

"I still have two," Ed answered. Bretton heard the word "still" and assumed it implied Ed had lost a child or more. Ed reached down and tapped two of the small boys. "These are my son's children. He has another boy in the fields. He pointed to one of the girls. "This one is my daughter." My other daughter lives in Maseru. She has a job with the government."

"What about these other two?" Bretton asked.

"They do not have any family left. They live with us."

Good man, Bretton thought. He considered asking more about their circumstances but Ed's wife was pushing Bretton onto one of the chairs in front of a plate of steaming vegetables Ed's daughter had just brought in from the kitchen rondavel. She was clearly miming that he should eat. Bretton was worried that no one else was eating and that he would be eating all the food they had prepared, but Ed sat with him and more food was brought in by the daughter, another plate of vegetables and two bowls of corn meal. The other children stood near, watching Bretton while he and Ed ate dinner.

"My wife wants to say she is sorry we have no meat to share."

"Please tell her this is the dish I wanted to have. I came to Lesotho to learn how the Basotho live and this is very good. I can see she is a good cook." Ed translated and Bretton added, "It is wonderful for me to have *moroho* and mealies. At the college I hear of growing these things but I cook for myself and do not know how to prepare them so I never learn what they are like." Ed translated again and then told Bretton she was happy to show him.

"Maybe, Ed, I should be honest and say I do not know how to cook anything well so it is wonderful just to have a good meal."

He laughed when he translated this time.

"My daughter can come and live with you. She is good cook and can do many other things for you."

"I am sure she has learned well, but I am used to living by myself and like it even if the food is not good."

"I show you my fields," Ed explained, "after we eat. You can see I follow the contour to stop erosion. And I'm teaching other farmers here how to plow properly for soil conservation."

Bretton lingered over his food as long as he could to extend the meal, taking small bites but never pausing for long between bites, giving the impression of continual engagement. He was being closely observed and wanted to convey his genuine appreciation, regardless of how it affected his palette. There was an undercurrent of conversation among the smallest children but Ed did not speak and Bretton could not think of anything to say. He remembered the comfort Basotho have with silence in social situations and relied on that to convince himself all was going well.

Suddenly, Ed stood up and said, "Come to the field, please, Ntate."

Bretton scooped up the remaining mealie paste and stuffed it into his mouth. "I am coming but I must see your wife first to thank her for the meal."

Ed nodded to show he heard Bretton but did not accompany him to the kitchen rondavel where Bretton made a small show of appreciation to a surprised and embarrassed wife before running outside to catch up with Ed and the children.

Ed strode uncharacteristically quickly up the slopes to the first level of contours. There he carefully explained what was grown in each field, how often they were fallowed, and who owned the neighboring fields. He pointed to the valley below to indicate where he had fields there and what he did with them. From their stance on the first constructed contour, they could see out to the plain that extended into Maseru. There were a few low mesas visible on the plain. A sad pattern of deep gullies, dongas, showed the tendency of the local soils to erode at the base of the mountains. The scene was entirely in shades of brown but for the deep blue of the cloudless sky. There were things growing below them, but they looked dusky too. Perhaps at harvest time, something would be truly green. He made passing reference to the fields near his home where his wife grew the family vegetables. Ed went on and on, by far the longest he had ever spoken in Bretton's presence. Three villages were visible along with a dozen separate households the size of Ed's. Nearly all of the buildings were round. Those on the higher slopes were made of rock and straw while the ones lower down tended to be made of mud and tin.

Ed was proud of his farm although he had no animals and no mechanization. He had knowledge and muscles. He explained that he was finished now with the mines and could put all his effort into building the farm. He needed to finish at the college first, he admitted, and the time at the college cut into what could be done on the farm, but the college was giving him ideas of how to use his time once it was devoted to the farm. He had some money for hogs saved from his work at the mines. Here he lowered his voice even though they were far from anyone but the children who spoke no English.

"I had some extra money, you know, from setting the fuses up in the gold city. I should give some of it to my chief, but he does not need it and I have many children to feed-- you see that."

"Did you ever raise hogs before?"

"No one in this village has ever had hogs. I did not even think of them until I went to the college. My education will be very valuable. My wife knows what I am doing. She is very pleased but she will not speak of it. She thinks it will not happen if she talks of it. Maybe she thinks I should not say anything out loud either. I think it is all right if I speak to my *Sekhooa*. It is not like talking to a Mosotho."

"I am no Mosotho. I am pleased you tell me of your plans and I think they are good plans." They talked about how many hogs he could afford to buy and how he would use the meat and how he could grow the operation into a truly commercial level with sales into the market. Bretton saw problems in the business plan, like transporting meat without a vehicle over the route he had taken there, but he also suspected there were ways to cope he could not imagine.

"It is good that you are the farmer and I am the teacher because I could not survive on my farming skills, Ed."

"Maybe you could study at the agricultural college," Ed suggested and Bretton had to laugh out loud.

"I will take you to my chief now," Ed announced. Bretton saw that it was a long way to anyplace and he worried about getting back to his car, especially if any problem turned up when he got back there. He said it was time to return, but Ed suddenly looked very worried and politely insisted on a very quick visit. In traditional areas of any culture, quick visits exist only in the imagination. It took thirty minutes to work their way across the rough ground to the headman's hut and another fifteen minutes for the boy in that hut to find the chief. He seemed very pleased and duly honored for Bretton to visit him but lacking a common language, their conversation was as short as ritual permitted.

The sun was sitting atop the hills when Bretton finally managed to shake hands with Ed a final time and wish him and his people well. He jogged back to his car and got there before dark, but there was a coterie of boys waiting for him to point out the unfortunate circumstance of his having a flat tire. On the other hand, he was fortunate that one of the boys knew someone who had a tire pump, a fact he communicated effectively through mime. Bretton thought of mentioning somehow that a pump would not fix a puncture but he supposed there was no puncture. In fact, he hoped they had merely let out the air and there was no more trouble than that. The boy came back with a bicycle pump. Bretton was skeptical that it would be adequate for a car tire, but it did work well enough to make the tire look full. The boys asked for no money for themselves, but they indicated the owner of the pump needed some compensation. One rand made them happy. Bretton gave them another rand without attempting any explanation. He understood he was contributing to the odds of the next traveler facing the same scam but it did not bother him. They had done little harm compared to what might have occurred. He was not feeling kindly toward the boys and resented that they might believe they had tricked him, but he resented more that he might be angry over what was a small inconvenience. Giving them the extra rand was to tell himself he was in control of his emotions enough to behave generously.

At the last moment, when he had the car started and the headlights came on, he did feel sorry for those boys in their sparse clothing, staying in the cold, dark mountain air with little prospect for anything in the upcoming season as entertaining or remunerative as his accidental visit had been and he was glad he had given them a little more than he had to and that they would be happy for a while as a result of his having passed by.

The ride back was not as amusing as the ride there. His headlights lit the road and, on corners, the featureless dry slopes beside the road, rarely showing any people or buildings. No lights shone brightly enough from the villages he knew he was passing to reveal the presence of homesteads so the drive felt more remote than the ride in. The disoriented feeling was as important as any rational assessment of uncertainty about the return route in causing him to turn aside when he first saw a light. It was a single electric bulb, powered by a small generator, that signaled a shebeen[6]. He thought he was on the right road, but everyone here would know the way to Maseru and he could proceed more securely and enjoy the trip after a quick consultation.

He turned off the headlights and used only the fog lights while parking the car so he would not announce his presence too much before going inside. There was no sign at the door and he hesitated to go inside without knocking. He was pretty sure it was a shabeen, but not a hundred-percent sure. If he were wrong, what harm could there be in going inside uninvited? He might offend someone but they would understand immediately he was a foreigner and not familiar with the place. He was accustomed to the security common among young, healthy, white men and had found Basotho especially deferential. He did not want to appear arrogant by barging in but he felt safe.

The door was just unpainted plywood on leather hinges. It did not latch but it could be secured by a chain running through a hole in the door and a padlock. Inside, there was a long hallway with no door visible. It

---

[6] A place illegally selling liquor.

bent to the right where light and sound were dimly leaking from a door he could not see. Bretton could hear music ahead of him and he went on as if he were confident of what was around the corner. Again he opened a closed door, again made of unpainted plywood, emphasizing the slapdash construction of an informal enterprise.

His first impression was relief at finding the place was a shabeen, as he had promised himself it must be. He had never been inside one although he had read of them in novels and newspapers. They were shady places in South Africa, outside the law, but succeeded on being refuges from the daily grind of the large working class. Those in Lesotho, he imagined, were pale copies. Nearly every business lacked the legitimization of official papers and there was no apartheid to resist. Of course there was no guarantee of food safety, but he would not test their hygiene, only their knowledge of the way to the capital.

The room's purpose was illustrated by a long, bare table that served as a bar and several smaller tables with cloth tops. More unmatched wooden chairs than needed were scattered around the room which was much larger than Bretton had expected. The chamber was brighter than he expected too. Apparently there were no windows since no light had been visible from outside other than the single bulb at the first door.

The patrons should have been his first impression. Bars the world over need to be assessed first for who else is there. It was exclusively male but for the bartender who was a solid, stolid matron who looked him over directly and then kept a casual eye on him. Surprisingly, no one else showed any attention to him after an initial glance, as if white men coming in alone were a common occurrence. Bretton took it well, interpreting their feigned indifference to his being no threat exactly because he was alone. This was their place; he was the outsider dependent on their goodwill, a position familiar to Bretton since moving to Africa and the way he preferred to be viewed.

The obvious thing to do was to go up to the bar although it felt odd to stand behind a table only as high as his thigh. The woman came to him and smiled at the joke he seemed to represent to her. She greeted him loudly in Sesotho with a phrase he did not recognize. He felt the rest of the room laugh at the joke although he did not actually hear or see any reaction.

"*Lumela, Mme.*" He was not sure of the proper etiquette for the situation. Should he ask after her family's health? He decided his demeanor would be sufficient to show his good intentions. Besides, he knew the Sesotho to ask directions. "*Ke batle ho ea Maseru.*" When he said it, he was not sure it was proper or polite, but he was sure his accent had been well honed in talking with the students and all she really needed to hear was "Maseru."

She answered with a long phrase he could not understand at all and he was sure she knew he could not understand her so the joke was continuing. When she finished, he saw it was his role to cease the pretense that he could speak Sesotho although he truly felt sorry that he could not maintain it. Usually it was enough that he tried Sesotho.

"Can you show me the way to Maseru?"

She walked away as if he ceased to exist, more precisely, as if he had never been there. It was treatment Bretton had never experienced in Africa. He was not even being offered the opportunity to buy a drink. His first inclination was to object, to demand her attention if not her answer, to buy a drink even to make his point. But Bretton was not prone to rash action and the heat under his collar dissipated before it got too high and he leaned on the table with both hands, looking at the shelf of glasses on the wall ahead of him. It felt to him as if he were being watched. The room was quieter than when he first walked in. He was disoriented even before he walked in the shebeen but now he did not even have an idea what to do. He did not need directions to Maseru. He was unsure of the way, but Lesotho was a small country without many roads and he would work his way back eventually. His immediate concern was how to exit gracefully. He considered called out good-by to the proprietress, "*Sala hantle*," but he had just enough pride to skip that step before turning to leave.

He turned but did not take the first step toward the door because a large, very fit Mosotho was blocking the way. He had not seen a Mosotho before who looked so physically intimidating although he was wearing a broad smile. He clapped Bretton on the shoulder.

"Buy you a drink?" he asked.

Naturally, this greeting put Bretton at ease, but his ease lasted for only a single moment. He answered, "No thank you very much. I need to get back to Maseru," and another large, athletic Mosotho appeared on the other side of Bretton... with another broad smile.

Bretton had not looked closely at the figures in the room but now he saw three more oversized Basotho.

"Yeah, we're police." It was said with pride, but the reputation Bretton had heard about police was no basis for pride. The policemen crowded up close, chatting amicably with Bretton although apparently only the one who had spoken first knew English. Given that

English was the language of formal education across Lesotho, its absence spoke loudly about the police backgrounds.

They clearly wanted him to drink something and kept offering him their half-full glasses. This was not unusual behavior in Lesotho or anywhere else in the world although Bretton was not accustomed to it since he did not frequent bars. Whatever they were drinking, it was all the same-- no one suggested there was a selection of delicacies.

The English-speaker quickly worked through the standard questions: Where are you from? Why are you in Lesotho? What do you think of Lesotho? And because he answered these question in Sesotho: Where did you learn Sesotho? He answered this last question with his most sophisticated sentence, which he had memorized when he was taking his language class and practiced many times since it always impressed his listeners. With perfect accent and ease, he said the equivalent of "I am aware I do not speak Sesotho well but I like to learn it." They all laughed at the irony of saying this in good Sesotho and crowded close for the opportunity to supply Bretton's beer. If Bretton had been looking for company, he might have enjoyed the situation. He was, however, tired of struggling to be courteous and entertaining without the language skills to communicate beyond the opening amenities. And he was uncomfortable with the physicality of his new, loud friends.

He tried to leave, but they would not consider it. He took a sip of beer, just to show himself at ease. He could not argue since he could barely speak to them. Bretton felt more like the joke they were enjoying than the honored guest they seemed to pretend he was. He doubted he could stay long enough to bore them. He had made himself clear so he needed to try something more aggressive. He slapped the nearest fellow on the back and pushed his way toward the door. Before he had taken two steps, ignoring whatever they were saying, two of the police rushed in front of him and blocked his way. They were smiling, but they expected to control the situation. They knew he wanted to leave and did not care or, if they cared, it only made them more sure they wanted him to stay. Bretton toyed with the idea of pushing his way past them, making them restrain him overtly, calling their bluff. He could not see that they wanted anything more from him than power over him but there was not much of an audience for them, just themselves, the bartender, and a couple drunks. They were not themselves drunk, not very drunk anyway. Bretton would have worried more if they were more drunk. He figured they retained some rationality. They might be accustomed to the freedom to bully and intimidate, like police in most poor countries, but they were not accustomed to doing so with white foreigners. He was not even South African, which would have made him more vulnerable. He wondered if it was time to play his "citizen of Rome" card. He looked into the eyes of the two in front of him and then to the laughing one who spoke English. He was not looking back at Bretton, apparently confident that his partners would keep him close. It was too dark to read anything in their eyes. Their posture was ready for confrontation although Bretton read it as a sporting sort of tension, not a deadly one. He prepared to be angry but he hesitated. If they did not back off in the classic fashion of bullies under a challenge, he would have no more cards in his hand. He was not desperate yet, not too scared to act thoughtfully.

In Sesotho, he gave his name and his Sesotho nickname. They liked that too. Then he asked for their names, hoping this would make them feel a little more accountable. Later he would be able to say who they were. They answered, each in turn and each with some smart remark Bretton could not comprehend but he had used a few words of Sesotho and might have created some doubt in their minds about whether he understood them and whether he would remember who they were when the daylight returned.

Suddenly the room changed and Bretton was no longer the center of attention. The woman behind the bar said something that touched it off and they all looked in the same direction as if the band were about to come out. One of the policemen wrapped his arms around Bretton as if to ensure he did not escape while their attention was on this new diversion. The English speaker started to scream. "This is for him! This is for you, Mister Bretton!"

Bretton could not see what they were talking about. His view was limited by the weight of the man hanging on his back and the way the husky Basotho insisted on standing against him.

The English words came through the hubbub to his ear.

"Don't worry about anything. We will pay for her. She is for you."

Slowly the small, close crowd parted and the fattest Mosotho woman Bretton has ever seen stood five feet before him. Lesotho is the land of bald, fat women but the women were hard working and never obese. Except for this one. He looked to her face. Although the room was not well lit, he could see her well enough to tell she was not especially young and would hardly be judged beautiful in any culture. But she was plenty fat and, apparently, available.

Bretton had not the least interest in having sex with anyone and he feared these fellows could enjoy being insistent about his providing some kind of show for them. He laughed and leered along with the others.

"Are you serious? May I have her? Right now? Here? You have a bed somewhere?"

He addressed himself to the English speaker who was very pleased with himself for being in the middle of the entertainment. He translated for the others and answered Bretton, urging him on.

Bretton licked his lips and stuck out his chin to show he was getting interested. They cheered. He made a motion to the English speaker to have him come close. It was too noisy to whisper but Bretton spoke into his ear as if to have a private word. "Do you know where I have been all day today? I have a young lady in the mountains, *mapeacecorpo*." This is a way of saying a "Peace Corps" person in Sesotho. He had to make his lover to be an American because it might anger them if he had a Mosotho woman. "Two times today. Once after dinner. I am finished for tonight. Do you understand? *U tsebe*?"

The policeman shrieked and told everyone what he heard, saying much more than the few words Bretton had given him. The fat woman laughed and came up to Bretton to wipe her hand across his face, somehow making that into a lurid gesture. Bretton shook his head and smiled, unsure what he was indicating thereby except that he was relaxed.

"You know, *Abuti*, this is really bad beer. You have got to get some German beer up into these mountains." Bretton started a new show of unconcern for the circumstances.

The English speaker translated and then raised his glass. "German beer! Here's to German beer!" They all emptied their glasses except Bretton who raised his glass and then pushed it away disdainfully.

"I need a real beer. Anyone want to go to Maseru with me to get some?"

Bretton spotted a reaction from one of the police who apparently understood English or at least this essential part of it. His offer provoked a quick exchange among the police. He had found a chink in their brotherhood. They were no longer unified in torment of him. Another loud discussion ensued, threatening to become angry as they clearly had some who wanted to go and some who wanted to stay.

Finally, the English speaker announced, "We will go with you, but when we get to Maseru, you must buy the beer.

"Let's go!" Bretton called and led the group outside. His car was designed for five at most: two bucket seats in front and a bench seat in back. Peugeots are not especially wide. They squeezed two into the passenger bucket seat and four into the back without complaint. Bretton was not himself crowded and he followed their instructions on the road back.

By the time they got to Maseru, it was past 2 am. Bretton did not know any shebeens or bars in Maseru and doubted any were open that late. His passengers led him down a maze of dirt roads to a place on the fringe of the town that looked like an all-night drug store. He bought six liter-bottles of beer, one for each of them and sat them in a row lit by the light outside the shop. They all clambered out of the car to claim their bottles. While they were opening them, Bretton called out "*Salang hantle!*" meaning "stay well" and drove off. He imagined they were chasing after him and calling for him to stop but that was only his fantasy of having mastered a difficult situation. In fact, they scarcely noticed his leaving which they had expected anyway.

XVII. <u>Bretton Meets Pheta (1983)</u>

The Principal called Bretton into his office in the second week of classes. Bretton expected it was just a meeting to get to know each other better. He was not worried about what the Principal might have to say about his work. It was clear he was performing above the usual standard of faculty at this college even though he knew less than any of them about local needs. Thus he was surprised when it turned out that the Principal suggested something unpleasant. He assigned Bretton to be the faculty advisor for the first year agriculture students. Essentially there were two programs at the college, one for girls in home crafts and one for boys or girls in agriculture. Since these were two-year programs and the agriculture side was the larger one, he was the advisor for more than a quarter of the students. This was much more than he could handle. He had to design all his courses since none of them had a syllabus from when they had been taught before. Furthermore, he did not know what a faculty advisor should do and he thought this weakness was entirely reasonable since he was his own first term at the college. The idea was so bad, he could not see why he would be asked to do this unless the Principal was trying to make him fail or to ask for less work in order to take him down a notch in prestige.

Bretton suggested that others would be better able to guide the students. The Principal answered that he had been chosen by the students themselves. It was obvious they had not chosen him for his ability to help them, but for his distinction of being American and having a PhD, although both those characteristics probably indicated he was less able to understand their needs. The Principal sat quietly looking at Bretton, awaiting his acceptance of the task. Bretton thought his boss looked smug although he had not said anything concretely wrong. Bretton thought he did not care about prestige in this place far from everyone he knew but he accepted the assignment as if it was no special challenge to add it to everything else he was doing and his suggestion that others would be better was just being diplomatic. Meanwhile his mind raced ahead to what he would need to do this and he thought it best to begin by talking to the other faculty advisors, so he asked who they were. Alan was the other agriculture student advisor. Mosele Mahasa was the advisor for the second-year home craft students and the Principal could not recall who was the first-year advisor for them.

Alan went over to his neighbor's house right after work to ask him what being an advisor entailed. Alan said it was nothing at all, just another empty ritual on which he had not expended any effort in the three years he had the title. "But you know all the second year students already, don't you?"

"Sure, I know them."

"And they ask your help on things outside of your classes from time to time?"

"I suppose so. I never thought of it as being their class advisor, but I guess you could say it. Probably all the faculty that have been around a few years get those questions. If something comes up, come over here and ask me. Maybe I have seen it before."

It was a kind offer that Bretton cashed in less than a week later. The students seemed to take the class advisor role seriously. A contingent of six students came to him when he was in his office and boldly asked if his office mate could leave for a few minutes to give them privacy. They claimed that one of the teachers, a certain Ntate Pheta, had started an affair with one of their classmates and was giving her test answers. They called him by his first name, contrary to the usual custom for teachers, because he was very young. Bretton did his best to display deep concern and to assure them he understood this was a dire charge that needed remedy if the situation was as they suspected. He asked what evidence they had. They seemed more certain of the affair than of the test answers, but had no real evidence of wrongdoing. Apparently, the girl was boastful and her test scores backed her up, but she was careful enough to avoid saying anything direct that could be quoted against her.

Bretton went to Alan and asked his advice. Alan thought it plausible that Pheta was involved with one of the girls but he had no advice about what to do except to stay out of it. "This is for the Basotho to work out." It was not the support Bretton had hoped to find.

He went next to the Principal and told him the story, leaving out the name of the accused and the accusers. He would reveal these if asked but he was not asked. The Principal was exactly as helpful as Alan, offering nothing that could be called advice, instead merely concluding whatever action might be taken would be within the authority of the class advisor.

Bretton nearly laughed out loud at this perversion of his add-on job.

This brought Bretton to meeting Pheta. He was immediately impressed by the affable young man who jumped up from his desk to shake Bretton's hand and offer him a seat. His courtesies ("Glad you came by, Dr. MacNamara; I wanted to meet you; I have heard you will be a very positive force for the college"; and "I hope you can explain some maths problems for me; I teach calculus at night to promising university students who want to get into graduate school in America, but I struggle with parts of the text.") were so excessive, Bretton suspected Pheta knew what had brought them together.

Bretton did offer to get to know his colleague better in good time but refused to be distracted for long from his original purpose. However, the idea that this young man could be tutoring calculus on the side brought up intriguing questions about why he was at the agricultural college. It was an advantage that Bretton did not know Pheta so he could explain the accusations objectively without trying to accommodate Pheta's personality or history. He was also aided by Pheta's introductory remarks because they showed he was bright and fluent in English so, again, Bretton could focus on stating the situation directly.

Pheta neither denied the charges nor confessed to them. He just shook his head while nodding to display something Bretton could not interpret. He assumed it meant Pheta was not pleased to be having the conversation. Pheta looked up as soon as Bretton finished his description and gave a look as if he had asked a question. Bretton felt it was up to him to say something to resolve it since Pheta was not going to defend himself.

"I told the students they had not given me proof of anything at all and because of that, I did not mention anyone's name to the Principal. I really hate to be involved in this at all but the students appeared sincere to me and I would not want them to believe we allowed one of them to be favored for any reason outside the classroom. I am sure you agree we need their trust in order to do our jobs."

He waited for Pheta to respond. All Pheta did was nod vigorously to show his agreement and the stare at Bretton to encourage him to continue.

Bretton had not decided what to do but his next words laid out his position as if he had thought it through properly.

"I will tell the students I have spoken to you and that I feel assured there will never be another test with anyone getting unfair help. Do you give me permission to say this?"

"Yes, of course, Dr. MacNamara. Please tell them not to worry about that in my classes."

"Naturally I will also say they should come back to me only if they have better evidence of some misconduct. I will explain that the effect of an incident like this with good supporting evidence would destroy more than the career of a teacher since the story would certainly become known outside the college and be a humiliation."

Pheta agreed heartily with this remark and then Bretton wished him well and said he hoped to get together another day to talk about calculus which may have been the oddest social date Bretton had ever proposed.

XVIII. <u>Mosele III (1983)</u>

Bretton stood near the door of the grocery store to wait for Mme Mahasa to finish her shopping. His excursion to the hardware store and his brief exploration of Ladybrand had killed about fifteen minutes and she was finished very soon after he arrived. He watched her take her items out of her basket and place them on the checkout counter. She was very methodical and placed each item so the price could be read without further handling. The clerk piled the items without any effort to bag them. Bretton saw that Mme Mahasa had put a large cloth bag on the counter so he presumed the store did not provide paper bags. Suddenly he felt like a spy to be watching her without her knowledge so he stepped forward and began to place the items in her bag. When the clerk had rung up everything from the basket, she asked Mme Mahasa to take off her blanket.

"Why should I take off my blanket?" Mme Mahasa asked, although the reason was obvious and the clerk gave the obvious answer without any show of irony.

"You can hide things under there."

Mme Mahasa did not raise her voice when she answered, "I will not take off my blanket."

The clerk placed both hands on the counter and stared at Mme Mahasa, as if that would make her change her mind and open the blanket. Bretton wanted to say something but he did not know what to say. He wanted to support Mme Mahasa. If he said something to show that he vouched for her honesty, it might have gotten her past the clerk but she might have objected to his interference. She must have been in this market before. Surely she knew how to deal with this small town clerk.

Mme Mahasa took out her money and asked "How much is it?"

The clerk said "Take off your blanket first." The clerk saw that Bretton was waiting for Mme Mahasa and looked toward him as if to suggest he resolve the matter, presumably by getting Mme Mahasa to take off her blanket. When he did not act, she offered a small compromise. She turned back to Mme Mahasa and said "Maybe just open it up."

"One does not need to undress in order to buy one's groceries."

They faced each other silently for just a few more seconds before Mme Mahasa asked Bretton to empty her bag. He put her items back on the checkout counter while Mme Mahasa watched him and the clerk stared at Mme Mahasa. Then Mme Mahasa led the way out of the shop. The clerk did not utter another word.

Bretton thought he might have been more supportive somehow. He hoped he had respected Mme Mahasa. The clerk might have done more if he were not there. Or he might have said something powerful and Mme Mahasa would have her groceries. It was hard to tell what might have happened if he had spoken up. When they were seated again in his car, both in the front, Bretton asked if he could go back and buy some things Mme Mahasa really wanted. They should not miss the chance to get what she needed.

"I do not need anything in Ladybrand," was all Mme Mahasa would say. Bretton started the car and went out of town a short way. When they were out of sight, he pulled to the side of the road.

"I have a map. There must be another town we can use," he suggested.

"Thank you, Ntate, for bringing me. I no longer want to give them any of my money. Please let us go back to Maseru."

Bretton learned later that it would have been a long drive to the next town. Mme Mahasa probably knew that. He decided much later, after he had lived there some time, that people like Mme Mahasa did not go to South Africa often and did not have much experience with the clerks. He had much to learn about the complicated social relations in southern Africa. He would never understand them well, but it was so clearly obscure to him that he was afraid to even guess at what might be appropriate and preferred to hang back and watch. Still, he was at an age where he was consciously shedding his childish behaviors. Hanging back might be worse than saying something stupid. Mme Mahasa had far more potential as an ally than as a critic. From Bretton's perspective, the whole trip was not to help Mme Mahasa so much as to get to know her, to befriend her. Watching her embarrassing treatment in the grocery store had not advanced his purpose.

After a silent ten minutes of brooding, Bretton noticed he was drumming on the steering wheel, revealing his nervousness. He broke the ice anew. "Mme." He spoke boldly, having made up his mind to be an adult, beyond his well-practiced student mode. "What should I have done back there? I am too inexperienced to know but I know I should have done something. You tell me."

"It is South Africa. You are American. There is nothing for you to do."

"I did not think being American left me with nothing to do. Maybe it is not a fair question for you.

What should I have done if I was a white South African man and a colleague of yours, standing there?"

"I should not have come here. We know we are not welcome."

"We are just people, all of us. I know you fully understand this, Mme. I have seen you in meetings and with others. You do not care if I am American. You do not even care if I am a man when it comes to my rights and responsibilities. Please help me learn how to meet those responsibilities in this place."

"I cannot tell you what to do in South Africa. And it is not my job to say what your responsibilities are."

"No, of course it is not your job. I need help. You are a senior member of the faculty. Have you not thought about what someone like me should do? Were you not thinking I should have done something back there?"

"I do not think of people like you. I do not know many Americans. We have no more of you at the college."

"You know plenty of Brits."

"I do not think of what you should do. I do not think about you at all."

"Oh, listen to you! You are not as tough as you think you are. We work in the same school. You know who I am. Sure, I am not important, but you think of me once in a while. You wonder what I am doing in Lesotho and sometimes you wonder if I might be of use. I am not quite like the Brits. No better, obviously, but better in certain significant ways than most of the South African whites, we both must agree.

"I see everyone at the college respects your opinion." he continued. "They know you and listen to you. I do not know you much but I do respect you, not just in the way I must respect anyone, but an additional amount, like the others do, for your obvious hard, careful work. Let me be your student. Teach me, when it is convenient for you, like right now, how to be a good teacher at our college."

"I do not know how you should act. You are proper enough already. You have more education than any of us. What can I add? The staff do not respect me as much as you say anyway. I am a woman."

"Lesotho is run by women. Africa is run by women. Any fool could see that."

"This is true but it does not make it easy and it does not mean we get respect from men. You see that the Principal is a man and the Education Minister is a man and the Prime Minister is a man. The King is a man too, of course. We have a queen but we hardly see her. I am young and already at the top of my career."

"Really? In Lesotho women are sometimes the boss. I understand it is not as often as they deserve, but enough to show it can be done. You should be the pathbreaker."

"I don't need to hear from you how much opportunity is staring me in the face. Did you know you have the advantage of color, money, nationality, sex, education, height, youth, brains and who knows what more. I hardly know you and I can see this much. You want me to spend my time to teach you?"

"Mme, we are not competing, you know. We are colleagues. I was only asking for you to help me, when convenient, to be better at the job we both have, teaching the students at our college."

"If I tell you to do something, will you do it?"

"You know, I think I will. Our students do not do everything we ask them to do but they know they should. I would like to be at least as good as that. Try me."

"Will you argue with me in staff meetings?"

"Oh yes, when I think I have something to add. I believe we should speak up with our ideas. Not insist on them, but argue? Yes. Respectfully. You know, listening to the points of view of others and granting they may know more facts or have better understanding or generate better ideas. Arguing is a respectful process; should be anyway. At the college, the Basotho staff usually have more relevant facts than me and better understanding of circumstances and of possibilities. It would be wildly inappropriate for me to aggressively promote my views very often."

"You speak up as if you had been here all your life."

"That is a mistake. I do not think I should give that impression. So you see, you are teaching me. For that I thank you and I will make a great effort to avoid sounding like that."

"You are not wrong. I did not mean that. You are always right, I think and it is good to have you advising the college. Only you sound so confident all the time. It makes everyone listen to you. It would not be the same if you were a woman."

"Well, I have never been and will never be a woman. We have to use the tools we have. Not to the point of arrogance at our good fortune. There are, you know, some advantages to being a woman too. You have some different tools."

"You think we should use our tools to get our way."

Bretton sensed she was about to be offended that he was suggesting she be sexy somehow. There was a thought behind his words of how he had been maneuvered by women through their attractiveness although it had not occurred to him that this was a tool for Mme Mahasa. It was not hard to explain his point less offensively. "For example, as a woman, you can speak more easily with the women who are most of the farmers in Lesotho and better understand what they face and what they need. Our college could not succeed without those kinds of insights."

Mme Mahasa felt there was something unsavory in Bretton. She did not shrink from distrusting him for being a white male and, apparently, rich by the standards of Lesotho. She had not seen him do anything wrong yet but there were many untrustworthy people whose particular failures she had not seen. She held back from rejecting him. She was fair-minded and saw the possibility that his slippery words could have truth behind them, however, she was not open to starting some kind of friendship or some teaching role. So she looked out the window at the passing veldt. With the window of the car rolled down, there was a roar in her ears and she did not feel the need to continue conversing.

Meanwhile, Bretton felt he had been too formal, too academic in his language, as well as being too trendy in his thinking. Even so, he was pleased that he had made an effort to know her and hopeful that the olive branch might be accepted in the future if something came up. They had not come to terms on how to relate, but it was a satisfactory opening. Becoming part of a community like the college would require many more awkward openings.

When they neared Lesotho, Mosele asked Bretton to stop the car so she could sit in the back. The South African border guards checked Bretton's pass against a card file of trouble makers and did not find his name. They hardly glanced at Mosele's passport. After they crossed the bridge they came to the Lesotho checkpoint. A young boy wearing only his underpants lifted the gate without any further inspection.

XIX. Palesa (2003)

Bretton looked past the pool to the city below and the low mountains beyond that. Maseru was a city by Lesotho standards but would have qualified as no more than a medium-sized town back in his native Ohio. The pool was nice by any standard and the view was better than any he knew in Ohio. Dusk was approaching and the smoke of cooking fires, fueled by coal, was building a long grey cloud over the houses. It was too low to obscure his view of the mountains and the sunset. He was glad he was not breathing the air below. Even without industry or automobiles, Maseru generated and endured the pollution of poverty, like London in Dickens' time. It would be worse in winter when more coal was burned for heat than for cooking.

No one was in the pool. Bretton thought he might enjoy the exercise of a few laps but he had not brought any shorts and did not want the bother of making some arrangement. He sat in a chair with a webbed seat and pulled up a plastic table to hold his papers. A few South Africans were lying on towels, apparently not having noticed yet that the sun was nearing the horizon. The dry air of Lesotho would cool quickly and chase them indoors. Bretton had collected some government reports to update himself on official statistics. It would improve his credibility to have these in his head. He would only cite data that were relevant to the discussions and would not shift the discussion to areas in which he knew some numbers but he was sure there would be occasions when mentioning the official numbers, with due regard for the difficulties of data collection, would strengthen his arguments while keeping his opinion well respected.

A waiter came by. It was M. Phaki.

"Good evening, Sir."

"Sir? I am not used to that, Abuti. *Khotso, pula, nala.*" This was the most traditional and formal greeting, meaning "Have peace, rain and prosperity."

M. Phaki laughed to hear this familiar language from his old teacher.

"But I am the servant now. I have come to take your order. Would you like dinner? Or a drink for starters?"

"I don't know. Are these lights coming on soon? I will stay here a while if it is bright enough to read." Lights were strung all around the pool six feet back from the edge at the height of a man's head.

"The sun is nearly gone. I will turn on the lights now. It will be very bright."

"Then I will have a drink. What do people get when they sit out here?"

"Daiquiris and margaritas are very popular."

"Not with me. I'll have a Castle. No glass, thanks."

"Very good, Ntate. Did you know we have Maluti Beer now? It is made in Lesotho, not from maize, a real lager."

"Is it good?"

"No. It is cheap."

"I'll stick with the Castle, then."

"Will you have dinner with us tonight?"

"Yes, I believe I will. Something simple. Bar fare would be just right. I'll come inside when it gets too cold to read out here.

"Are you going to see any of your friends while you are here?"

"Yes. I will visit the college to see if anyone I knew is still there. I did not keep in touch with anyone so I don't know who might remember me. I hope to run into some of the students, like you. I won't remember their names."

"They will remember you. But all the expatriates you knew are gone. It has been many years."

"Oh I would not be looking for any of them."

"Ntate Alan came back for a couple years to run the dairy but he left too. If I see any of the students should I tell them you are here?"

"Thanks, no. I mean you can tell them but they should not try to come up here and visit. We did not know each other long. I was only here a couple years."

"I could find some of the Basotho staff."

"I already saw Ntate Pshoene. He said he is married to Mme Mahasa now."

"Yes, he is a big man in the government."

"I think he is a serious man and does good work."

"Yes, very smart and hard working. Do you want to see Mme Mahasa again?"

"That would be interesting. She and I took a trip once and I got to know her a little even though she is a very private person. I might have dinner with her and her husband one of these days." Bretton wondered if she would be more open with him now. She was well established, being married to a big man, maybe more confident. Maybe it was just her permanent personality to keep people like Bretton, foreign colleagues, at a distance.

"Should I find Palesa for you? I know where she works now."

"Ntate Phaki! What a question! Did I seem so interested in her?"

"Sorry. I just thought you might want to say 'hello'."

"I did like her back then. It was a long time ago."

M. Phaki did not make any more suggestions. He waited a few moments for Bretton to say more and then nodded to himself as he went back to the bar to get a Castle for his former teacher.

Bretton drank his Castle slowly, almost sipped it like a cocktail. It was just something to add dimension to the dusk while he focused on work. Unfortunately, no bathing beauties came out to lie by the pool. The lights came on and the dusk passed quickly as it does in tropical latitudes. It was just Bretton and his reading and his beer for an hour. He took a few notes although he did not expect to ever look at them. The act of making them helped him to remember the high points in the data. He would carry the notes with him in case someone challenged something he said. Then he could look up the source of the information. As a technical expert, he did not allow others to challenge his authority without a firm response. M. Phaki checked on him a few times to see if he wanted another drink, but Bretton smiled and motioned him away without further conversation.

After an hour, Bretton was getting bored and decided to regard himself as hungry so he went in to the bar. As he approached M, he tried to formulate a greeting in Sesotho but his repertoire of phrases did not fit the situation. He could be more or less formal, or adjust for the time of day and even a little humorous in greeting but everything he had learned was intended for seeing someone for the first time in a day, not for seeing someone who had a conversation with him an hour earlier. He wanted to be friendly since he had pushed M off when he came out to the poolside the last few times. He used English.

"It is always this quiet during the week?" Bretton sat at the bar.

"It is early. They will start coming in from the casino around ten."

"Is the casino busy during the week?"

"There are always some people. Of course there are more on the weekends. We have music in here on weekends too."

"I see some Basotho going into the casino wearing blankets and bare feet. They do not look like they can afford to gamble."

"Some Basotho use all their money this way. They do not lose much because they do not have much. No one would give these men any loan either."

"So it is not the Basotho who start to come in at ten?"

"No, it will be white South Africans. Boers speaking Africaans."

"Do you speak Africaans?"

"I learned some at the mines. I can take their orders but not have a conversation with them."

"Did you say I can order dinner from here?"

"For sure. I will get you a menu."

"No, I don't need a menu. Can I get a hamburger and chips?" Much of the world was adopting American English. Lesotho had never been colonized but it had been a British protectorate and first learned English to deal with Brits in South Africa so they still thought fried potatoes were "chips," and called American potato chips "crisps."

"Of course. Another Castle now?

"Do you have sparkling water? I'll have that."

"Very good."

Bretton pulled out his papers while he waited for his dinner. It was too dark to read them and he did not want to read any more. He realized he should have eaten in his room. He could have found something more interesting to read and had the light to do it. He had wanted to show some camaraderie with M although he was not sure why he should bother. He just seemed like a nice fellow who deserved a little company. They did chat a little until someone else came in: two white men in t-shirts. They sat at a table and talked quietly while they drank shots. The hamburger was not long in coming. Bretton ate quickly although he made an effort not to appear in a hurry. He enjoyed the food, its flavor being enhanced by the decadence it represented to his diet.

"Abuti," Bretton called out. Should I pay now or do you want to add it to my hotel bill?"

"There is no charge, Ntate Mac. It is on the house."

"*Ka nete!*" which is a Sesotho expression Bretton picked up without ever learning its meaning. It was used to show surprise, perhaps like "really!" in English when used alone. "*Kea laboha, hahoolo.*" He knew how to say "thank you." He knew the hotel was not buying him dinner. M was trying to be generous. It would be expensive for him unless he had kept it off the books in the first place. Bretton did not want to be a party to that. "You will let me leave a tip, right?"

"I cannot stop you," M laughed.

Bretton handed him a twenty, more than enough for the dinner and M laughed again when he realized what Bretton was doing.

"Will you be having dinner here tomorrow?"

"The future is a mystery to me, including tomorrow. I have no plans for myself but I think the many people who consider themselves my boss have ideas for me."

"Good night then. Enjoy the rest of your evening." M did not follow the odd response from Bretton but the actual answer did not matter. He was just being polite, as he had been trained by the hotel.

"And you too," Bretton waved on his way out of the bar. He walked up the stairs to the ground floor, admiring the immense chandelier over the lounge as he passed it at eye level. The hotel was built into the side of a mountain so the level with the bar looked out over a grand view to the west even though it was below the main entrance on the east. His room was one floor higher. He had never noticed a stairway going up from the lobby so he took the elevator.

Upon exiting the elevator, Bretton hesitated because he had not thought about which way to go to his room. *It's to the left*, he recalled, in the direction of the sunset since he had been able to look down on the pool and the town from his window. He went to the end of the hall and turned right. Halfway down the remaining hallway, across from his room, sat a woman. Her legs were straight out in front of her, like the women in the market selling tiny piles of fruit. The woman did not turn toward him until he was close. The thick carpet had kept his approach quiet. She jumped up when she realized someone was there. She looked at him. They regarded each other for a moment. She was not dressed like a hooker or as assertive as a hooker would be. She was not in the uniform of the hotel staff, but wore a wrap-around dress in an African print, a style that would have been common even on his earlier trip. He recognized her in the same instant she recognized him. She must have known he was coming there so she should have recognized him first unless it was only coincidence they were at the same place.

"Palesa!"

"Thabo," she answered quietly and lowered her eyes. That was the name she always called him and the students used behind his back, using his real name out of respect when addressing him. It was a common name meaning "happy." Bretton had not heard it in ten years but he had been proud of it when he lived here.

"It is wonderful to see you!"

She raised her face halfway. "You have come back." And then "You will not stay for long?"

"I don't know how long. Maybe a week."

"Please go inside your room." She looked up the hallway as if nervous to be seen with him.

She kicked off her sandals and sat on the bed, her bare legs stretched in front of her. They were scarred and did not inspire the lust they might have ten years earlier even though they had never been ideal in his view. He liked her best in jeans and she knew it. She continued to keep her face down. This posture was not typical of her before. Bretton did not think she had become demure; he guessed she was hiding her blind eye from him. It was mostly white, perhaps due to a large cataract or to some kind of deterioration Bretton could not name.

Bretton went to the refrigerator. "What would you like to drink? Cold beer? Water? Soft drink?"

"Beer" she answered. He took out a water for himself. He handed her the bottle, thinking she could not have changed so much that she would want a glass for her beer. He sat in the wooden chair by the desk.

"How have you been, Palesa?"

He did not want to hear how she had been. He could not imagine she had done well in the past decade. She did not look happy or especially hearty. The story behind that peculiar eye was not a good one. She had retained her youthful shape although Bretton doubted she saw that positively since she had not liked it as much as he had before.

"Sit beside me, Thabo."

Bretton stood up but did not go to her.

"How is your daughter now?"

She did not answer.

"Is she going to school?"

When she did not answer a second time, Bretton feared he was pushing on an uncomfortable issue. Life was often short or harsh among the Basotho.

"Do you have any more children now?

"My daughter is well, thank you. I have no man and no more children. I did not come here to talk about my children. Sit with me."

Bretton considered staying where he was but thought they could talk quietly if they were closer. As he crossed the small room, she began to unbutton her blouse. His mind did not race back to the party where she had bared her breast in front of everyone and everyone laughed at him for thinking it significant. It went back to the night she asked him to meet him in her rondavel and he knocked at the door and heard her say "*kena*" which means "come in." It was almost completely dark in her rondavel, a little starlight through the windows suggesting the space within. She had then said "*tlo koano*," come here, in Sesotho. She knew he only knew a few phrases, but the meanings of many more phrases were so obvious to her, she always expected him to understand. Fortunately, this was one of his phrases and he followed the voice a few steps until he felt a sheet hit his face. He remembered she hung a sheet in front of her bed as if to create a room behind it. Her voice had come from the bed. She was naked, waiting for him under her quilt. He felt her and understood. He undressed without any more words and lay beside her. Her breasts were the softest things he had ever sensed.

"Wait, Palesa." How could he say he felt no desire for her? He did not want to insult her or her poor eye or her battered legs. In truth, the eye did bother him. It was a reminder of the distance between them, of the poverty she endured and that he would never have to face. He wondered if he should feel guilt for her circumstances, but he had asked himself that question thousands of times in dozens of countries where nearly everyone was worse off than him by a large margin. He always countered in his mind with the fact that the reasons for his personal good fortune were beyond his control. He could not possibly adopt all the needy people he encountered in a career devoted to work in poor countries. Maybe, however, he could have helped Palesa. She had been the special one in his youth.

"We just met after all these years. Let us talk."

"You talk too much, Thabo. I am your wife. When you are in Lesotho, I am your wife."

Bretton could not think of anything to say to her although he wanted to answer, to reassure her somehow and words did flood into his consciousness. *No, Baby, you are not my wife. As much as I once wanted you, it never entered my mind to marry and you knew this very well. On the other hand, the way you said that, "when you are in Lesotho," shows you are using the concept of "wife" informally. I imagine you mean it more in an economic sense than a romantic one. Our past relations always contained a silent and essential quid pro quo, didn't they? Is that essential to your understanding of marriage in Lesotho? I could be convinced it is a widespread practice. The importance you accept for brideprice toward getting and staying married is hard for people like me to understand. It is also hard for me to believe you do not know what people like me think on this subject. You have been around us for many years now. Maybe I was relatively new to you back then; maybe that was a part of my appeal, but there have been two decades of Americans and Europeans working with you at the college since then and none of them would differ greatly from me in how we used the concept of marriage. We used to talk, Palesa. Don't you remember? I told you stories. You did not find them entertaining although you tolerated them. They should at least have shown my efforts to connect with you intellectually. And you talked; I know you remember that. Talking was overly important to you. I saw it as your sexual fetish. You were too consistent in turning whatever conversation was underway into some form of complaint that carried you to tears before our petting could become serious. Afterwards, you made you a plea for payment, always minor, but always payment, usually one large bottle of beer but a couple times something larger that you had in mind before we had sex, new jeans once, remember that? You mentioned the brand and the shop where you could get them even though those points held no meaning to me. The requests for beer were amusing. Even in your economy, it was too small to constitute payment for borrowing your body. It was more like an old movie that marked the dissipation of passion by smoking a cigarette. It sometimes occurred to me that you wanted some payment, however minor, to prove you held the upper hand, that I wanted you more than you wanted me. Now, after all this time when you could hear all of my accomplishments around the world or could tell me your troubles, if that is what you wished to do, you are proposing we go straight to sex? In the era of AIDS? Are you proving you trust me or checking whether I trust you or just being foolish? I should warn you about AIDS even though you have doubtless heard an abundance of warnings already. Palesa, if I ever loved you, I should use this moment to ensure, at the cost of our relationship, that you remember the dangers of unprotected sex with multiple and concurrent partners, as we say clinically in our foreign assistance program.*

While Bretton's thoughts wandered, Palesa continued to disrobe. With only one dim light on in the room, Bretton could not see her clearly. He could see her movements enough to know what she was doing. Suddenly he realized his silence could be read as accepting her offer. His delay was making it harder to back way kindly.

"Palesa! Please wait. You must stop that. You make me want you just as my memory makes me want you, but not at this time and place. We need to know each other again first." He was, of course, lying. He saw no chance of their getting together again.

Palesa turned her back to him and quickly put her clothes back on. When she turned around the fire in her one working eye was so bright, it lit the dark room like day. The room did not catch fire only because she spit her words so actively it put out the flames that would have consumed him.

"You don't want me anymore. You did not ever love me. You never said that word because you did not love me then. Now you do not even want me because you have slept with more beautiful women. You have a new girlfriend in Lesotho and you will see her tonight and you want me to leave so you can be with her. I am too old for you now."

She finished buttoning her blouse and Bretton stepped close to her to embrace her. She pushed him away and thought better of it and came forward with her fists flying at his face.

"You tell your friends you slept with me and I was not good enough for you. You said you did not want someone fatter but then you found someone fatter and that is what you like. And you give this girl money for whatever she wants because you like her better but I know you will not marry her either."

"No, no, no." Bretton could still not think of what to say but he could see he had to say something. It would not be the truth, which was that he might have been induced to jump into bed with her if she were the same girl he knew ten years earlier. It was not her age that bothered him, but her broken eye and his broader knowledge of poverty and AIDS. Any reassuring lie he could conceive felt transparent. "I have no girlfriend in Lesotho." This was true, at least. "I have not met with any girl in Lesotho since I left you. I do not even have a wife or a girlfriend outside Lesotho." This also was true since he used the present tense. "It is hard to love a woman and have to leave her." He felt like genius for finding more truths beside the point but soothing, at least to himself. They were fighting with their hands with her trying to hit him and him catching her blows to keep them ineffectual. He considered letting one in. Perhaps he deserved it. Perhaps it would calm her. He could make clear he intentionally let her hit his face. She was strong and might make a mark. That would be all right too.

She managed to contact him a few times. Some were firm although none did any harm. It was enough to express her opinion so she stopped her attack before her frustration became too silly.

Did you ever love me? The first question he thought brought no answer, only more questions. *Do you think that does not matter, that a woman is not supposed to love in the same way? Do you now want to recover our younger years, rekindle our flame, or capture some wealth? This passion would be excessive if your goal was a liter of beer.*

Palesa fell back on the bed, breathing heavily and staring at Bretton, staring with her one good eye. Bretton sat beside her without touching her. She was too angry to sob but tears flowed from both eyes. Bretton wondered if this was a sign she was ready for sex. Apart from her past pattern, she looked anything but sexual. He reached to her thigh and gripped it to feel its firmness. She did not respond and calmly said "E-e." Bretton had forgotten how to say "no" in Sesotho. He took his hand away. She turned her face away from him. He imagined she had realized she was crying. Bretton felt sympathy. He adjusted his weight on the bed, aligning his body near her without quite touching. He could see no reason for her distress. They had not communicated in twenty years. Regardless of what unspoken promises she heard when he was there, she could not imagine he would be her husband now, no matter how temporarily. He had always been annoyed by her senseless tears except for the fact they led to sex. He was surprised to find that he was feeling a desire for intimacy with her. It was, to him, completely inappropriate and, because of AIDS, a completely impossible risk, but he reached out tenderly with his gentle lust.

Palesa sat up immediately upon feeling him and said "e-e" decisively, and then watched him closely as she maneuvered to the side of the bed and stood up. Bretton saw in her caution the experience of fighting off a man or men from unwanted sex. He still wanted her but would not be such a man. He laid back on the bed and looked at the ceiling.

"How can I help you, Palesa?" he asked. In their former relationship, he never offered her anything. She would tell him what she wanted and he would either give it to her or not. Her requests were never large and he usually met them. Bretton wanted the painful encounter to end and was trying to hurry it along by making an offer. In fact, he was likely to grant something much larger than before. He had more resources now. Besides, there was no danger of seeming to pay for sex now.

"My life is very hard, you know. You know this. Much harder than yours."

Bretton thought it a complement that she credited him with some understanding but it was undeserved. Of course he knew her life was hard and harder than his, but he could not imagine what problems she faced at the moment. Was her income secure? Was her family starving? Did she or someone she loved have AIDS? "I would like to help you."

"You cannot help me."

"I can do something, Palesa."

"I will never take anything from you. Stay away." And then very sharply "*Sala*."

The normal way to say "goodby" is for one person to say "go well" and the other to say "stay well." "*Sala*" meant "stay." Bretton had never heard it without it being followed by the word for "well." He would not say "go well" for it might sound as if he were sending her off so without any more words, she turned her back and went out, closing the door quietly behind her.

Bretton thought of jumping up and watching her depart, maybe even walk her to the hotel exit. He might try again to give her something. But he agreed with her. There was nothing he could do for her, nothing that he would do anyway. He continued to lie on the bed in the dark for another 30 minutes when his emotions had cooled and he was simply bored with his own thoughts. Then he rose, turned on the lights, and brushed his teeth before settling in with a book for an hour before falling asleep.

XX. ANC Party (1983)

One day about two months after Bretton had begun teaching, the college Principal came by Bretton's office and shut the door. Bretton offered a seat but his boss said he would only require a minute.

"Do you know Phyllis Naidoo? No? She's big in the ANC in Lesotho. Maybe you'd like to go to her party. If you want, I can get you in."

Bretton was very proud to be invited to an ANC party although he did not know what sort of party it would be.   The African National Congress held a mythical stature among anti-apartheid activists in U.S. universities. The head of the party was in jail and the acting head had spoken on his campus to promote the international boycott of South African business.   In Lesotho, he had taken every opportunity during classes and in faculty discussions to show his support for majority rule in South Africa, but few ever said much on the topic.   No one had reacted to his comments. Everyone assumed he would support democracy since he was American but Bretton sensed that the Basotho were tired of the subject and preferred to ignore it. It was a fact of life in the neighboring country-- they in Lesotho were independent and free. Of course the politically active would be fully conscious of the burden apartheid placed on Lesotho but Bretton had not met anyone politically active.

He suspected the party was designed to raise funds since he had been invited and who was he to them? They might think he had money and maybe he had a little more than most of them, not enough to fund anything but enough to pay his way at a party. Someone

217

had given someone the impression he was sympathetic enough to be invited-- that was something.

He carefully underdressed for the event. It might be a party for fund-raising but Bretton had not seen anyone in Lesotho who dressed well, if "well" meant in the manner of formal America. It was important to wear a tie when meeting with local officials. Even on the hottest day, they would be wearing tie and jacket, but that was not sufficient to be well dressed in the American sense. Even the Minister of Agriculture, whom Bretton had met several times, wore pants that were too short, as if they had been handed down from a smaller older brother, and his cuffs were threadbare. His jacket showed that it had been worn despite inducing perspiration. Apart from the differences in taste and style that are inevitable with such long-standing cultural differences between continents and hemispheres, there was a different appreciation of crispness. The Basotho had a very logical position that what you wore was your statement on rank and occasion. Details were not of the essence while in Bretton's experience, Americans were very much concerned with the specific features of style, specifically that they demonstrate newness, expensiveness, or both. A party with the ANC was no place to prove his familiarity with the latest American trends or to display his wealth. Short sleeves on a white shirt and a tie would be too humble, maybe asserting a communist identity, perhaps not unwelcome at the party but not Bretton. He opted for a striped shirt and an unassuming tie. A jacket would have made him pretentious in addition to being impractical. He was young but actually did teach at a college so he could be professorial. The party was his chance to make some political contacts, not a place to meet interesting young women.

Bretton struggled with an arrival time. He wanted to ask his boss when he should arrive, but his boss had never shown sympathy for Bretton's misunderstanding local standards. He was reluctant to ask his Basotho friends because he was not sure he should tell anyone he would be at an ANC event. He had not been told it was secret but it might have been assumed. He decided it would be more awkward to arrive late and possibly suggest thereby that he thought he was important, than to arrive on time and merely look naïve.

So he drove to the address he had been given and then faced the question of where to park. The house was of a common sort in a nondescript neighborhood near the center of Maseru. There were no cars parked nearby so he drove a block away and walked back. He was five minutes later than the time he had been given. He walked to the door and did not knock as it was already open. Just after he entered a woman came up to him and handed him a glass of wine and introduced herself as Phyllis Naidoo.

It did not surprise Bretton that she was not Mosotho-- she would most likely be from South Africa if she was an ANC leader-- but he had not considered that she would be "Asian," that is, Indian like Gandhi. She came across as educated and gracious, and made Bretton comfortable in a moment. He was less comfortable after she moved away to greet someone else and left him standing with a glass of wine in a large room already quite full of well-dressed people actively engaged, he imagined, in the kind of conversations he aspired to join.

219

He stepped near a trio of middle-aged white men. He noticed that, with the addition of him, all the white men at the party were together. They did not look as awkward as he felt, but he was not going to settle in with them, so he drifted past them as if he had someone to meet on the far side of the room. *Who looks involved but not in a way that would make him unapproachable?* Bretton asked himself. And then, *Why are you acting like this is your first freshman mixer?* As a result of his first mixer, he had learned that he was just like everyone else in his insecurities, his desires, his frustrations, or so it seemed when he talked about it with the freshman men in his dormitory. Of course it was just that he was typical of the eighteen-year-olds of his class and sexual orientation and country and region and race and education. But it had been reassuring to hear they had nearly all felt uncomfortable with the women they met at the mixer, women like themselves but for gender, and what gender did to people in those days, in the 1960s. And he had used that knowledge of his fundamental normalcy to project confidence in later social situations with the happy result that he actually found a few dates with girls he had met at parties. Still he was never smooth in those situations and did not seek them out. And none of the girls he met that way ever turned out to fit well with him. He needed something more to form the basis of a relationship, not merely shared background and desire for companionship.

Here at his first ANC party, and it was a party, not a meeting or a clandestine assembly, he wanted to feel like part of the scene, like an adult who was part of the solution to one of the world's great injustices. If only he had something to offer the proceedings... He stepped close to a thin man nearly as young as himself who was studying the cheese plate.

"Hey man, I mean, *lumela ntate*," Bretton ventured, hoping his apology for using only the most common Sesotho greeting was modest rather than stupid. "I'm new to Lesotho." The young man looked up at Bretton, rolling his eyes without lifting his head.

He muttered "I'm from Zimbabwe," and reached into the bowl of crackers as if he had revealed an important detail.

Cool! Did you fight in the revolution? Have you trained for the struggle in South Africa? Do you know Mugabe? What's he like? Maybe you are too young for those things. Was your family abused by the white authorities? Bretton thought but all he said was "Cool. I'd like to get up there one of these days. See Great Zimbabwe, you know."

The young man rolled his eyes toward Bretton and made a small sound, almost a word, but his mouth was full of crackers and nothing intelligible came out.

Bretton looked around while the young man's attention was directed again at the bowl in front of him but no group attracted him in any obvious way. *Damn, I've met upperclass coeds who were more courteous to freshman than this guy,* Bretton thought, but he said, "What part of Zimbabwe is your home?" The question had the advantage of implying Bretton knew one part of Zimbabwe from another and the disadvantage that he might have to admit he knew nothing of Zimbabwe beyond the international headlines. *Why should I be tested on Zimbabwe?* Bretton wondered silently. *I am living in Lesotho and hoping to support democracy in South Africa. Zimbabwe is ahead of the game right now.* Majority rule had come two years earlier, the so-called "independence" from Britain. Bretton knew this, a point not known to all Americans although it was probably known to all Americans living in Lesotho. He waited for the young man to answer, clearly looking at him to force some recognition of the question, meaningless though it was.

The young man swallowed conspicuously and said, "That's my father over there. I'm just here for a snack."

Bretton took this as a complement, an indication that the young man saw Bretton as a participant. Bretton parted company with a condescending courtesy "Welcome to Lesotho, *ntate*" and then he wandered to the first group he could find with enough physical space nearby that he could get close enough to listen in. *I've seen this kind of party before and I will not be defeated by it*, he resolved, thinking now of being shot down by women in bars as well as in college events whenever he was surrounded by strangers. He had gotten past that in his graduate school years, he thought, although it might have been that he had fewer occasions where he was surrounded by strangers. Coming to Africa as the only American teaching in the agricultural college, he saw that he better become adept at meeting new people. He leaned into the group. They were speaking a language he did not recognize, not English, Sesotho or Africaans. He guessed Khosa but there were more possibilities than he could name. He nodded his head and smiled broadly to show he could not follow them but he did not speak. One man smiled back and said, "Excuse us. We all live away from home and do not get to speak our language very often. I miss my tongue almost as much as I miss my wife."

I'm in! Bretton thought to himself. *See how easy it with a room full of generous people,* and he said aloud, "Please do not let me get in the way, but I came here to meet people working on our issue, you know, and this looked to me like the most intelligent group."

"You have good instincts, my friend. Is that an American accent?"

"Yes, American. And new to the region so I will not be showing you my accent much tonight. I am here to listen mostly. But let me ask, where is the home for your language?"

"We are from Transkei," another man answered. "Do you know it?"

"I know that was the home of Mr. Nelson Mandela," Bretton replied, pleased that he could use the one name he knew in the anti-apartheid movement.

"Yes, he is from the village of Mvezo which is not far from my own village although I never met him. He has not been home in a long time."

"You probably have missed the chance to ever see him," Bretton answered after a respectful delay of a couple seconds and was pleased to hear a small laugh from one of the men.

No one spoke and Bretton worried that he was spoiling their conversation. He would not slink away. He had been invited to this affair, and he was going to be part of it. "When I go to Transkei, what should I see," he asked.

"You should not go. There is nothing there for you."

"My friend, do not listen to him. There is nothing there for us. You may go to Coffee Bay and see the beautiful rocks out in the sea and play in the waves. There is a rock wall with a hole in it. Very beautiful."

"And why is there nothing for you?"

"We cannot go through the Republic. We are banned, you know."

"Our families have forgotten us. We are only trouble for them."

"We do not swim in the ocean anyway."

"I do not believe your families have forgotten you. What can they do while you cannot return? I would be proud to be banned in South Africa although my family would not understand it. I hope to be banned someday."

"You are American, no? It does not matter if you are banned. All you will lose is the chance to see the waves passing through the hole in the wall. You will never lose your family. I do not think you will even be banned but if you did, how would it matter to you?"

"Yes, I am lucky that I do not have to face apartheid in the way you do. I want to be banned to assure myself I am on the right side."

"And once you have won this badge, how long will you stay here?" They seem to be politely taking turns asking Bretton to justify his presence at their party, if not their conversation.

"I am no good at looking very far into my own future. I never expected to be exactly here, for example."

"What are you doing here?"

"To Lesotho? I came to teach at the agricultural college."

"Do you know more about agriculture in these mountains than the Basotho?"

"Look at my hands. I am not a farmer. I am more specialized. I know more about a few things. I can teach them to account for their inputs and use them more effectively. I can teach them to monitor the markets to get the best price or to change what they are growing or how they grow it to be better off."

"It's all right, my friend. The Basotho need some professors. But you won't get yourself banned for any of those things." And then that professor said something in Xhosa that the other two men found humorous although they did not look toward Bretton as if it had anything directly to do with him.

"We serve as we can, right?" said Bretton although it was not a very strong political position amid these presumed revolutionaries. The three men were silent again. Bretton had not yet learned that silence was an acceptable form of interaction in this part of the world, so he worried that he was in the way of something they might be planning that was important. In addition, he was uncomfortable trying to make small talk and he had already said enough to regard the interaction as successful. He decided to pull away. "Thank you, gentlemen, for your time. I am new here and learning my way around. Maybe I will see a little farther into the future after I have learned more about this place." He was about to walk away but none of them had answered him with any small courtesy so he shook hands with each and gave them his first name. They responded respectfully and said their names but they were too strange to remember.

That left him floundering without any apparent purpose again. He was not close to a cheese plate, but he spied one in the next room and made his way to it, hoping to see another group he could join. "One more conversation like that and I can leave feeling the evening was good," he mused.

The other people seemed to know each other or, at least, to know some of the others. The hostess did not offer any introductions. She probably had no idea who he was. And then he saw, miraculously, a young white woman sitting alone on a sofa, holding a wineglass but hardly moving. He was not trying to pick up anyone so it would not matter if she met any minimum standard of attractiveness. He knew from experience this was an opportunity to grasp immediately. Someone would take that spot on the sofa momentarily. Yet he had not quite the confidence to sit beside her. His good fortune held further when he saw there was a dining room chair nearby. He pulled up beside the sofa and introduced himself, "Hi, I'm Bretton. Just moved to Lesotho. Really pleased to be meeting some people with the ANC."

"From America, I guess. Capetown," was all she said and Bretton assumed that she meant to say she could tell he was from American and that she was from Capetown. She wore a skirt and sneakers, a look that made no sense to Bretton but which was becoming popular among working women of the First World around then. He like the strength she projected in her posture and the fine features of her unadorned face. If he were trying to pick up a date, she would be a fine choice, he told himself although he immediately promised to stop thinking in those terms. She did not look his direction, even when she spoke to him. Presumably she identified his country of origin by his accent. *Rude*, Bretton thought. *She is rude in any language.* But he had faced rudeness in attractive women before. He would not press his case, neither would he give up at the first discouragement.

"What brought you to Lesotho?" he asked cheerily, too cheerily for the venue.

Now she looked at him. She wore a sneer as if he had insulted her. "What do you think? Isn't it obvious?"

"Obvious? Not to me. As I said I am new. Unless you mean you had to get away from apartheid."

She huffed an acknowledgement that she had heard him and looked away again as if they were in front of a play and he was whispering over the dialog. But her huff suggested he had found the obvious explanation. He thought to say there were lots of places to go to get away from South Africa. "Why Lesotho?" was not a stupid question but instead he asked, "What made you this way, that you see the obvious when most white South Africans don't?"

She softened. Bretton suspected she liked this question and he was surprised she did not have a ready answer, sarcastic or otherwise. While she hesitated, he added, "Were your parents more insightful than most, or someone else who led you away from the dominant interpretation?" He could have suggested other possibilities but stopped himself before he became obnoxious.

"I don't know," she finally answered in a whisper. Then with a fuller voice, "No, my parents are like the rest. Nothing happened to me when I was a baby or anything. I always knew our laws were wrong. It was always obvious. I have no idea how my family or the people I grew up with can be so blind."

"In America there were people even before our independence from Britain who knew slavery was wrong, who knew it completely and had no doubt and could not see how anyone could fail to see it. But there were not many of these. Over time there were more and some of them even knew women ought to have the same rights as men, and that took even longer to become obvious to many. It is a pleasure to meet a person who sees beyond the fictions she has been told."

"There is nothing for me to do in Lesotho. I have no career. I cannot afford to go to college. I have no friends from the past. I have to fight apartheid for my own good, not to help others. My bad prospects are my greatest asset. I am not any good at fighting; I don't even know if I am willing."

"There must be others like yourself in South Africa."

"Yes, of course. It is hard to find each other and harder still to do anything together."

They were interrupted by a pat on the back from Bretton's boss who called him "morena," which means "chief" and was formerly used to address white men. Bretton stood up quickly to show respect and called his boss "morena."

"Morena, I am glad to see you could come tonight!"

"Morena, I can't thank you enough for inviting me. The room is full of good people."

The young woman had not stood up and had turned her attention away. Bretton tried to reengage her. "This is my boss, Ntate Wilson." She did not turn toward them as if she had not heard or not understood she was being addressed. "Excuse me. I never did hear your name Miss," he said loudly so she could not ignore them. She turned toward the two men and raised her hand to shake with Wilson. "Caroline" she offered and Bretton added "From Capetown."

Wilson nodded to her as he shook her hand and then tilted his head toward Bretton in a conspiratorial way. He held her hand a few extra moments although his attention had shifted to Bretton. "You should get to know Mme Nydoo. This is her house you know. She is a brilliant woman." Then he dropped Caroline's hand as if to contrast her with their significant hostess. Caroline did not acknowledge Bretton when she rose to move away. Bretton called to her and she turned her head just enough to show she heard him and she favored him with a very subtle wave of her hand. Meanwhile, Wilson made a dismissive gesture in her direction and pushed Bretton toward the other room to introduce his friend. The rest of the evening Bretton stayed close to Wilson and listened to talk lacking any political content. It was much easier to be led by Wilson, to be shown off as the young American who worked for him, than to work into a real ANC conversation. Bretton told himself the evening was a success, a minor one of the sort he should hope to have when he was just getting started. At the next ANC party, his face would be known, he would have more local experience as a base for discussion, and he might even have found some way to contribute beyond teaching farm accounting. He was on Mme Nydoo's invitation list. Like many events in a new environment, the evening could be interpreted as full of promise but his only real contact was Wilson and Wilson had not shown any actual interest in ANC issues. It would take some time before Bretton realized the extent of Wilson's disinterest. More importantly, he never heard of another ANC party so his plan to build on the foundation built that night was frustrated.

XXI. <u>Bretton Is Co-opted (1983)</u>

Bretton lived alone and said he liked it that way. He would actually have preferred to live with a wife to keep him company and share his meals and ensure him regular passion, but he denied these things were true because he had no sense he could do anything about it, not while living in Lesotho where the women were rarely conversant in English, and where they avoided him out of fear or mistrust of his alien aspects. He developed a pattern in the evening of reading books for an hour or so. That was about the pace that tired his eyes and led him easily into sleep. He washed quickly, put on his bed clothes, and warmed up a glass of milk before he started to read, settling into his one soft chair. On the night of December 8, he passed the halfway point of a Graham Greene novel set in West Africa. He did not concentrate very closely on the novel because he kept visualizing himself in the role of the main character, a British spy in the guise of a minor government agent. How would the story go in contemporary Lesotho? Would everyone know, or at least suspect, he was a spy? That had its attraction. He would be seen as something much more than a teacher of accounting. He tried to work the story in his mind into a form that brought a woman into his bed, but, unlike Greene's hero's situation, and the real life experience of Greene himself in West Africa, Bretton did not live in a community of expatriates with bored wives and maturing daughters who might be seduced by some adventurer.

The wanderings of his mind made him read over a paragraph several times to pay more attention. It was peculiar that he could silently "read" the words without comprehending anything while his attention was elsewhere. What was going on in the brain with the words he read? He could feel himself framing the words. He could spot an error in the text and still recall nothing of the content when he reached the bottom of the page. It was not yet ten o'clock when he gave up on reading, earlier than usual but he had to admit he was not reading well enough to enjoy what he was doing. Maybe he was unfocused because he was more tired than he realized. He continued to fantasize about being a spy, hoping it led him into a dream. The Graham Greene novel gave him a more credible scenario than the 007 movies with its highly flawed central figure who had no exotic training or skills but was in a position to learn something secret.

His fantasy did not turn into a dream, as far as he could recall when he awoke. That it was still dark though only two weeks from the longest day of the year made him suspect he had not been tired enough when he went to bed. He usually slept through to the alarm at 6:30. He lay still for a few moments, suddenly completely alert. He considered getting up and making himself another cup of hot milk. It was actually only one o'clock in the early morning of December 9, a date whose importance to Americans for the attack on Pearl Harbor was about to reverberate in local history.

Bretton noticed a popping sound. He thought at first it might be hail hitting his neighbor's tin roof. It seemed possible it might hit his neighbor before it reached his own roof. He heard more sound, but it came and went too much to be hail. It had to be real machinegun fire, not nearby, not very far away. Then he heard the crump sound of an explosive. And then a group of explosions.

None of it sounded close enough to be threatening him immediately so he went to the window on the east side of his house and looked toward the center of town, toward Maseru. It occurred to him the noise might be a celebration. The explosions could be fireworks, the shooting could be soldiers, only soldiers had machine guns-- they could be drunk. It was too irregular to be an organized celebration. He could not see Maseru directly from his window and nothing in the sky above town corresponded with the sounds. He went outside and looked for his neighbors. He lived in a compound of matching houses for the college senior staff. There was no light on except for his own. More oddly, he could not see any of the fires normally maintained all night long by the guards at all the houses but his own.

He had never hired a guard, never saw any need for one and never trusted that one would provide any protection if an actual thief showed up. Now, however, he wished someone were around who knew if there was any benign explanation for the noises. He had a cart he used in his garden to haul dirt or weeds which he now leaned against his house so he could climb on it and reach the roof. His tin roof had a smooth edge he could grasp easily while he swung one leg over the edge to one side. He clambered up. The roof did not slope much so it was easy to walk to the highest point although he worried it might be too weak to hold his weight unless he kept to the sides, over the walls. From there, he could see the rooftops of Maseru. There were no tracers rising into view when the machine guns fired. When the next explosion came, he saw the flash well before he heard the crump. He watched without seeing anything to go with the sounds and then it was quiet for a while. A fire was burning where the explosion had been and then suddenly a flash came up somewhere closer and a louder crump and the machine guns chattered again.

It was time to react more than to watch. Knowing what to do required some minimal understanding of what was going on and he had gathered all the facts he could afford to accumulate. This was not a celebration and it was not entirely localized. Bretton knew there was a revolution in progress in Lesotho. The Lesotho Liberation Army had blown up a few public places in the past year although nothing since he had arrived. He lived in the college staff housing with an equal mix of Basotho and foreigners. Normally the nearby community included guards, gardeners, cooks, and nannies who tipped the balance of numbers heavily toward native inhabitants but the apparent absence of guards made him wonder if the Basotho had fled, knowing something was going to happen this night.

He could see that he, as a foreigner, might make a good political target. The LLA was not opposed to foreigners or to Americans specifically as far as he knew. In fact, he understood their whole *raison d'etre* to be based on the suspension of democracy by the current Prime Minister, surely an issue consistent with American values. Of course, he was working for the current government and his country was supporting it with foreign aid. All substantive arguments aside, if the friend of one's enemy is one's enemy, Bretton could be a target of the LLA.

He clambered down from his roof and went in the house to gather some things to get through the night in seclusion. He rolled up his blanket, picked up his flashlight, and went into the kitchen. It seemed he ought to get something more. He took a can of cola from the refrigerator and went outside again. The sounds of violence continued. They echoed from the concrete block houses on his street such that he could not tell where they originated or if they were closer than before. The glow in the sky over Maseru seemed brighter. Maybe the fires were growing.

He crossed the street and trotted quickly though the neighbor's yard and into the maize field beyond. He worked his way between the rows of knee-high stalks to the opposite side. From the edge of the field to the river was only twenty or thirty yards. He could cross the border if the attack came close. There he spread out his blanket. When he lay down, he was out of sight. He shivered from the tension and from the sweat of tension cooling his brow.

He awoke to the heat of the sun on his face. The solar disk had just risen above the height of the maize, shining on his face and his toes but not yet reaching his body. He was cold since the dry air holds the summer heat very poorly at night. He lay still to listen first. No sound reached him, not a bird or a cricket or the crackle of a fire. He marveled that he had slept so soundly as to need awakening by an external signal. The scent of maize was heavy, as if he were in a loft full of new hay bales. The odor was familiar from his childhood of playing in barns, building fortresses, and jumping into piles of straw. The memory helped him to relax. He sat up and rotated his head in all directions to be sure there was no one nearby, no rebel soldiers about to search the field or set fire to it. Then he shifted his attention to the homes on his street. All was quiet and intact there. Just to give himself some time to wake fully and to hear if he was in the middle of a temporary lull, he drank his can of cola, resting on one arm to keep a low profile.

The walk back up the rows of maize was dramatic, slow and intense like a scene shown during the opening credits of a film. He looked at his feet stepping rhythmically among the unnaturally regular stalks of growing maize. This simple repetitive sight contrasted with the complex possibilities in the silent street ahead. He looked forward to see any motion or light, indoors or outside, that would prove he was not alone in this corner of this tiny country.

He knocked on the door of the first house he reached, the one across the street from his. It belonged to Ahmad, the distinguished Iraqi with a wife and two kids. No one came to the door. He walked around to the large window facing the street. Everyone on this street had the same floorplan. The window opened to their living room. He showed himself and tapped. Still no one answered.

As he crossed the street to his own side, he looked carefully at all the houses and saw nothing except excessive silence. He knocked at the house next to his and the door immediately opened. This was his British neighbor, Alan, who ran the college dairy. He had a large pistol in his hand.

"Get in, Bretton. What did you see?" he said quickly.

"Nothing. No one is around. Not even the guards. What do you know?"

"I know they better not come here. I'll make someone pay for it. We came here to help this bloody country but we can't stop them from blowing themselves up."

"Yeah, there were plenty of explosions. I saw some fires last night from the roof of my house. Couldn't tell where they were though."

"You were on the roof?"

"Just for a minute until I decided they might come here. Then I slept the rest of the night in the maize field. Seemed safer than staying in the house."

"We stayed here. Going out to the field sounds like a good idea."

"You can use it next time. Did your guard leave last night? Was it before the gunshots?"

"I don't know when he left. Maybe he's still here under the maid's bed or something."

"Does the telephone work? Can we get through to the Embassy?"

"No phones. I get a dial tone but it doesn't work."

"You've been here longer. What do you think it was?"

"LLA, a coup, South Africa, CIA, I don't know. I don't know why anyone would bother fighting over this town."

"Alan, show some respect. You live here. You believe it is worth helping."

"It's a job, you know. Not one that pays enough to get shot."

"What are you going to do now?"

"Can't wait for the phone to work. My contract may expire before that happens. Can't wait for the Embassy to come by to explain things. No one from the Embassy here was smart enough to get into a first-rate college. Can't wait for a clarification from the government. They wouldn't do it and I wouldn't believe what they told me anyway. Let's go to the school; see if anyone shows up for class this morning. Good chance the students know what's what."

They walked together to campus, a mere few hundred meters from their street, going through the Eucalyptus woodlot behind their homes. No one was in class and none of the Basotho faculty showed up but the students were milling around outside the administration building as if waiting an announcement. Bretton did not know how the students got their information but they seemed to know what had happened in the night and they were not scared for their own safety.

"It was the South Africans," they said, proud to be teaching their teachers.

"They came in helicopters," claimed a boy named Oscar but others said he was wrong; that was only a rumor.

"I saw one of the choppers myself," he cried loudly. "I saw six men in uniform get out. I was in Ha Thamae last night. That's where they were."

The students lived in dormitories on campus but Maseru is a small town so they could be anywhere in the town on a given night. If Oscar could not convince the other students that he was an eyewitness, Bretton was not going to take his story seriously.

"It's true that it was South Africans," said a girl called Khodu. Bretton knew her and thought she was bright and level-headed. "I was in the house next to the USAID Director's. I saw SADF soldiers march in uniform up to her house and they surrounded it and then just waited for an hour and left. No one shot anything there. We all thought they were guarding Mme Boorady."

Bretton whispered to Alan, "What's SADF?" and Alan answered, "South African Defense Force. Who is Mme Booradi? Is she someone political hiding at USAID?"

"She's the Mission Director for USAID. If it was South African military, they might have been protecting her from the fog of war. ...Trying to keep it a local incident."

"I heard everything was over in an hour. Whatever they did, it was done and they left," said an older student Bretton recognized but did not know. The other students accepted his words. It was interesting to see the students in this peculiar situation, to see who was outspoken and who was respected.

"What did they blow up? Was anyone hurt?" Bretton asked. Alan avoided asking any questions because he did not feel students should be explaining anything to him.

No one answered Bretton at first. The students were quiet, and looked around among themselves for a spokesperson. The older student shook his head to indicate he did not know and then, one by one, a dozen students gave their uninformed and inconsistent opinions.

"We should check to see if all our students are here," Bretton suggested to Alan.

"Nothing we can do if someone is missing anyway. Wait until Winston shows up. He'll do whatever the Basotho think is needed."

Palesa reached from behind Bretton and took his hand into hers. He looked back startled. He was surprised at anyone's touch in this moment and doubly surprised she was even present. She did have a light step to accompany her graceful movements. She continued to hold him while she spoke without looking up, "Ntate Pheta says he needs to see you. Follow me. Not close." She dropped his hand and walked between the nearest pair of rondavels and off toward the piggery. Her hand

and her nearness felt a little sexy even if everything else about the situation made such ideas absurd.

"Alan, are you going to stay here until Winston comes in?"

"No, you're right. There's no reason to hang around. These kids told us everything they heard. I need to get back to the house and help Helen. Maybe the South Africans did it and maybe they're gone but that just gives a chance for the local thieves to get active. I should be standing guard. You want to stay with us today?"

"Nothing in my house needs guarding." Bretton watched Palesa departing. She never looked back. "I'm going to check the animals." Alan should have been the one to check the animals, at least the dairy herd. If he thought about it, he would realize Bretton would not know how to do anything useful if there were a problem.

"OK. Come by when you're done. Let me know if you hear anything more."

Bretton walked around the row of rondavels and headed along the trail to his house just a short way before cutting through the light brush by the trail and climbing the hill up to the piggery. At the top, he saw Palesa waiting for him. She pointed to a certain small shed.

He knocked on the door of the shed, knowing it was unlikely anyone had ever knocked there before. Nether pigs nor tools would have answered. No sound came from inside. He looked to Palesa to get a signal that he had understood her gesture, but she was gone. Inside the shed was dark, a few shafts of light coming through cracks in the walls lit illogical portions of the stalls and tools. Bretton could not understand anything in the room until he heard Pheta's usual upbeat voice and saw a movement approaching.

"Ntate Thabo! *Le kai.*"

It was an ironically normal and polite greeting, meaning "How are things with you and yours."

"*Re teng,*" Bretton answered, meaning "We are well." "What the hell are we doing out here, Pheta?"

"It's about the raid. We need pictures for the press. You have a camera, a good one, right? You have film? This is for the ANC, Thabo. You want to help, right? Take pictures for us. We will get them to the international media. People need to know what happened last night. They won't believe us without pictures."

"What did happen? What do you know? Are you part of the ANC?"

"It was soldiers: SADF. They killed some ANC in Lesotho; what they could find. Goddam Lesotho police went around the other side of the mountain just at dark to stay out of it. Goddam Leabua Jonathon knew about it. Where is your car? You must drive us to take pictures."

"OK Pheta. Let's go back to my house."

"No. Nothing is safe now. It is best if you go back alone. I will meet you at the college gate. You go there now and wait for me. I will be nearby."

"So you are part of the ANC, Pheta."

"No man. I'm Mosotho. That is a South African thing. But my friend wants you take some pictures. Please let's go now."

They visited three sites that had been hit in the raid. Bretton took pictures like a crime photographer and worried whether his camera settings were proper. He had only black-and-white film and that made him a little more comfortable because it was more tolerant of errors.

At the first place, Pheta jumped out of the car ahead of Bretton and held Bretton's hand as they worked through the crowd of angry onlookers. Pheta's confidence impressed Bretton although he was not certain it was merited. This was not a good day and place to be a white male in Maseru. The tension he felt and the part of it that was directed toward him made him feel he was doing something, that he was taking some small risk on behalf of the cause. He was excited to be the ANC photographer on the day it was needed, even if he would face a mob with only Pheta to protect him. But there was no mob. He had some ugly looks facing him but the Basotho did not automatically place him with the SADF. And no one said anything angry directly to him all day.

He photographed walls that had been chipped by machine gun fire to show the bullet marks and again to show the damage in relation to the house. He went inside and saw two pools of blood and a blood-soaked blanket. The victims were gone. Bretton could not tell how many there had been and he did not ask. He was not a journalist collecting the story, just an amateur photographer filling in. There was very little furniture. The neighborhood was relatively prosperous and Bretton interpreted the bareness of the rooms as an indication this was a warehouse for ANC refugees. Someone might have been sleeping on the blanket, maybe several people crowded together. He hoped there had not been many people here. Pheta keep close, kept physically in contact with Bretton but he hardly watched the work. His attention was always on the other people, presumably looking for danger, presumably for danger to Bretton.

His touch was as much to follow Bretton without watching him as to communicate to anyone that Bretton was there under Pheta's protection. Pheta spoke to people a few times. It was always in Sesotho so Bretton could not understand anything. He listened to the tone of the conversations. They were neither friendly nor angry. Bretton assumed they were just the simple explanation that these were pictures needed for the outside world. At least that is what Bretton would have said if he were playing Pheta's role.

The second site showed a greater disaster. The targeted house was still smoldering, its concrete walls a ruin without a roof, the windows smashed. There must have been more furniture in this house since there was so much ash although it might have just been the remnants of the roof. Some of the roof beams were still overhead, charred and smoking. The whole place carried the potent stench of unfulfilled fire, of wet ashes, of obliteration. Bretton reminded himself his pictures were not for solving a crime; they were to inform and inflame the foreign media. He could not see anything personal enough to incite pity or dramatic enough to arouse an editor to place the story closer to the front page. The charred frame looked like a stock photo of a fire, maybe less interesting than the ones he had seen before because of the smallness of the house. Then Pheta tugged Bretton to the back door and pointed to the neighboring house. A crowd was gathered there as well. The soldiers had allowed their gunfire to stray into it.

"Let's take some over there," Bretton suggested.

"No," countered Pheta. "They do not want any visit. Some injured people are still inside. They are ANC. This house that was exploded and burned was a mistake."

"That is a story the media will tell! I won't bother them but we need to get the context." And Bretton took a few shots to show both buildings in the same frame to accompany the story and he tried to sneak a few of the grieving families at the doorstep. Then he remembered the crowd he had been avoiding could be photographed to show its anger and he turned his camera to the on-lookers. Of course someone else would write the story. If it was written by the ANC, Bretton would be satisfied he had done his part.

The third site had the largest crowd. Maybe that was because it was later in the day and people were bolder about leaving their homes and hiding places. One wall of the house was collapsed, blown outward. Bombs or grenades must have been thrown inside. The heavy damage could be shown in a photo but Bretton figured the shot with two houses was the one that would be picked up by the press.

Pheta did not seem to be asking anything, but he listened in on what others we saying. This group did not seem as angry. Maybe the latecomers were just the curious. "No ANC here," Pheta said. "Some had lived here but they moved away more than a month ago. Two children and their mother were inside. Just Basotho. Very bad."

"All this is very bad, Pheta."

"Terrible, Ntate Bretton."

"Where to next, my friend?" Bretton asked.

"We cannot do this anymore because it is getting dark. It will be too dangerous."

"I cannot take pictures in the dark anyway. Who gets the film?"

"I will show you."

Only two paved roads went out of Maseru in those days except for the one to the border. They took the road north, toward Roma. Bretton had never driven that road at night. Everyone said it was unsafe: drunken drivers, stray sheep, LLA roadblocks. He was glad when Pheta told him to turn just before they reached the end of the Maseru settlement. They went into an area that was dark at night, having no electricity, with mostly tin-roofed, mud buildings for people who could not afford cement block. No effort had ever gone into building the dirt road they took; it was just a pair of ruts that formed after sandaled feet, ponies, carts, and motor vehicles had worn a pattern among the shacks. This was the neighborhood where Bretton had gone to have his flat tire fixed, but he could not recognize anything specific. It all looked about the same in every direction.

"Turn off the lights," Pheta commanded, leaving Bretton to notice how quiet Pheta had become. It was still dusk and Bretton could see the road. He drove slowly, barely faster than a walk, not from uncertainty, but because it was so rough he did not want to break an axel. A few more turn-heres and turn-theres, and Pheta finally said "OK, stop."

They went to a house more substantial than the others nearby although it was only 10 meters long and half that in width. Its cinder block walls and tin roof were substantial if not glamorous. Pheta knocked on a solid wooden door. Bretton saw a curtain flutter on a window and saw a glow from inside, probably from candlelight.

The door opened and Pheta entered without a word from anyone inside. He pulled the door almost shut behind himself and spoke in low tones, sounding like English, for a moment before opening the again and pulling Bretton inside.

"Bretton, this is my friend from ANC public relations. You have the films? Just give them to him."

Bretton handed over the small bag of film. "I am terribly sorry for the attack last night. I hope it did not harm too many people and I hope it does not set back the ANC significantly." Bretton offered sympathy along with his pictures. A middle-aged man took the bag, felt the weight of it, and passed it quickly on to someone behind him. In the dark, Bretton could not see anything of the second person.

The man reached out to shake Bretton's hand and said "*Amandla.*"

Bretton answered "*Awethu.*" It was the first time he had used the slogan of the ANC: "power" followed by "to the people." He was not positive he had pronounced it right. He had practiced under his breath when he heard it on the radio, hoping for an occasion exactly like this. "If you show me the pictures after they are printed, I can explain what each one is showing. I think I can point out two or three that will be the most useful."

But no answer came back. Pheta tugged Bretton back out the door and said. "Come on. Time to go." Bretton took a couple steps backwards and the door closed. A clank suggested that the door had been barred rather than locked.

"Back to the college," Said Pheta in his relaxed, cheery voice. "We did a good day's work today."

"I hope so, Pheta. I'm afraid there were not many interesting shots, the ones newspapers would use. The best ones were late in the day at that last place. I hope there was enough light for them to come out well."

"Oh come on, Ntate! I've seen your photos. They're really nice."

What Pheta had seen was some of the portraits Bretton had taken. He had taken dozens, maybe more than a hundred, for the students and faculty and even at times for friends of students. He took them all the same way. There was a brick wall near his office with privacy and indirect light. He always took one shot with the subject looking serious since they all claimed to want that and another shot after he told a joke since they all ended up preferring the shot with a smile. He was no good at telling jokes in any culture, but the Basotho were very generous with their appreciation and whenever they recognized that he was trying to make them laugh they quickly obliged with a chuckle. These snapshots were not photojournalism although the distinction was not worth proving to Pheta.

"Am I ever going to see those pictures? Can I help explain them to somebody?"

"Sure, you can see them in *The Guardian* next week."

They drove slowly for a couple hundred meters before Pheta said it was okay to turn on the headlights.

"We should not be out at night like this," Pheta said softly, as if to himself.

"Pheta, this was your idea, not mine."

"Not my idea either," he answered.

Bretton concentrated on navigating the rutted shadows and Pheta helped by remaining silent until they were about to drive up the steep final fifty meters before the paved road and Pheta said suddenly. "Stop here!"

Bretton hit the brake. "What? What did you see?"

The back door of the car opened and someone got in quickly.

"It's all right," said Pheta. "Drive on. Let's go."

A woman's voice from the back seat said "Thank you for coming. This whole thing sucks. We will need you tonight." The voice had the accent of English in southern Africa but not the lilt common among educated Basotho women. It sounded familiar.

"Is that Capetown behind me?" Bretton asked and the women answered, "Good guess, America. Drop off Ntate Pheta and then turn right at the paved road." Turning right would take them away from Maseru.

XXII. Refugee Sanctuary (1983)

"What about that, Pheta?" Bretton asked. "You want to get out here?" He expected Pheta would say it was the right thing to do, but the question made it sound as if Bretton were making his own decision and it gave him some time to think about the situation.

"I'm done here. See you at tea tomorrow. We're won't talk about today, right?"

"Whatever you say, Pheta. See you."

After Pheta had gotten out of the car, Carolyn did not move up to the front seat and Bretton could not see her in the rear view mirror. He turned around and saw she was slouched down.

"C'mon. Turn right," she said as if he were one of the servants she may have had growing up white in Capetown. Bretton fought of the temptation to answer "Yas'm." Then he fought off the inclination ask their destination and to suggest that she did not need to keep up the mystery in order to seduce him if that were her

247

game, but if obedience was what she and the ANC needed, he would go along.

They went over the first pass, the one that took them out of view of Maseru. Then Bretton pulled off to the side of the road. Before he had stopped, she demanded "Why are you stopping? Keep going."

"What are we doing? Driving out here at night, especially this night after the raid, I need to know more."

"First we have to pick up some people. ANC leaders. The SADF is looking for them for sure. Four guys. Good men."

"OK, maybe we can do that. Then what? Where do we take them? Am I supposed to cross the border?"

"Of course not! You could never get through in a car like this. If they wanted to cross, they would just walk. No, we need to hide them."

"I don't need to know where they will hide, but where will I take them?"

"They told me you would help. Can you be trusted?"

"I will never give up a secret against apartheid. Even so, it is better that I do not have secrets I do not need."

"I was thinking you could hide them at your house. You have extra rooms, right? Servants' quarters?"

There was an empty room of the side of Bretton's garage for the housemaid he had never hired. It had a bare lightbulb hanging from the ceiling and a thin mattress rolled up on a bedframe of noisy springs. The room was identical to the tool shed attached to the opposite side of the garage although Bretton often wondered if that room was built as a residence for the gardener he had never hired.

Bretton did not answer her question because it would sound as if he was agreeing to her plan.

"They can't stay at the college. There is no privacy there. It's a very tight place. We could not get in there without a bunch of people knowing it and we would not even know which ones saw it. And if they were there, they could not take a breath of air without someone noticing the tiny breeze they had made. You need a better idea."

"I was afraid of that, that you were not serious. All right. I have another option. It's not as good for them but it is better for you. Just pick them up. They are not so far off. Less than half the way to Roma."

Bretton drove the car back onto the road and accelerated toward Roma. "I know where Roma is. It's pretty far for this time of day. I'll go. I want to help. I guess I have to trust you are not wasting my time and risking my health for someone insignificant."

Bretton gave her a few seconds to say something back and then continued in his mind: *I'm kinda glad you stayed in the back. If you were up here and I could see you, see into that lovely face I saw once before, I might not have been able to refuse your order.* With his hands on the wheel, his eyes on the road and her in the back seat, he could hardly threaten her with his attention. "You know," he went on since she was silent, "the staff housing at the college is no place to hide. Couldn't work."

"Yeah, I know. It wouldn't work. I appreciate the ride anyway."

The road so familiar in day was not recognizable in the dark. There were no lights in the villages to show their progress and no light in the sky but stars to show the profile of the land. The eerie boredom of the lonely, twisting road was far better than a disturbance by any of the kinds possible out here, away from modernity, where the SADF would love to find him, where the LLA would suspect him, where a government roadblock administered by undisciplined boys might see an opportunity for booty, where thieves without a political identity could be hoping for some foolish, relatively rich Westerner to pass within reach, where a herd of goats could leap into the road without fear of the rare threat of an automobile at night. Bretton embraced the zen of his task, of driving in a dark he had never known in America, hugging the constant corners for traction, always looking to the full extent of his headlights for rocks lined up across the road to stop him for some nefarious purpose, all with a strong, attractive woman in the seat behind him, possibly contemplating his blandishments.

His focus on the present moment allowed him to ignore the accumulation of moments that implied a growing distance from Maseru with the problem of getting back growing as well. He did not ask again where they were going or where they would take their unfortunate passengers. Lesotho was a small country. The trip would have to end soon, and eventually, it did.

"Stop here," the woman said simply in an incongruously small voice. She cleared her throat and spoke more loudly the next time. "No, this is not the place. Go around the next turn."

The road was all turns. The quick stop indicated they must be getting close but Bretton started a new set of worries when they stopped for a third time for the woman to look around.

"This isn't it. Keep going," she said, back to using her command voice and implying that it was his fault for not finding the pick-up point. Bretton had no confidence in his passenger. Had they passed the place she wanted? Could they find it in the dark? What was she trying to see out here where they could not see anything?

But the fourth stop was the right one. Again she said "Stop here," and she must have already been sure this time because she immediately got out of the car. "Stay here. This won't take a minute." She went down a steep embankment. She was out of sight before her footsteps dissipated into silence.

Bretton turned off the headlight but kept the motor running. Then he locked the car doors. He drummed on the steering wheel and spoke to himself aloud, "Goddam! This is goddam stupid to be out here. You should help the ANC, fight apartheid, but this is goddam stupid. You don't know this woman and she doesn't know what she's doing. You should have insisted on knowing what she expects to happen. She needs you. You have leverage. Is it just that she is so damn good looking you want to impress her, want to believe her? You think she is going to sleep with you because you followed her, let her be the leader?" The sound of his own voice calmed him. His thoughts felt less frightening when made absurd by speaking them. He heard voices, male voices, coming up the gravelly slope beside the road and then someone tried the door handle and there was a knock on the window. Bretton turned on the light inside the car. A little light shone off the faces at the door. He did not see the woman. Two or three or four men were tapping and talking to him in something other than English. He was pleased that they were not wearing uniforms and were not especially young. Then he heard a tap in the driver's side window and the image of the woman looked back at him without speaking. He rolled down the window.

"Open the fucking door," she said, not indicating any prospect of accompanying him to bed once the adventure was over.

She climbed in with four men, three of whom had to sit in the back with her. It was tight in his blue Peugeot, but not so crowded as to be unsafe.

"Hi, I'm Bretton," Bretton offered to lighten the mood and to apologize for being slow to open the door. He shook hands with the fellow seated in the front and then turned around to the back.

The woman said "You don't need to know their names. You just need to know they need a ride tonight. Really need it. These are men who will make a difference."

Bretton would not be cowed entirely and he smiled in the dim light and went ahead with the ritual of shaking hands with each one, accompanied by small courtesies: Pleased to meet you... Happy to help... The men were dressed in urban clothes and would not pass for Basotho from the villages. They answered him with shy voices in simple English but each of them had a strong grip and communicated thereby his masculine camaraderie. Then he turned off the inside lights, turned on the headlights, and asked where to go next.

"Back to Maseru," Carolyn answered and then added some personality which Bretton hoped was more than an effort to co-opt him further, "the big city with the bright lights."

"Oh good, I know the place. It is not far, I believe."

The four men spoke gently among themselves. They filled the small car with the personal fragrance common among traditional people in warm climates. In this case, the odors may have been more the result of a long day on the run for their lives more than their customary condition.

As they neared town, Carolyn began to give directions to Bretton, "turn left here, turn again," until they were on the road that would have no more turns before passing through the college gate. Bretton stopped the car. He was not anxious about sitting on this familiar stretch near his home. No homes were nearby to see the car had stopped and to wonder why. "We're not going to the college. They will not be, would not be, safe there."

"There is no other place."

"The ANC has friends, contacts, in Lesotho. Don't you know how to tap into that network? Look how many Basotho were at that party."

"Some people are doing other things. This is a very bad time for us. Some people are not sincere and just want to look like they are helping. Some people say they can be counted on but we can't count on them. It is your turn right now. You have to take these men. Sure it will not be safe for them at your home. It is not safe for them anywhere. You have no idea what they have been through, what they have already done, not just last night but for years. I know these men, all of them. I know their names and I knew their families, and I can hardly believe what they have seen. Do I have to tell you of the abuse they have experienced? I am not important in the ANC but I am committed to it and I have my job and my job right now is to help these men. My cell; do you know what that means? They are not looking for 'safe.' They just want to survive long enough to get back in the fight. The fight they are doing is much more than driving them around one night, you know. And they cannot decide not to fight, to 'go home.' This unsafe life is the only life they have; probably the only one they will ever have."

"Caroline, can he take us to the Holiday Inn? The border is easy to cross from there. He is smart; he is right. It would too dangerous to take us into his home..."

"No! No fucking way, goddam it! You can't cross the border now. The SADF is all over it since the raid. It's not just me guessing about that. We have reports on it. This foreign bastard is going to hide you for as long as it takes to have a reasonable chance for you. I am negotiating with him, not you. Just shut up and let me do my job. It will be miserable enough for you at his house. And you, foreign bastard, what do you want? What would it take to get you to do what you can do?"

"Let me think a minute. Maybe I can do something." Without much hesitation he continued, "Capetown Carolyn, get in the front seat and everyone else lie down in back. If I come in late like this with a woman, the guards and busybodies on my street will think they understand. I'll turn on the stereo. When the lights are out, we can move our friends inside the house."

"That's good. Now you're helping. I'll stay 'til morning. Feed the gossips. Pheta will contact you when we can move then on. We'll have to set up contacts on the other side. You just go to work like normal. No one will come to your house, will they? You have a girl friend?"

"No, they will not be in the way of any girlfriend. I'm still working on that part of life. You want to hear about it?"

The man who spoke before answered, "Yes, you will tell us of the girls you are knowing. We will have time for your stories and they will be better than ours."

XXIII. The Funeral (1983)

For the first days after the South African attack, it remained in the forefront of every mind in Maseru. A few were taken up by the facts of the invasion. With very little formal news reporting and substantial skepticism about official accounts, they sifted through the rumors and eyewitness accounts to piece together some kind of sense in it and then, typically, passed on their findings and interpretations. There was no reason for much embellishment as the actual events were so extraordinary. They tended to focus on the Basotho side of the story, on the rumor that the police and/or the army had left Maseru early in the evening before the raid, apparently aware it was coming and giving it tacit or even overt, if secret, permission. Certainly there had been no official resistance within Lesotho to this invasion. Was that merely the smartest thing to do in the face of overwhelming firepower or were the Basotho authorities in active collusion with the apartheid government? Various inducements could be imagined that might have appealed to Leabua Jonathon but it was dangerous to speculate about those possibilities and there was not a shred of evidence on which to base them. Some struggled to accept that their loved ones were gone forever. These people usually did not concern themselves very much with understanding why it had happened. In southern Africa at that time, Basotho had learned to expect abuse from the world.

Others struggled with the proof of mortality that death always brings to the living. Some worried that another attack would come and feared they would never be able to feel safe in their homes again. Some wished everyone would stop worrying so much about something that had passed quickly and mostly affected South Africans, from another country entirely than Lesotho, so they could get back to playing football seriously again. This last group was very small and consisted entirely of young boys who knew well enough to keep these thoughts to themselves.

Bretton sensed that all he was hearing was unreliable. No one who was an actual witness was talking to him. His students had grown remote, as if he were part of the problem. They did not suspect him in any way; they simply were insecure and stayed close to their most familiar companions. If he had been better able to understand them, he would have seen they were treating each other with unusual reticence as well. The attack seemed to implicate informers within Lesotho. No Mosotho would say anything positive about the apartheid regime but they suspected one another in direct proportion to how little they knew a person.

Pheta neither overtly avoided nor sought out Bretton and when they spoke in each other's presence, Pheta hardly mentioned the raid. Bretton thought he was a good agent of the ANC. Palesa made no reference to the raid either. She did avoid Bretton and he was not sure why although he suspected she did not want to be associated with him if he were caught some day as having been involved, no matter what he had done.

The resident foreigners, other than South Africans, also hung close to each other. They avoided the shopping district downtown but huddled in the hallways at the college and invited each other over in the evening for drinks when they would go over anything they had heard or imagined. The drinks were more to fortify their decision to stay in Lesotho than to lubricate their conversations. They prized information from their Embassies, assuming for the most part, other than Bretton, that those sources were reliable. The Embassies dusted off evacuation plans and set up a "call tree" to make everyone feel in touch. The British, as the largest expatriate contingent and the one with the strongest colonial history, viewed itself in a leadership position. Roger saw it as his particular responsibility to guide the young American, Bretton, into proper behavior in this moment, to reassure him the Western powers stood behind them and the crisis would pass.

Bretton was skeptical of the American Embassy reassurances. Obviously, the Embassy would not have figured in the presence of actual ANC refugees, probably operatives, in his home. The telephone, his link to the "call tree," worked less than half the time and he did not know the Embassy staff socially. Their major instruction was to keep away from everything related to local politics. Nothing derived from that formal institution could offset the chaos he felt through his role in the aftermath. He remained viscerally disturbed that he had been absorbed into the turmoil, and could not recapture any faith that the near future would ever again arrive in the reasonable ways it used to come. Unlike Roger, he had not grown up with images of his nation's military power securing the safety of its citizens abroad.

After a few days, classes resumed at the college, which seemed to Bretton to be a transparent and probably immoral pretense that normality might return although he could not see what else the college should do. It was irksome that the Principal, a Mosotho chief, might agree with Roger's British position that the event was over even before the funerals, that it was a South African matter even though Basotho were killed too, that it was a small invasion by historical standards even if it was not small by Lesotho standards.

"Bretton, you holding up well enough?"

"I'm OK, but that's hardly the question. I was not targeted. Do you think our students will be able to focus on their studies?"

"Good one, Bretton. As if our students ever focused on their studies. You don't have to worry about them. They have lived next to South Africa all their lives. They weren't targeted either, you know."

"The Basotho nation suffered in the raid."

"They expected no less."

"They have not been invaded before. Not since South Africa became a country. Used to be the Queen, your queen, guaranteed some kind of protection to this country."

"Well, that deal is off the table these days. It wouldn't have happened if we were still in the protectorate business. I'm not sure the Basotho care all that much about the thing you call an invasion. They kind of resent the anti-apartheid activists hiding in Lesotho in the first place. They understand those guys knowingly endangered the Basotho."

Bretton admired Alan's courage to say aloud something so despicable which he suspected was being thought by other expatriates. As for what the Basotho were thinking, he could not be sure. The comment helped him to form his own thoughts: *The South African activists were not on vacation. They were not even refugees to escape the regime. For that, they would have gone farther away. These were patriots working to resist apartheid, an ideology that was holding Basotho down, not as harshly as it hit South Africans, but just as surely.*

"I don't know any of the students very well personally, but I have come to know some of the local staff. They seemed completely apolitical to me and yet I know for certain they felt involved."

"Oh how could you know this? They just said something to show off to you 'cause they know you like to talk against South Africa. It's OK. You're American."

"I know they felt involved because I saw them get involved."

"They 'got involved'? What the hell are you talking about? Who did what?"

"It's their business. I shouldn't say. I think they showed courage."

"Bullshit. You weren't even there. You weren't any part of it."

Suddenly Bretton was transported into a fantasy stored in the back of his brain where old dreams and forgotten childhood heroes lie unbidden for years. He was being challenged to show he was not exaggerating his accomplishment. He had a real experience to throw in the face of his accuser, he was at that moment facing more danger than Alan had ever felt and yet he was about to modestly keep his proofs to himself. He was forced into modesty by the extreme stupidity it would require to explain what he knew of Palesa and Pheta just as a boast, or to reveal the awful secret of who was hiding in his bedroom, but he could imagine he was choosing to be ethical. It was a move Gary Cooper would have made in any number of Westerns or in Sergeant York, not a move Rambo would have understood.

"Yeah, I wasn't there but I know the Basotho at all levels understand how apartheid hurts the South Africans. Even back in the mountains they know it. No place here is so remote the travesties are unheard or unappreciated. The relatively well informed and thoughtful ones also know it is holding back Lesotho's opportunities for national development, but that does not diminish their sympathy for the resistance."

"You are a romantic. Africa will tear that out of you soon enough."

"Not a romantic. The story is too stark to be missed."

"You don't know them. They don't care what happens in the Republic. They barely care what happens here. Look at the revolution they're having, the LLA and all that. Kinda weak war, wouldn't you say?"

"I don't hear much about that. It seems to be happening out of town except for the occasional bombing." They were drifting away from Bretton's opportunity to boast that Palesa had come to him to help the ANC. He wanted to enjoy the rare chance to not boast aloud, to have a connection to the Basotho that this semi-colonist did not have. But he could not enjoy the moment knowing they did care and they did suffer. The Basotho were generally uncomplaining about their lot even though they had a bum deal.

"Are you going to the funeral?" Bretton asked.

"Now your naiveté is getting to the danger level. You can't go to that. First of all, it is not about you Americans just like it isn't about us. But what's important is that is fuckin' dangerous. You're talking about the war between the ANC and the RSA. That is no joke. No telling what will happen. Funerals are the worst place. They don't honor their dead. It's an excuse to make their points. It is smart to have a little fear around here. If the funeral speeches accomplish their purpose and whip up the crowd, us white people fast become the target. The mob won't check your passport. You're right about one thing. Apartheid reaches us here."

Bretton did not feel like arguing. He could hear some validity in Alan's words but the only words he could form in response were personal insults. *Wimp. Pussy. Racist.* He wished he had a better vocabulary in this range of meanings. Nothing that came to mind was quite right to say at the moment. He did not want to believe Alan was right. There was nothing to be gained from Bretton's bringing up their human duty to fight oppression, at least when it was blatant and nearby and affecting their friends and their students. *But*, he wondered, *how exactly is going to a funeral, a dangerous funeral, fighting oppression?* It would only be symbolic and most likely no one would care if he were there, not in a positive way. It would be better, he thought, to make himself available to the resistance, as he had done, and to do what they asked, within reason, as he had done. And yet he felt hypocritical to stay away from the funeral. He did not want to stand with Alan on this and he did not want to appear to Alan or himself to have accepted Alan's rationale.

"I see what you're saying, Alan. Not much to be gained from participating." He wanted a parting shot but was not clever enough to make an effective one. *Not much chance of picking up a girl at a funeral for 42 people. The drinks won't be free. You never struck me as a man to care about being on the right side of history anyway.* "So you don't think any of the college expatriate staff will be there?"

"No reason for 'em to go. No, we've all been in Africa long enough to stick to our own business. Except maybe you. You're a slippery one. You're thinking about it, aren't you? You want to be where the action is. Probably disappointed the shooting was in town instead of out at the college, right?"

"I know it won't end apartheid no matter what I do," Bretton answered, looking Alan in the face. "For my own reasons, I expect I will go."

Bretton did not care what Alan thought of him. He was not worried about saving face if he decided later not to attend the funeral. He had not been in Lesotho as long as the others at the college. It made good sense to feel out their opinions in case it was a stupid move, useless or prone to misunderstanding. If it were dangerous, however, so much the better, he thought. He did not mind a chance to test his commitment to principle. It was a test he had rarely faced.

The next day he left the house early and waited on the trail from expatriate staff housing to the college until the next teacher came along. It was Alan, dressed in his khaki shorts and long socks, like a Boy Scout. The Boy Scouts were a British invention based on Lord Bayden-Powell's romantic memory of the Boer War.

"Morning Alan. *U phela joang*?" asked Bretton.

"English is all I use. They understand it.," he answered. His tone was more matter-of-fact than surly, despite his words. "'Tis a beautiful summer morning here."

"Still hard for me to say it is summer when it is December."

"I hope the damn students show up today. They need all the classwork they can get. Funeral's tomorrow you know. They might use that as an excuse to stay out. Figure we won't say anything."

"If they stay away, there is not much we can say, not that would matter to them."

"Right you are, Bretton."

"So Alan. Are you going to the funeral?"

"Me? No, I haven't changed my mind. And why would any of us do that?"

"Solidarity. The students might like us to show our support."

"sure to be a dangerous place, especially for whites. The students know we are here to support them. They don't care if we make some kind of small statement about South Africa."

"It's not all about South Africa. There will be a dozen Basotho being buried, some of them just children. If they died in a natural disaster, we would show our sympathy for them."

"Maybe. No, I'm not going. No one will be going to some local funeral. It's not a religious ceremony. It will be political."

"Hmm," responded Bretton after a few more steps along the trail. He had nothing more to add.

The students did come to classes that day. It was a normal day in all objective respects but to Bretton it felt different. He could not see any odd behavior, but he felt tense in front of the students and the Basotho staff. He wore a mask of normalcy that was so distorted from his side, he could not see through the eyeholes clearly enough to know exactly what was in front of him. Everyone interacted with him and each other as if it were an ordinary day and everyone knew it was not, that the world was different now. It might be normal again someday. Time would weaken the memory of the raid, would replace the insecurity with confidence if nothing like that happened for a while. Bretton saw that a ceremonial ending to the raid, a funeral, could help in the process. He put it out of his mind for the duration of a class in farm accounting and then went to the college Principal.

"*Khotso Ntate. Ho joang?*" It was a relatively informal greeting.

"I'm fine, thanks," The Principal answered in English to prove how comfortable he was in that language. "What brings you to my office so early in the day?"

"I just wanted to ask you about the funeral tomorrow. Do you think there would be any problem if I go?"

"Why would there be a problem? You should go. Everyone should go."

"I don't think any of the expatriate staff is going."

"You're probably right. In fact, you probably know better than me what they are doing. But you should all go."

He did not sound surprised that the other expatriates were not going. Bretton was pleased that his boss took it as reasonable that he, Bretton, would be the one foreign member of the college staff who would be doing the right thing.

"Anything else?"

"No. Thanks. *Sala hantle.*"

The college was closed on the day of the funeral. Bretton did not speak to anyone on his way to the football stadium where it would be held. He was not especially early but there was still room for him to sit on one of the concrete benches that rose in concentric steps around the oval, as in the Roman coliseum or innumerable cheap small college stadia in America. It was hot when he arrived and was only destined to get hotter and less comfortable as the day advanced, and he baked in the large, breezeless cement oven.

The crowd was subdued while they waited for the dignitaries to arrive. Most people, but not Bretton, filed past the row of coffins. They were built in a matching style of varnished wood with just the head open for viewing. A large medallion shone on the headboard in addition to a pair of smaller, ornate brass latches that would be used when the head piece was put into place for the last time. They matched except that some were smaller, the children not needing a full sized coffin. Twelve of the 42 dead were Basotho. The name of each person was handwritten on a piece of paper loosely attached at the top, not as finished in appearance as the rest of the coffin accoutrements.

It seemed appropriate to everyone that the ANC play the major role in the ceremonies. Most of the dead and injured were South Africans in exile. They and their

ANC brethren in Lesotho were the targets of the raid. The Basotho victims were sadder in an ironic way, caught in the deadly ineptitude of the SADC. Bretton wanted to talk to Carolyn about this. He wanted to tell her his idea that the South Africans might have been entirely willing to include some Basotho victims, to punish Lesotho for allowing the ANC refugees to stay, or viewed another way, to discourage Lesotho from future cooperation with the ANC, or viewed yet another way, to spread terror.

The names of the dead were read out. The crowd was quiet but Bretton sensed that the Basotho had friends and family on the concrete benches. Of course, some of the ANC were ethnically Basotho and spoke Sesotho at home. The national borders of Lesotho, like most in Africa, did not correspond to cultural lines. The names of the ANC victims read out did not match the names they had been given by their families. Most lived under pseudonyms. Their families knew who they were but the false names helped hide the relatives of the targets. Even as martyrs, they were not publically recognized.

Bretton looked over the crowd to find a familiar face. He knew dozens of college-age Basotho and a handful of older ones, but he did not spot any in the stadium. No one looked back him—he felt no resentment for being white. He felt invisible, as if they, the people who belonged at the funeral, the people who were suffering personally, did not comprehend his involvement. There were other whites. Foreign diplomats sat in the shade behind the King. A few were from the press. He could not tell who any of the others were; missionaries he suspected. He failed to spot Carolyn although he was sure she was there somewhere.

He was sure there were South African agents in attendance; probably not white ones. Maybe those agents were wondering what Bretton was doing there.

When the 42 names were read, Bretton was reminded he had no good source of information on the raid. In the face of conflicting rumors, he had decided the BBC report was the most accurate. It has said there were five women and two children caught in the cross-fire. They implied the rest were ANC operatives. Yet Bretton knew gender did not define who was in the ANC; he had met women at the ANC party, including the hostess of the event. Maybe Carolyn had been targeted. He should have been skeptical of the BBC report. It had said, like the Rand Daily Mail and the Voice of America, that it was a "successful raid."

Lesotho's Prime Minister spoke in Sesotho which Bretton could not follow at all. He was enthusiastic and dramatic. When King Mosheshoe spoke, he was more subdued and the crowd was more animated. Bretton already knew the king was more popular. People said it was because his authority relied on traditional values rather than a coup against democracy. Bretton thought it might be easier to be popular when you do not have power and its resulting responsibility. He would not have said this thought aloud as he was not certain of it and knew it could be offensive.

A young Ace Magashule speaking on behalf of the black South Africans of the Orange Free State, commended Basotho support in the liberation struggle as one of the frontline states against the apartheid regime. "You told us not to despair and we are who we are today because of you. We fought for this freedom together, and this is all because of the Basotho and all others who fought for freedom," he said. 7

Oliver Tambo spoke. Bretton had heard him once before back when Bretton was still in college. He was the President of the ANC while Nelson Mandela was in prison and lived in exile in Mozambique. The South African newspapers said he would be killed if he showed up at the funeral but there he was. Although he spoke in English, Bretton could barely understand him due to his strong accent and the broken speaker nearby that mangled the words. Nonetheless, he was impressed with Tambo's presence. While the Prime Minister, Jonathan, wore a white dashiki and dripped with perspiration, the slender king and Oliver Tambo both wore sculptured facial hair and dark suits which seemed to have some internal air conditioning.

Tambo listed the other massacres by the government of South Africa and some of the martyrs of the struggle. Bretton recognized more names than he had expected to know. Tambo offered the ANC's Freedom Charter as an alternative to apartheid. He said the Charter calls for "a democracy in which the majority decides, but it is not a black majority we are looking for, it is a majority of the people of South Africa as a whole." Bretton was most moved by his repeated assertion that the struggle against apartheid was one for all people. "...They have fallen to the bullets of a common enemy of the people of this land, the people of South Africa, and the peoples of the world... Far from intimidating the people of Lesotho, the butchers of Pretoria have united them and risen them in their anger which expresses

---

7http://sahistory.org.za/article/speech-funeral-maseru-december-1982#sthash.V8VyKQZm.dpuf

itself in their determination to defend their sovereignty and independence. Their murderous crime has lifted this nation from its geographic circumstances and planted them in the hearts of the nations of the world, winning it the support and solidarity of mankind."[8] Bretton's eyes flowed with tears knowing that mankind was not solidifying in support of this struggle. He knew the coffins in front of him would not be remembered in New York or Washington past the weekend and would never even be heard of in most of America.

Leabua Jonathan had been relatively cozy with the white South African leadership. He might have been merely reflecting the regional balance of power in which Lesotho was almost completely impotent, but over time he had formally broken with the regime. Rumors surrounding the raid suggested he had cooperated but the public face he presented was unambiguous. Jonathan said the ANC soldiers were not in Lesotho as refugees but as his people. South Africans needed to learn that South Africa belongs to the whole continent.

Bretton sat among 35,000 strangers who never gave him a glance and he was proud to feel he was one with them. Under the surface, he knew he was there temporarily, that he was not going to be refused an education, a place to work or access to a hospital or a chance to vote, but he felt at that moment the pain of unfairly, far more than unfairly, losing members of his race, the human race, and the threat that loss implied to the people he did know and love. In that moment he loved the families of the ANC fighters and the Basotho

---

[8] http://www.anc.org.za/ancdocs/history/or/or82-9a.html

supporters and the Basotho who had simply been in the wrong place when the raid tumbled out of the SADF helicopters into the Maseru night.

XXIV. <u>Pheta's Last Trip (2003 &1983)</u>

Somewhere in a mountain village is Pheta's home with people who knew him as a boy, an especially lively and smart boy; and probably some girls who thought he was cute back when they knew him; and probably not his mother and father unless they had survived past the usual lifetime in the rural parts of Africa. Pheta had not been back to see these people at home, his people, for more than twenty years. The girls must have stopped thinking of him. They might have forgotten him altogether. His mother would not have forgotten. Does a mother ever stop thinking of a son who has passed before his time, before her? If she had survived all these years, had she forgiven him for throwing away his charmed life? If she had survived, could she forgive Bretton for what he knew about Pheta?

It is a good thing, Bretton thought, *that Lesotho is not one of those feud cultures where retribution is required for a murder.* Bretton knew, and he may the only one who knew, there was no jealous husband behind Pheta's disappearance.

Pheta had been Bretton's guide when he took pictures of the raid's destruction. And Pheta had taken him to Carolyn before he disappeared into the night. Bretton had seen him at the college the next day and no glance passed between them about their project together. Bretton did not tell him or anyone else about the ANC men in his house-- that was a step beyond

Pheta's need to know. Bretton felt superior for the larger responsibility the ANC had assigned him. ...Until he heard a tapping at his bedroom window on the night of December 12, the third night after the raid. Three of the South Africans were sleeping on the floor of the bedroom. Bretton had not been able to talk them into using his bed. They slept in the same room so any sounds they made that might be heard from outside could be attributed to Bretton.

The tapping did not awaken Bretton, but one of the ANC men was on guard duty and he called Bretton to look out the window. Bretton pulled back the curtain and looked out. It was too dark to see anything. He doubted the person outside could tell he was at the window. He found his flashlight and held it at arm's length so he would be less of a target himself and shone it through the window. Pheta was there, smiling as if he were getting into a party. Bretton opened the window and whispered, "Go around to the door." Bretton told the ANC men to stay in the bedroom and he went around to the front door. Pheta had raced around the house and was already there.

"It's time," Pheta whispered as soon as he had closed the door behind himself. "We go tonight; right now. Everything is ready. I will take them across the border."

"What are you talking about?" Bretton asked. He did not know Pheta well enough to trust him with his life although he may not have any choice in the matter.

"You know. The men Carolyn gave you that night. She sent me to get them over the Caladon River."

"Then what happens?"

"I don't know what is next. Someone is there to meet them tonight. Carolyn said the whole reason she liked them coming to your place is the river. You're close to it and there is nothing on the other side near here. Just some fields for maize or cattle. Her friends know where to meet us. It just that we have to go now."

"What time do we see them?"

"I don't know. I don't even know what time it is now. Carolyn did not tell me to come here until a few minutes ago. I came straight to you. What's the matter? Why aren't you getting them?"

"Pheta, this is dangerous business. I'm a little scared by it."

"You don't have to do anything. You already did a lot. Now I gotta do something; take 'em over."

"Wait here a minute," said Bretton. His mind was full of possibilities, all but one of which was bad. He could not think of anything he could do other than what Pheta asked but he wanted at least to ask the ANC men what they thought they should do. He did not get a chance to ask them. They came out of the bedroom ready to leave, having overheard most of the conversation with Pheta. It had begun in whispers but their voices had unconsciously risen as they talked. It was all too simple. Bretton had been feeling the stress of his role in this affair for two days, anticipating some dramatic finale and now it was ending in a single stroke, leaving him free to live his life as before, except that he would have a little more pride and the hope of running into Carolyn again under favorable terms.

The four men came into the living room. Bretton turned off the flashlight so they would not be visible from outside. He asked Pheta, "Is the moon out tonight?"

"Oh no, it's really dark. Is there a path down to the river?"

"Yes, don't you know it? The bank is very steep but there is a place with some steps." When Pheta did not immediately say he remembered the steps, Bretton saw his personal peace would be delayed a few more minutes. "I'll show you the place. But the river is deep here. There is a better place to cross farther down. I could take you there."

"It has to be here. Carolyn said they would be met on the river exactly opposite the college farm. Right across from your house, she said."

"It's all right. We can do that. It is deep here but not very wide. Do you know how to swim? Do all of you know how to swim?" All five of them answered in the negative.

"OK. That's all right too. I have a boat down there, a raft really. We built it for this river. It'll hold all of us." *Dumb luck that I have this boat*, he thought. *Carolyn was not entirely right in her arrangements.*

Bretton went outside first. He carried his flashlight but kept it off. It was very dark although the lights of Maseru reflected off the haze enough to show the street a little. Their eyes were already adjusted to the dark since they had not turned on any lights other than the indirect glow of the flashlight. He went back to the door of his house. "Stay close. It is dark and we do not want to have to shout to find each other. We will go down my driveway, between the two houses there and straight across the maize field. The maize is still low, so we will bend over when we go through. On the other side is a sand road and then the trees at the top of the river bank. No one is ever down there. We can walk along the road until I find the steps down. At the bottom, there is a sandy place and the raft is tied up there. Stay together. I won't go too fast. Pheta, you know the area some. You follow at the back." His speech needed something to wrap it up. "Everyone ready?" They whispered responses but he shook the hand of each one to give them a chance to ask questions. The concern over quiet was more for Bretton's benefit than theirs. If no one had found them yet, there would be no one close enough to respond to any sounds in the night. But someone in the next few days who heard about noises this night might piece together who had helped the ANC. His ambition to fight apartheid was no secret. If the men were caught in the area, he would be a suspect. It was best for Bretton if they were not caught.

They made it easily to the sand road. They had walked, not run, bent over in the maize, altogether not a strenuous five minutes from the house and still every one of them was panting. Bretton walked along the edge of the road and looked back at the small group to see if it was conspicuous against the light sand, but he could barely see them even as close as he was. He focused on finding the steps down to the beach. He marched his group along the road, no more than five minutes more, until he as sure they had gone too far. It all looked so unfamiliar in the dark. He told them all to wait while he went back to find the way. On this pass, he could concentrate better because he was not worrying about the others. He went back for five minutes and still did not find the way. He normally went to the beach from his house so going toward his house made it even harder to find the path. He turned around and looked a third time. Somehow, it seemed obvious on this pass. He found a stick and stuck it upright in the road, and went on the find his group. He walked past them without seeing them until Pheta called his name. Pheta had actually whispered it once but too softly for Bretton to notice, so he spoke out aloud. Not very loud. Bretton thought he should have run out and grabbed his arm rather than make any noise.

The beach was extremely dark, being below the steep embankment and under the trees. Lesotho was semi-arid and had very few trees but the river was a separate ecosystem from the rest of the country, cooler, moister and far greener. Bretton had to use his flashlight to find the raft. He warned the others to shade their eyes so they would not lose their night vision. It did not take long to find. The "beach" was small so Bretton knew about where to look. Finding the poles for pushing through the water did not take long either but only because he had the flashlight.

Bretton positioned one man next to the river to prevent anyone from falling in accidently in the dark. Bretton knew the bank was steep going into the river except at the beach. Then he assigned one man to hold the poles and rope so the raft did not drift away. That left three to drag it to the beach. They were not in a race this time but the task was made hard by the darkness. Bushes and small trees blocked the way. The raft was too heavy to lift. With more noise and grunts than Bretton wanted, they got the raft onto the beach where it slid easily into the water. Bretton guided it out far enough that it could float with the men on board. He held to the rope in addition to the man assigned to that task. The current pulled at the raft. The water was high. Bretton guessed there had been some showers in the mountains although the skies had been clear all week in Maseru.

They climbed onto the raft one-by-one, with Bretton getting on last. Their weight lowered the raft onto the sand. Bretton sat on the edge and pushed with his legs but the sand was too weak to give him any traction. "Move your weight to the other side, away from me. Don't fall in. Sit down on the raft. They moved and suddenly the raft was afloat, just as it ought to be. Bretton was tempted to raise a cheer.

He asked for a pole and one was handed to him clumsily, banging him in the face. He felt a scrape on his cheek but nothing to impair his thinking. Up on his knees, he pushed toward the South African side. The river was deeper than it had been in the race and most of the pole was in the water before it hit the bottom. More troubling, he could hardly see the river to know which way to push. A panic overtook him and he became angry that the others were doing nothing, just waiting for him to get them through. He took a deep breath and looked up. The sky showed dimly between the trees, enough to mark the route of the river. Three pushes with the pole and the raft ran into trees along the South African shore. Pheta grabbed a branch and the raft came to a halt. Bretton shone the flashlight briefly onto the shore to let them all see how to get onto the land. They were on the inside of a bend and the water was moving slowly under the raft.

"Don't forget," Bretton reminded Pheta, "you need to go back along the river, upstream to find your contacts. We probably drifted 50 meters in the crossing." He worked the raft around until the end with the rope was near a tree and looped it twice around a sturdy trunk. "All right, my friends. Leave the raft one at a time. If you all go at once, that side will dip under the water. Best of luck to you!"

The first two got off when the shouting began. It was in Africaans. Bretton could not understand it but he could understand the anger in it.

"What are they saying?"

"They are saying 'stop' or they will shoot. But they haven't even seen us yet." Then Pheta turned his attention to the three ANC men waiting on the dark shore. "Wait here a minute. Then go upstream. I will take these bastards for a race down the river. If they catch me, I'll say I had a date with a woman on that farm." He jumped off the raft, nearly dumping the last of the ANC men into the river. Bretton managed to balance the raft enough to keep himself on top of it. Pheta headed off to the left through the brush. "What? What did you say?" he called to the presumed border guards and kept moving noisily downstream.

The guards shouted back in English but the words were indistinct through their heavy accents. Pheta kept calling in a questioning way. The voices moved away. Suddenly the guards started to shout louder and altogether. A few seconds later the first shots were fired. Pheta's voice could be heard, giving himself up. Then another barrage of shots. Then silence. Bretton waited for thirty seconds. A soft voice came from one of the ANC. "We go now."

Bretton realized the stream would push him downstream, toward the guards. He pushed off hard to get back to the Lesotho side as quick as possible. A few pushes with the pole and he hit the riverbank. It was soft where the raft hit, muddy. The raft spun around. Bretton slid off as quietly as he could and paddled to the shore. He could not climb up the mud so he drifted along until he found a branch hanging into the water. He pulled himself up and then stood for several minutes, listening. He could not hear anything upstream. He heard subdued male voices fairly nearby on the opposite shore. There was no confrontation. Pheta was under their control or he was dead.

≪ ≪ ≪ ≪ ¤ ≫ ≫ ≫ ≫

He hoped somehow he would see Pheta at the college the next morning. When Pheta did not show up, Bretton hoped to hear from Carolyn. If she had no report on the escape, she should have had some questions for Bretton. She could have said something about how his photographs had been used. On the weekend, he saw two of his pictures in a French magazine article on the raid. They were marked as ANC pictures, which was fine with Bretton.

XXV. <u>Last Meeting with the Ambassador (2003)</u>

After sticking to informal meetings throughout his Lesotho sojourn, Bretton finally made an appointment. First he checked to see when the economist would be out of the office and then asked for a meeting during that time with the Ambassador. Bretton saw this as his last meeting but he did not tell this to the Ambassador.

"Thank you for coming by. I am very interested to hear if you made any progress with Pshoene. You have been here a week, I think. He has not shown any movement yet, you know."

"I think we can wrap up my part today."

"Yes? That's great. Is he going to just give in soon or does he want something more?"

"Of course he wants something. I am not certain what it would take. I have not given him my proposal yet but I have discussed the whole picture with him a few times and feel confident I can move him, maybe even this afternoon so I can leave on the weekend."

"OK, tell me what you think he wants. I doubt we can arrange anything for him today. For one thing, I would like our economist to hear what you have to say. He is not here today."

"I heard you are a fan of the Roof of Africa rally."

"That's one of the perks of being stationed in Lesotho. Great thing for the country."

"Will you sponsor a bike again this year?"

"Well yes, I think I will. It was a personal expense. The Embassy could never buy in, obviously. We placed well last year. Got my name on the bike and on the uniform. It was good publicity for the U.S. I take it you follow the race."

"No, I don't. It came up when I was at the Chinese grocery in town and overheard a customer explaining to the Basotho clerk that the Americans thought the race was more important than the welfare of the Basotho."

"Who was this customer? That is complete bullshit!"

"Of course it is, but it is a story circulating these days."

"One Chinese spreading rumors. I wonder if he works for the Embassy."

"I checked into that. He is not officially employed by them. Anyway, I heard him say the road improvements the Chinese are offering are being opposed by you to protect the Rally."

"I do oppose the road but that has nothing to do with the Rally. It is a waste of money to build up a road on the far border of the country. Besides the Rally does not have to use that part of the road anyway."

"Do you know Smitty? Of course you do. He is the representative of the Rally in Lesotho. He has met folks here in the Embassy a number of times, right? He told me the road improvements would certainly hurt the reputation of the Rally by making the region accessible. They like having the event in a place where the starting line is hard to reach."

"The first part of the race is right here in Maseru."

"Sure, and we both know that is not so easy to reach either, but what he means, of course, is that the hard-core, off-road portion of the event benefits from being in a remote location."

"That can't make such a big difference."

"I don't know anything about marketing these things, but I am sure you are right. I was up in Butha-Buthe this week and talked to folks about how road improvements would affect them. Now I don't know about marketing an international race, but I do know something about African rural development. It looks to me like it would be a pretty good thing up there."

"Is Pshoene putting you up to this? I knew he wanted that Chinese funding."

"The Chinese are not offering money. They are kinda like us in that way. They are offering a road and that's all."

"The Chinese are not like us. They are doing it to provide work for their own people."

"True in small part; this is not an employment program. All the work in Lesotho could not put a blip on the employment state of China. Just like none of ours promote employment in Lesotho although they give work to Americans."

"You think that road is just what Lesotho needs?"

"I doubt it is the best possible thing for Lesotho but Lesotho needs a lot of things and I would put this on the list of reasonable options."

"That's between the Chinese and the Basotho."

"The Basotho Ministry of Commerce is reluctant to accept the road improvements while you are speaking against it. They fear you will make their government less popular. The public voice of the American Ambassador is very well respected.

"And I will speak out against a waste of money."

"Yes, public waste is critical in a poor country like this. But speaking of waste, how much does sponsorship of a bike cost?"

"You are getting out of line here. What I spend with my personal money is not any of your business."

"Depends. I want to make sure you are protected from these rumors I heard. Depends on how substantial the discount was that Smitty gave you for that sponsorship. The payment by each of the sponsors can be obtained from Smitty. He says he does not give out that information normally, but I worry someone may think he has or that someone may induce him to show something."

"I don't follow what you want here."

"I think we can agree the Chinese project is not so harmful to the Rally and does some good for Lesotho. You know that fantastic photo the Rally uses of the endless switchbacks going down the escarpment? The road improvements will not change that view. It would be great if you could make this point to Smitty who has sincere concern for the welfare of Lesotho too. This would remove any chance for rumors. If you are supporting the road, there is nothing to be gained from a story that you had a really good deal on the sponsorship."

"I can't say the road is a good thing for development on the say-so of one short-term consultant. I need to bring in our own economist."

"I thought it might be better to do this without him. He has not heard the rumors so let's stop them before anyone else hears them."

"I think you are trying to blackmail me."

"There is nothing in this for me but there is for you."

"What you call 'stopping rumors' that only you have heard?"

"No, that is not what I mean. I may be a short-term consultant at the moment, but most days I am a Washington bureaucrat. We have an unpleasant reputation but we serve some functions. In my bureaucratic role, I can help you with the education program you wanted. I saw it was hung up on the U.S. side over how to alter the approved plan for HIV money."

"Can you get that freed up?"

"I doubt it but that is not what I would want to do anyway. Wouldn't it be better to get additional funding to cover the cost of your program?"

"There is no new money. You can't claim to bring that."

"Nonetheless, my proposal is to deliver to you a budget increase earmarked for the ed program within a week or two. Only after that you will tell Smitty how much good the road improvements will be for this country he supports and which supports him. I am sure Mr. Pshoene at that time will embrace the program that will bear the name of the U.S. Ambassador for the next five years. Longer if it is renewed."

"You will deliver funds before I do anything?"

"Yes, of course. There is no reason to trust I could get funding."

"How will you do that?"

"Frankly, Mr. Ambassador, your program is not large in relation to the cracks in the Washington budget that we bureaucrats manage."

"And you trust me to help the Chinese?"

"No, I trust you to help the Basotho... especially when the Chinese are ready to raise rumors."

"But they will not do this in the next couple weeks?"

"That's right."

"How do I know that?"

"I guess you can't. How could you stop them if you wanted to? But it costs you nothing to wait until I get your project funded. To be clear, the education project is yours. It is your initiative. It could not happen without you, the Ambassador, behind it. I know I am a bureaucrat scrubbing out a crack and no one cares about my week back in Lesotho."

"Something doesn't feel right here."

"I know. You are not used to getting so much for so little. Let me say it straight out. There's just you and me here. I like your education program. I will get it funded in addition to your present budget. No one will resist it at USAID any more. These deals are already made but for my 'go-ahead'. The budget will take a couple weeks to get to you. I will stop it unless I hear you have backed off blocking the road improvements. I suggest you clear that with Smitty. Whether you get a discount on a bike this year is of no concern to me. Pshoene will support the ed program after I see him at dinner tonight. Is this good enough?"

XXVI. <u>Dinner with Pshoene (2003)</u>

M explained where Minister Pshoene lived very precisely since he knew Bretton would be walking there from the hotel and would have no help. M assumed no foreign visitor could find anything on his or her own. Bretton was not certain he could remember the directions perfectly but he was not worried. He paid close attention to the start of M's explanation so he was sure to get to the right neighborhood. Once there, he could get guidance from anyone.

Pshoene and Mosele lived in the second best part of Maseru, with homes that would have fit in an American suburb, except for having better flowers, and security walls with glass shards and barbed wire on top. Diplomats lived in the absolutely best part of town, along with a few well connected Basotho and, in their servants' quarters, many working Basotho who weeded the gardens, cooked the meals, washed the clothes, tended the children, guarded the night, and did anything else the relatively rich asked.

Pshoene's guard was looking out for Bretton but was surprised when he turned up on foot and he was surprised at how well Bretton greeted him in Sesotho. Their conversation never went beyond the greetings so he was left with the impression Bretton was fluent in the language. Bretton did not mean to misrepresent himself although he was aware that his skill was often misunderstood to be far more extensive than it really was. He did not mind leaving this illusion since it seemed to leave a sense that he had respected the Basotho.

Both Pshoene and Mosele were dressed in their best for dinner. Bretton expected this and had worn a jacket and tie. They were an odd looking couple, she being much larger and significantly younger than him. Her movements projected strength while his spoke of frailty. Nonetheless, they seemed perfectly matched in personality, both so serious, even severe. They had both struck Bretton as admirable for their professional dedication although jealous people said each was too ambitious. Neither was popular in the form that gets one invited to young people's parties but both were respected for their work. Their opinions had dominated the college whenever the Principle would take direction from the faculty.

The woman who worked for them served wine but that and the clothing were the only concessions to Western styles in entertaining. Mosele was cooking dinner herself and the couple explained early in the evening that they regarded Bretton as a friend rather than as a professional responsibility. Bretton leaned over and kissed Mosele's hand in response to this announcement. It was not a gesture he had ever made before nor was it a local custom, but Bretton acted spontaneously to show his appreciation of their declaration.

Mosele soon went into the kitchen with her wine glass, leaving Bretton and Pshoene to talk alone in the living room. It was furnished with several matching upholstered chairs, some small tables and a larger table supporting a 21-inch television. It appeared to Bretton that they ate their dinners at the table with the television and he wondered if it was on during meals. The room could be distinguished from a lower middle-class house in mid-America only by the smallness of the television and the presence of a coal-burning stove to be used for heat in winter.

Bretton was itching to tell Pshoene of his proposed resolution of the problem that brought him to Lesotho, but he sensed protocol required, even in relaxed Lesotho, that they socialize first, especially since he had been awarded the rank of friend. This was difficult since Pshoene was always focused on work. He would have been called a "wonk" in America.

The personal question that came to mind for Bretton was how Pshoene and Mosele had ever become married. He did not ask it because he wanted to save it for a time when they were both in the room but he could not get it out of his head. Did they fall in love? Did someone notice their similarities and bring them together? Was it a marriage of convenience, to share living expenses and professional contacts? Was Mosele his only wife? Bretton had assumed when he was teaching at the college that Pshoene was married because of his age and he vaguely recalled meeting his wife once. Single women in career positions were much more common than men so he had assumed Mosele was unattached.

They could sit in silence comfortably for a few minutes, sipping the wine, but Bretton would need to speak up eventually. It was absurd to rely on Pshoene to initiate small talk.

"I'm off to Windhoek tomorrow. Have you ever been there?" Bretton asked. He could go on indefinitely talking about the work in Namibia without impinging on the issues in Lesotho.

Pshoene answered negatively in a single word, two syllables in Sesotho, but his expression implied he was interested in whatever Bretton was going to do with it. Bretton did not think it was appropriate to talk about himself except as a last resort to say something.

"You have risen to a high level of responsibility in the years since I left. Does it take you out of the country often?" Asking questions reduced the potential for monologue. Bretton was sure Pshoene never traveled for tourism, but he was likely to represent Lesotho in some international fora.

This question worked well for its purpose. Pshoene named the various international trips he had taken as Minister of Finance: some for seminars, some for short-term training, some for consultations with regional counterparts. Each of these gave Bretton room for questions, important since Pshoene tended to volunteer very little without prodding, so the time passed until Mosele was ready to serve dinner.

She came out with two plates of white starch that Bretton assumed was mealy-meal, i.e., corn mush, and set them on the large table. Bretton worried that she was eating in the kitchen and leaving them to their business so he jumped up as soon as he saw the plates and went into the kitchen to help with the serving. The third plate was there-- her plan for it was unclear but she said nothing when he carried it out to the table and then brought up a third chair to it. He stood by the table while Mosele brought out the main course, a meat sauce that would be poured over the mealie-meal. He found a bowl of cooked greens in the kitchen and used one more word of Sesotho that he suddenly remembered, "*moroho*?" As far as he knew, the word meant no more than "vegetables," but it was used a lot so he thought it would apply as a question of whether he should take the bowl to the table. Mosele answered "*e*," to respect his use of Sesotho while she gathered the silverware and glasses for water. Meanwhile, Pshoene was sitting at the table silently watching Bretton help his wife.

They served themselves beginning with Bretton, followed by Pshoene, and began to eat. Bretton made a motion to show he was smelling the food appreciatively. Neither Mosele nor Pshoene thought complementing the cook was meaningful.

Bretton took out the question he had held in reserve: how had they advanced from colleagues into spouses.

"When I left in 1985, I was not aware you two had any thought of coming together. When did things change?"

Pshoene gave a precise outline of their courtship, presenting it almost sweetly, as his initiative against all logic that she would be available to him. Mosele followed with her view of it, that she had expected to never marry since she knew so well what liabilities men were, but she saw that Pshoene was like no other man and she was very much complemented by his interest in her.

Bretton's thoughts reverted to the day he had driven Mosele into South Africa and he wanted ask her what impressions she had back then, but he doubted the truth would be complementary to himself and might embarrass Mosele. He had nearly forgotten about those days twenty years before. Coming back to Lesotho had brought out more guilt than nostalgia so he abjured reviving the times further.

The room was silent again. It was acceptable to let the stories of courtship echo separately in the three of them, however, Bretton was again the first one too uncomfortable with the silence to let it continue indefinitely.

He asked Mosele if she went home often. He expected that asking her if she traveled outside the country would only bring out the differences in opportunities between his host and hostess. Fortunately, his question introduced a topic Mosele liked and she spoke of visiting her family every weekend and how they were living. She was proud of the conveniences her urban salary had provided. Bretton followed up with simple questions about where her mother lived and what the place looked like. Then, after another silence, she spoke up again, thoughtfully reflecting, as if noticing it for the first time, that those regular visits to the mountains had kept her in touch with the way of life in rural Lesotho, an essential input to her teaching at the agricultural college. She noted that she had now lived in the capital city for twenty-five years and was married to a government minister so it would be hard for her to address the needs of her students unless she undertook some form of research. Standing in her mother's village, it was easy to believe nothing more than a few amenities had changed since she was a girl. That might even be what her mother believed, but Mosele saw that village work was more productive, with better tools than the hoe she had invented, more fertilizer, new varieties to grow, and new techniques coming from the agricultural college. The fields were larger than when she was a girl, mainly because there were fewer people farming. Efficiency reduced the work needed which was good because young people did not want to farm. Work in the mines had declined in quantity. The men were not all automatically going off to South Africa in the same way, but they were not staying in the countryside either. The changes were complicated. She did not understand them, but, she claimed, she had a husband who did and she could ask him to explain whatever she wondered about in these changes.

Pshoene responded to her verbal opening very modestly, acknowledging that he had seen more change than Mosele since he was significantly older than her but he denied understanding the important question of what changes were coming next or, even more importantly, how to affect the coming changes, even though that was the challenge the Prime Minister and the people of Lesotho had issued him.

Then Pshoene backed away from the questions his wife raised for him and reflected on how her background had helped her as a teacher of Basotho home crafts. He had been an orphan back before AIDS made orphans commonplace throughout southern Africa. Unlike Mosele, he had no family support to help him get established or to guide him through the years. He regretted that he had not built close personal friendships to replace the role of family when he was young, but he attributed whatever success he had to this same isolation. He had become independent very early in life and had never looked for help from anyone. He claimed the self-reliance that was forced upon him by his circumstances had protected him from corruption when he began to work at the college. He had no conception that anyone would or could help him personally. Furthermore he claimed the limited ideas he held for achievement made him a good person to be second-in-command in his government career, second to the office director, second to the bureau chief, second now to the Prime minister. No one wanted Pshoene to be in charge of anything or to spend much time in his company, but everyone was content to have him implementing what a more able leader envisioned.

Eventually there was nothing more on anyone's plate and Bretton had refused several attempts by Pshoene and by Mosele to accept more so Mosele passed around a bowl of toothpicks and they all cleaned their teeth to confirm the end of the meal. Bretton saw it was a time for transition and he brought up his plan.

"Ntate, I believe the Ambassador will make clear he has no objection to the Chinese road project. It seems to be a reasonable form of assistance for Lesotho."

"And does the economist agree with this?"

"I do not know what he thinks. I did not include him in the planning I did. I found enough of a challenge getting the Ambassador's support. I think I understand the reasons for the Ambassador's previous remarks on the road and they did not originate in an argument about the economic benefits of this infrastructure."

"I see. And the Chinese have convinced you this is a good idea."

"Not at all. I did not meet with their officials."

"But you hired Han! I gave you an invoice and you paid."

"Yes, he helped me. I interviewed some Chinese unofficially. You did not ask me to negotiate the Chinese assistance, only to understand the Ambassador's objections."

"But you are not explaining his objections."

"Yes, I think it is better that I do not explain them too much. Please accept that they are ended."

"And you think I should support the education project?"

"It is a small thing. The Ambassador wants to do something on his own for Lesotho."

"But I know USAID does not want to do it."

"You will find them supporting it now. They hesitated because they thought it was competing for funding with their own ideas, but the Ambassador got additional funds from Washington and they are all happy together."

Mosele broke in. "The Ambassador, the economist, USAID, China, and Lesotho are all in agreement now. No one is fighting anything. You did not change anything but you were there when each of the objections went away. It that right?"

Pshoene continued to look at his wife, slowly nodding his head to show agreement with her implication-- that something did not add up.

"Right. I am the fortunate person to be bearing the news. There will be a small delay. The additional money the Ambassador is getting from Washington will take a couple weeks to arrive. I expect the Americans will be quiet during that time. You should not approve the education program until you hear it has its new funding. USAID will give you a call about that. You know Bill Friese over there, don't you? He can set it up. I have seen him do good projects in other countries."

Mosele held her hand on Pshoene's arm, as if to keep him quiet while she formed her thought. He looked at her, waiting. Finally she said softly, "The Ambassador suddenly likes the Chinese idea and USAID suddenly has money for the new education program. I think you are our hidden hero, Ntate."

"No, no ,no, no Mme, please so not speak of me that way. My trip to Lesotho has reminded me and proven to me anew that I am not a hero although I have been to places that have needed them and to places that has had them. My reward for this trip is to be allowed into your house as a friend. I can accept that. It is as much as I deserve. My tiny assistance is no more than a day's work. I do not make anything or grow any food or teach anyone. I am well paid to help good ideas move along. Nothing heroic in that since the particular ideas I facilitate are not the biggest ones or the hardest ones.

Pshoene put his second hand on top of his wife's as if to signal it was his turn to speak. He did not hesitate long. "You have brought us a good solution and you are right about your place in the world. You have a respectable position but you will not save us from the Boers or from AIDS or from ourselves."

Bretton stood up and bowed slightly. "*Kea leboha hahoolo*" (thank you very much). You have understood me."

"Do not forget you will always be welcome in this house."

"And you both will be welcome in mine," Bretton answered. "*Salang hantle*" (stay well, plural).

XXVII. Mapheta (2003)

On Bretton's second night in Lesotho, he did not want any dinner. The fruit he had saved from breakfast and a drink from the mini-bar in his room would be enough, but he went to the hotel dining room to look for M Phaki. The waiter on duty directed Bretton to the kitchen. M was sitting on a stool eating a bowl of something. M jumped up as soon as he saw Bretton, as if he were guilty about something. Bretton put him at ease and apologized for interrupting his dinner. He asked M if he could help find Pheta's family. M was anxious to help and assured Bretton he could find anyone Bretton wanted to see.

"But why," M asked, "would you want to see them? No one remembers Pheta. Except me. I remember him. I remember everything. He was one of the teachers at the college, right? He lived on the same street as you, down on the end of it. He was killed back when you were here. It was so long ago. It was a husband of a girl he was seeing. Pheta knew girls and they always went with him. He was very good looking, I guess. And he was always happy. Not at the end; he could not have been happy then. It was a few nights after the raid. He went out to her house and he got caught. His family was angry. At Pheta, not the husband. They said he got what he deserved. They paid back the brideprice but his wife could not stay in Maseru. I do not know if she went to South Africa or into the mountains. Maybe I could not find her if you wanted. I think they never found out which husband it was. Maybe it was even one of the married students at the college. They never found his body. Some say his sisters' husbands got together and hunted down the murderer, but I do not believe that."

Bretton had hoped the truth about Pheta had come out. Carolyn knew what had happened. He should have been in the pantheon of southern Africa heroes. "You can find his family?"

"If they are still alive. Lesotho is not so big."

"I would like to see his parents. If they are not still alive, I would like to see his sisters."

"They do not want to talk about Pheta."

"Maybe. I can ask. I may have something to tell them about him. I think he was not that bad."

On the third night of Bretton's visit back in Lesotho, he had the disastrous meeting with Palesa which he suspected had been arranged by M with good intent. On the fourth night, M ran out to the lobby as soon as Bretton came in. He had found Pheta's mother. Pheta's father was "late" and his sisters had apparently moved to South Africa with their husbands. The mother lived in the mountains but the road to the water project passed near her village so it would be possible to get there in an hour from Maseru. Bretton asked M if he could find someone to drive him to the village and M quickly volunteered to go along.

"You can hire a car and a driver from the hotel, but it would be best if I came with you to find her village. She is not a city person and she will not want to talk about Pheta. I can help. I knew him. I was his student too."

Bretton argued it was unnecessary but he liked the idea of having a translator he knew and who seemed to be trying to help. Bretton said he was not sure if he would go or when he would go but would decide something before the weekend when M had his day off. On Friday, Bretton had his last meeting with the Ambassador and made his arrangements to go back to Namibia on Sunday. That left Saturday free for this last detail. He thought it unnecessary to leave early since the drive was only an hour but he did not trust the estimate by M who did not ride by car very often and he imagined a farm woman of any age in Lesotho would be up with the sun, so they left the hotel at 7 o'clock.

The road was very good most of the way although the last couple miles were as slow as travelling on foot. The last section barely showed two tracks for wheels; it was just a wide, rocky, eroded path recognizable more for having no vegetation than for being flat. The driver zigged and zagged slowly around the largest holes without getting a ride smooth enough to prevent nausea arising in both Bretton and M. When M made an odd sound in his throat, Bretton looked back at him and knew he was close to spilling his breakfast in the backseat so he asked the driver to stop. They could walk the rest of the way. The driver would stay with the car and protect it from boys with bicycle pumps.

Bretton laughed at himself when his mind asked the obvious question, *How much farther is it?* and knew the inevitable answer would be "not far." When he had first noticed this tendency, he thought it was because the rural Basotho did not have a history of measuring distances or time and therefore did not make estimates in kilometers or hours. But in time he decided it was a cultural attribute, essentially recognizing that estimating distance does not affect the distance so the answer means "it does not matter."

They arrived in the village before 9 o'clock. The sun was already warm and the dew had burned off. The village was surrounded by maize fields with stalks already knee-high. Some girls were working in the vegetable plots inside the village. No boys over the age of ten were visible, probably because they were tending goats farther up the slopes. A half dozen small, barefoot children ran out of the village to greet Bretton and M, singing and running in circles around them. There was nothing for Bretton to see that would reflect the passage of time since Pheta was a boy here, however, his mother was fully aware of the time since then. She had grown old. Her son had left full of promise and then humiliated the family. Her husband had died. Her daughters had fled the disgrace of their brother. Yet she was not alone. She took care of four grandchildren so their mothers could work. The grandchildren ensured her daughters came home regularly. The daughters sent her money. They had been good to her and she could be proud of them. She regarded her old age as comfortable and her troubles as merely the normal course of affairs.

M asked the children which was the right rondavel and then Bretton went to the door and called "*Koko*," the polite way to knock. The rondavel was made of mud although there seemed to be sufficient stone around the village that it might have been used. Some of the buildings nearby had tin roofs but this one was made of thatch. It had been replaced recently enough that it was in good repair. The door was open, showing a polished floor inside, made from cattle dung. Bretton noted the leather hinges on the door were also relatively new and sturdy.

Pheta's mother came to the door and Bretton greeted her formally in Sesotho. He asked in Sesotho if she was Mapheta, and she answered very shyly that she was. M insisted on intervening to reassure the woman that this unexpected and unprecedented visit from a white man brought no trouble.

She invited them to come inside. Bretton did not recognize her words but he understood her gesture. It was dark inside the rondavel, with light only from the door and a single window. The grass roof hung over the door forcing Bretton to duck down as he went through. He had a thought of cutting a better opening for her and then thought how much better it would be if he got her a tin roof. That would not have cost much. He could probably get M to arrange it. She took some food from a shelf and poured water from a plastic jug into unmatched ceramic cups. M sat on a stool to leave the chair for Bretton. Bretton sat on the floor so Pheta's mother could sit on the chair but she pushed him until he got up and sat in the chair. There was no more he could say usefully in Sesotho so he spoke in English and had M translate a sentence at a time.

"I am Bretton from America. I used to work at the Agricultural College with Pheta. M Phaki was our student."

"Pheta is late," M gave as her answer, meaning he is deceased.

"Yes, I am sorry. He died when I was still living here."

"It was long ago. He had no children."

"Yes I am sorry about that too. He was my friend. He was a smart man and cared about his students."

"He cared about girls."

"I know he cared about his country and his family."

"Eat something."

Bretton was not going to eat anything from a village kitchen shelf but he took a little of the thick porridge with two fingers and pretended to eat it while actually passing it into his shirt pocket. He was sure she did not see this maneuver as she mostly looked down. He did not care whether M noticed. He did not even wish to drink the water but he raised the cup to his lips. M ate some porridge. They sat without speaking. Bretton thought this was acceptable. He tried to guess the age of Pheta's mother. Her skin was wrinkled on her face and hands. Her dark skin was not prone to wrinkling but she had spent all day for many years in the mountain sun. *Pheta was a little younger than me. His mother probably started having children younger than my mother but I do not know his sibling rank. She could be older or younger than my mother,* he thought.

"Are these your grandchildren?" Bretton guessed, referring to the faces peering in the doorway.

She called two of them inside and introduced them. She also had two more tending goats. "Pheta used to be a herdboy. They said he was a good herdboy," she added. Her statement sounded more matter-of-fact than prideful but it was hard for Bretton to judge her thoughts.

"He was a good teacher, Mme," Bretton added lamely. He was not even sure it was true. They had both worked at the college but had not worked together. Bretton knew him mostly from the weekend volleyball game the college staff played together. He scooped some more food into his pocket so his bowl would look used. He stood up, unable to find words to convey his thoughts or his reason for coming.

She said something softly that M translated as her saying she was honored by this visit. Bretton was pleased by that and embarrassed he could not tell her more. He was afraid to explain that her family had lived 20 years with this shame upon them when they should have lived in pride. He told himself he could not have explained it back when it happened because it would have endangered her family from the next attack by the apartheid government but he could not convince himself this was true. There was never another raid into Lesotho. Apartheid had fallen long ago and Bretton had been glad for that, had gone to see Nelson Mandela when he came to Washington, and had simply ignored the potential for what he knew to help Pheta's reputation. He had assumed Pheta's true actions were known, or he would have assumed that if he ever thought about it. The assumption would have been easy to make and hard to disprove.

On the ride back to Maseru, Bretton wondered why he had never spoken up about Pheta. *Probably*, he concluded, *I was thinking about whether I would become the target of the SADF,* although that was unlikely. *Carolyn knew and did not speak out. She was the ANC person. She knew better than me what was safe and what was right.* For the first time, it occurred to Bretton that maybe Carolyn did not know what happened to Pheta. Maybe all she knew was that she never saw him again, just as no one else ever saw him after that night. Bretton could not go back twenty years and grant Pheta the glory he deserved. He could not see how to right the wrong, a small wrong on the scale of the apartheid legacy. He thought of putting a roof on Mapheta's house. He thought of donating to the hospital in his name. Giving money felt like a filthy, guilty response. Doing nothing, as he had done for twenty years, seemed unforgivable.

There were ways to honor Pheta's memory. They would only be meaningful if they were public. How about getting others to donate to endow a scholarship to the agricultural college? Bretton had set up endowments and knew the mechanics of them. He began to calculate how much he would have to raise. This was a project within his skill set. The work of collecting money would be penance for the delay. Bretton might even look like an anti-apartheid soldier himself to tell the story of Pheta's last night. The truth was, Bretton had taken some risk back then; had followed his principles. He would look mighty modest for having never told the story before, but, on the other hand, he might look pretentious to tell it now. He had no proof of what had happened. Strangers might suspect he made it all up. It might appear convenient that he happened to decide to make his claim when he came back for a visit and all the people involved were long gone. Would Pheta's mother or Pheta's sisters be happy to learn he was a legitimate hero or angry that they had suffered 20 years under his false reputation?

The car broke down. The driver walked to the nearest village and came back with a "mechanic" surrounded by a dozen "apprentices" ranging in age from six to sixteen. "No worry" the driver said. He worked for the hotel so he would take care of all costs. It was not the cost of repairs that worried Bretton as much as whether they would actually be made. The "mechanic" had no tools with him at all. He looked under the hood and then sent apprentices back to the village to get whatever he wanted. There was a constant flow of boys between the car and the village. Bretton had no faith in the mechanic and thought of a back-up plan of walking to the main road and then hitching a ride to town. This was an impractical solution so he let the mechanic have his try. And after a couple hours, the "mechanic" put all the parts back inside the hood and called the driver back from his resting place under a bush. The car started.

M had fallen asleep in the back seat. Bretton was awake, antsy, physically uncomfortable with the springs of the well-worn seat poking his bottom and his back. He suddenly noticed his underwear had become clammy around his waist and he suspected it was due to the stress of his thoughts rather than to the warmth of the day. Meanwhile, the sweat on the neck of his shirt was evaporating and giving him a chill. The sun had set and the dry mountain air was rapidly cooling. Bretton rolled up his window and wondered how far it was to Maseru. Not far.

Planning, project design, good works for national development... these were Bretton' expertise. They could be applied to Pheta's legacy. If he used his own money or money he raised outside the government, he would have uncommon freedom in its use. He found it surprising this was not an attraction. He knew the rules and the options of a certain game in the bureaucracy. He was confident within the familiar parameters. It was just what he had already done on this trip to Lesotho. In a week, he had accomplished something. Everyone but Palesa was happy with him Even Pheta's mother saw the visit as an honor for her son.

He had a flight out tomorrow. There was no time to arrange something more before he left. He had work to finish in Namibia. Innocent and interesting Anjali would be there. He would need to concentrate on that work for a week and then fly back to Washington where he could take up the cause of Pheta. From there he would not have access to M as an agent to make some small improvements for Pheta's mother. She did not really need them anyway. Everything about Lesotho would be remote once he was back except for getting some funds for the education project. The next thing would demand his attention and it would be professionally irresponsible to dwell on a gesture to an event now twenty years in the past. Without the old woman sitting in front of him, looking down in her humility, clothed in her thin shift and rubber sandals, Bretton could not appreciate who would care to have him undertake this risk to his own reputation, to his own effectiveness at good works. The apartheid struggle had ample heroes. The minor ones, like Pheta, were lost to modern memory, even if they had, unlike Pheta, been lauded in their day. A leisurely shower in the hotel would wash away the ache of the long ride. He would work some lotion into this hands and face to erase the dryness of the day and change into fresh underwear and a crisp shirt to convert himself back into the First World professional that was capable of the neat resolution he had brought to the education project. Bretton's shoulders relaxed as he thought of the glass of red wine he would order at the bar from M's weekend replacement followed by the steak dinner on the hotel menu, an indulgence he had saved for his last night.

XXVIII. Library Visits (2003 & 1983)

Sunday morning Bretton woke before the alarm went off. He was wide awake, already feeling the pressure of meeting the airline schedule. He did not need to leave for the airport until noon, but he could not rest again until he was on the plane. He would shower and shave in fifteen minutes and pack everything in another fifteen. The familiar sense of moving to a new country and a new assignment kept him churning through the routine. There were no decisions on a morning like this: how he washed and packed and dressed was the same as always on such a day. He had plenty of time for breakfast. He already knew what he would put on his plate; what he would put in his pocket for later. The routine was disturbed by the lag between breakfast and meeting the plane. He had a couple hours outside the routine. He asked the hotel desk clerk if a driver was available to take him to the airport and to make a stop on the way. He would go out to the ag college to see if it had changed much and look at his old house to see if it was still there.

The driver pulled into the parking lot of the college. There were a few cars but no one was visible. Classes had probably started already, at 8:00, as they had twenty years earlier. Bretton could stick his head in to the faculty lounge at tea time but that was an hour away still and he might not know anyone anyway. The administration building looked shabby. It could have benefitted from some paint. It looked sturdy at least, nothing to pity about it. A new building had gone up where the dining hall had been. It looked like a dormitory. He stood beside the car and twisted around to see where the dorms had been. They had been razed and a well-tended garden grew there. It was partitioned into segments that might have been experiments or individual student plots. Another building was under construction nearby, a large one. It might be an assembly hall. It would not be a gymnasium. This was not like an American school.

The row of rondavels that had housed the non-teaching staff had been refurbished and looked better than the administration building. Bretton figured Palesa might still live in one of those. He looked at the one where he used to visit her. He could not believe she was still living in that one round room. The thought made him get back in the car before he met anyone. He directed the driver to go beyond the school, down to the road by the river, to where the faculty housing had been.

"Wait!" Bretton called as they were leaving the college grounds. They had reached a long, windowless building with wooden siding and a tin roof, like a large, prefabricated tool shed in the States. It bore a romantic appearance because of the grand entrance along a winding path through an allee of tall trees with colorful bark. He got out of the car to look more closely, thinking this place might reveal how much the school had changed since he left. He stood in front of it and recalled his first visit inside.

《 《 《 《 ¤ 》 》 》 》

In his second month at the school, Bretton had gone into the long white building they called the library to see if it really was one. Though it was early afternoon, no one was inside and he was surprised when he switched on the light to find a room with a long table in the middle surrounded by walls of shelves. It was immaculate; everything apparently in its place. The shelves were not filled with books, but there were more than he expected, enough for a school the size of this one. They were grouped into broad categories labeled with handwritten signs taped to the shelves: science, agriculture, poetry, current events, religion, etc. Most of the books were lying face up rather than standing on edge and in this way were spread over most of the shelf surface. Agriculture seemed the critical topic for this school so he looked at the titles there. Three copies of a book on soils of Lesotho written by a former faculty member were very impressive. He picked up the copy on top and noticed the cover of the second copy had a crease. Inside was an unmarked envelope containing a dozen seeds. He put the envelope in his pocket. The soils book had photos of dongas, eroded gullies, in Lesotho, and test pits that had been dug in the lowlands to show the typical soil profile. It was an excellent tool for agriculture students who might advise farmers after they left the college. Next to the soils books was a small pile of books on dairy science by another former faculty member. Those were similarly useful although they were about dairy husbandry in Britain. After these two finds, he struggled to discover anything else relevant. The books were generally donations from the first world, castoff remnants, out-of-date or inappropriate to the region, or too technical for the students here, or too simple for adults, or too esoteric. There were several sets of scientific journals, four copies per year for ten years or so, ending some years ago. Each set covered the same years. Probably someone had retired from professional life and donated all of them. He saw no card file of titles and no desk for a librarian to officiate over checking out of materials. And then he remembered he had simply walked in; the door had not even been locked.

The materials were not subject to theft, not like the television that had been donated to the student lounge. The doors to the lounge were locked for the first time on the evening of the donation and yet the television was gone by morning. Bretton had not been disturbed by the loss since he did not think any good would come of having a television for the students. He was bothered, however, by the reaction of the students. They were not angry enough. It was only what they expected. They claimed it had been stolen by the college Principal; nothing less than they had expected when the television arrived. The rumor was that he had not even sold it, merely put it in his living room where anyone could see it.

Bretton thought he might be able to obtain better books, books that the students would want to use. The students in this college were not likely to read for entertainment or to use references in writing papers for class, but it was not for him to prejudge the value of books to them. They probably never had access to such resources. Maybe some of them would use them. Maybe some of the faculty would benefit. Maybe even some of the Maseru community would use it. There was no public library in town although a few of the embassies had reading rooms to promote the culture and politics of their countries. He considered how he would find an appropriate American donor but thought that better books would require better security in the library and a librarian and other administrative funding that would not be forthcoming, not even from a donor.

Perusing the shelves, he espied a picture book of the U.S. moon landing. It was published by NASA. The phrase "coffee table book" came to mind. It would have little meaning to the students who were the putative patrons of the library. But the book did interest Bretton and he thought it might well be entertaining to an occasional LAC student. He sat at the end of the table and leafed through the pictures, reading some of the captions. *Beautiful shots, good quality printing, exciting stuff,* he thought as he went through it. *Must be nice to work with a Hassleblad.* He left the book open on the table as an invitation to the next person, hoping he could entice someone to appreciate the library.

After he left the library that day, he made some notes to himself about getting more appropriate books, what might be useful or entertaining or inspiring, but he never got around to doing any more before he lost the notes he made. There were other projects to undertake for the college anyway. No one ever showed an interest in the library during his time at the school.

But he did commemorate his one visit by planting those seeds he had found. First they were germinated in a row of pots he placed outside his office window where they could get sun for most of the day. He did not know what plants they were so he was not sure how to care for them and he watered the pots farther from the window more as an experiment to see what worked best. He was surprised when they all came up at about the same rate. They turned out to be Eucalyptus trees, not native to Africa but not uncommon in Lesotho. After a year, he transplanted six seedlings on each side of the path to the library. Even on the day he planted them, he did not go inside the library again.

« « « « ¤ » » » »

On the last day of his last visit to Lesotho, he would go inside again. He was extremely proud of the trees he had planted. They made the most beautiful view on the campus. The door was still unlocked. His eyes did not adjust immediately to the darkness inside and then he found the light switch. Cardboard boxes piled three high filled the first part of the room. They had all been opened and apparently all contained books. He looked past them to the shelves which looked as he remembered them. He maneuvered around the boxes and sat at the table in the middle of the room. There was one book on the table. It lay open to a photograph of a rocket launch. He dragged the book toward himself, leaving a track in twenty years of dust. A rectangle free of dust showed where the book had lain.

Bretton leafed through the book as he had done before. It was about the Apollo program which had ended in 1972. The book was published in 1975 and envisioned an era of continually expanding moon exploration, not how things had actually turned out.

He thought he heard a sound behind himself, possibly the driver had become impatient. A warm hand touched his head. He froze for a moment to decide if it constituted a threat. A second hand stroked the other side of his head. He turned around. It was Palesa.

"You are leaving now?" she asked and walked around the table to sit opposite him.

"Yes, in a few minutes."

Palesa said something in Sesotho with a questioning tone to it.

"Palesa, I never spoke much Sesotho."

"I know. You like to talk but you do not understand anything." She had summarized him well and he could not answer. "You will never come back."

Bretton was not sure if it was a question but he answered it anyway. "No. I do not think so." He reached across the table and took her hand in his. Her skin was rough. She had not been a farmworker but she had worked with her hands, washing dishes and clothes and whatever else was needed in her life.

"Do you have time to do something now?"

This was a question but Bretton did not answer her. He stroked her hand until she pulled it back and stood up. She took a few steps away and rested her weight on one of the shelves. Then she began to sing. Bretton had never heard her sing before although singing was universally practiced in Lesotho. He had heard it more than once for several days at a time building up to a wedding and he heard the students sing in the fields whenever they went out. Everyone but he had sung at the ANC funeral. He had never heard the singing in Lesotho accompanied by any instrument, but they always sang with full harmony. Palesa's song seemed to be a lullaby. He could not recognize any of the words. Bretton looked up at her and saw she was staring into his face. *Lovely voice*, he thought and nearly said aloud but held back because it might be disrespectful to interrupt her song. *Lovely face* he also thought.

When her song ended, Bretton asked if she remembered Pheta.

"*E*," meaning "yes," she answered.

"Do you know how he died?"

"A husband killed him. This often happens."

"No, Palesa. It is a long story. You know the night you took me to him, he was working for the ANC."

"I do not know about that. I only know he asked me to get you."

"Well, he was. And he had me take pictures for the ANC."

"I saw them. We all saw them in the papers. We knew they were your pictures."

"How would you know they were mine?"

"People saw you taking them." This made sense to Bretton. He had few secrets in Lesotho, apparently not even his affair with Palesa.

"On the night he died, he was helping some ANC men escape."

"The ones hiding in your house, you mean?"

"You know about that too?"

"Everyone knew. No one talked about it."

310

"Pheta took on the danger that night. He may have saved those men. He may have saved me. I heard him shot."

Palesa looked at Bretton as if there was more to be said. Bretton looked back. It was hard for him to look her in the eye and he kept looking elsewhere in the room.

"It does not matter now," she said at last.

"It mattered back then."

"*E.*"

"I saw his mother yesterday. I wanted to help somehow but, and you will understand this very well, I could not see how to help."

"*E*, you cannot help."

It is generous of you to say I cannot help instead of saying I am unwilling to help.

"I would like to help you, Palesa." *How pathetic. In a chance encounter on your last day I claim this?*

After another minute of looking at each other, she said "*Tsemaea hantle*" (go well) and added, "You know what this means?"

"*E, mme. Sala hantle*" (stay well). Bretton held his eyes on her as he rose and backed to the door. Palesa did not move except to watch him go to and then through the door. He turned toward the car, taking him out of her view. He sat in the car and looked at the rows of Eucalyptus trees gracing the way to or from the library as he departed for the airport and on to the next country.

CPSIA information can be obtained
at www.ICGtesting.com
Printed in the USA
BVHW071558010719
552377BV00009B/1019/P